PRAISE FOR LEE GOLDBERG

Ashes Never Lie

"Goldberg manages to give each of his four leads their due while keeping the investigation's fuse burning bright. This series deserves a long life."

—*Publishers Weekly*

"The sequel to *Malibu Burning* unites Goldberg's Ronin and Pavone police team with his arson investigators Sharpe and Walker in a clever, complicated story. With its witty banter and well-developed characters, Goldberg's latest procedural is tailor-made for readers who enjoy shrewd investigators in fast-paced dramas."

—*Library Journal*

"Goldberg overtly offers sly, knowing commentary on the state of today's media, even as he spins an engaging and exciting police procedural."

—*Deadly Pleasures*

Malibu Burning

"The author of the Eve Ronin mysteries returns with a fast-paced, over-the-top caper that entertains while keeping readers guessing."

—*Library Journal* (starred review)

"Goldberg returns to the wildfire he memorably chronicled in *Lost Hills* (2020) from a strikingly new angle . . . A businesslike thriller that shows how rewarding it can be to revisit the same story from a new point of view."

—*Kirkus Reviews*

"Goldberg's well-drawn characters will keep readers rooting for both crooks and cops, and he hangs everyone's fates on a clever, complicated con. The result is as explosive as a wildfire."

—*Publishers Weekly*

"Action-packed and captivating, *Malibu Burning* is a scorching-hot and fast-moving thriller that will have you sweating as if you're in the middle of a five-alarm fire. Once again, Lee Goldberg delivers a fast-paced, entertaining novel with well-constructed characters and an intriguing plot."

—Best Thriller Books

"Both fans and newcomers to Goldberg's work will enjoy the fast-moving, at times terrifying, tale and its close look at firefighting and arson-investigation techniques."

—firstCLUE

"Hilarious and touching, exciting and endearing. Highly recommended."

—*Deadly Pleasures*

"Lee Goldberg is one of the best thriller authors in the business and proves it again with *Malibu Burning*. He keeps things racing along at such a pace, and in such smooth prose, that it's almost impossible to stop reading in this novel."

—Rough Edges

"If *Malibu Burning* were a wine, we'd describe it as rich and full-bodied, with tasty top notes of humor and lightheartedness, a robust blend of experience infused with enormous heart."

—The Thriller Zone

"Lee Goldberg writes a scorching-hot thriller with his *Malibu Burning* that delivers on all the heat. Fast paced, the plot moves relentlessly to an unexpected climax."

—*Montecito Journal*

"Lee Goldberg knows how to write entertaining novels. His latest thriller, *Malibu Burning*, is a prime example. He creates a diversity of characters, throws them into some impossibly dangerous situations, and ratchets up the tension and suspense. Like a wildfire storming through the woods, I was racing to get to the novel's ending."

—Gumshoe Review

"This splendidly entertaining tale unfolds at a cinematic pace. Goldberg blazes new ground in his already storied career, treading on the territory of the great Don Winslow. Not to be missed for crime-thriller aficionados."

—BookTrib

"*Malibu Burning* is a blistering thrill ride full of Southern California thieves, cops, and firefighters, all facing high stakes and imminent danger. Superbly researched and told, fast-paced, and downright fun, this is Lee Goldberg at his best!"

—Mark Greaney, #1 *New York Times* bestselling author of the Gray Man series

"By turns tense and rambunctious, wildly entertaining, and breakneck-paced, Lee Goldberg's splendid *Malibu Burning* is pure storytelling pleasure from beginning to end."

—Megan Abbott, Edgar Award–, Anthony Award–, Thriller Award–, and *Los Angeles Times* Book Prize–winning author of *The Turnout*

HIDDEN
IN
SMOKE

OTHER TITLES BY LEE GOLDBERG

The Ian Ludlow Thrillers

True Fiction

Killer Thriller

Fake Truth

The Fox & O'Hare Series (coauthored with Janet Evanovich)

Pros & Cons (novella)

The Shell Game (novella)

The Heist

The Chase

The Job

The Scam

The Pursuit

The Diagnosis Murder Series

The Silent Partner

The Death Merchant

The Shooting Script

The Waking Nightmare

The Past Tense

The Dead Letter

The Dead Man Series (coauthored with William Rabkin)

Face of Evil

Ring of Knives (with James Daniels)

Hell in Heaven

The Dead Woman (with David McAfee)

The Blood Mesa (with James Reasoner)

Kill Them All (with Harry Shannon)

The Beast Within (with James Daniels)

Fire & Ice (with Jude Hardin)

Carnival of Death (with Bill Crider)

Freaks Must Die (with Joel Goldman)

Slaves to Evil (with Lisa Klink)

The Midnight Special (with Phoef Sutton)

The Death March (with Christa Faust)

The Black Death (with Aric Davis)

The Killing Floor (with David Tully)

Colder Than Hell (with Anthony Neil Smith)

Evil to Burn (with Lisa Klink)

Streets of Blood (with Barry Napier)

Crucible of Fire (with Mel Odom)

The Dark Need (with Stant Litore)

The Rising Dead (with Stella Green)

Reborn (with Kate Danley, Phoef Sutton, and Lisa Klink)

The Jury Series

Judgment

Adjourned

Payback

Guilty

Nonfiction

The Best TV Shows You Never Saw

Unsold Television Pilots 1955–1989

Television Fast Forward

Science Fiction Filmmaking in the 1980s (cowritten with William Rabkin, Randy Lofficier, and Jean-Marc Lofficier)

The Dreamweavers: Interviews with Fantasy Filmmakers of the 1980s (cowritten with William Rabkin, Randy Lofficier, and Jean-Marc Lofficier)

Successful Television Writing (cowritten with William Rabkin)

The Joy of Sets: Interviews on the Sets of 1980s Genre Movies

The James Bond Films 1962–1989: Interviews with the Actors, Writers and Directors

HIDDEN IN SMOKE

LEE GOLDBERG

THOMAS & MERCER

Text copyright © 2025 by Adventures in Television, Inc.
All rights reserved.

Published by Thomas & Mercer, Seattle

www.apub.com

Amazon, the Amazon logo, and Thomas & Mercer are trademarks of Amazon.com, Inc., or its affiliates.

EU product safety contact:
Amazon Media EU S. à r.l.
38, avenue John F. Kennedy, L-1855 Luxembourg
amazonpublishing-gpsr@amazon.com

ISBN-13: 9781662526466 (hardcover)
ISBN-13: 9781662526442 (paperback)
ISBN-13: 9781662526459 (digital)

Cover design by Jarrod Taylor
Cover image: © Cristian Todea / ArcAngel; © kampee patisena / Getty; © atk work, © M2020 / Shutterstock

Printed in the United States of America

First edition

To Valerie & Madison

AUTHOR'S NOTE

Fair warning, my friend.

If you haven't read my novel *Malibu Burning*, you might want to before starting this book because I give away the ending on page one . . . and much more about it as the story goes on.

But if you haven't read *Malibu Burning*, don't worry—you won't be lost or confused. This novel works as a stand-alone. There's nothing you already need to know to fully enjoy this adventure.

Okay, now buckle up. The ride is about to begin . . .

CHAPTER ONE

A Saturday in June
Hakone, Japan

The man with a stranger's face sat naked in the rock-rimmed volcanic hot spring, breathing the sweet scent of the yuzu fruit floating on the nearly still surface of the bath and listening to the soothing echo of water dripping into the *suikinkutsu*, an upside-down ceramic pot with a tiny hole in the bottom that was buried outside sometime in the sixteenth century. A cool, gentle breeze wafted in from the lush mountain forest and over the meticulously landscaped rock garden, a panorama framed in front of him by the floor-to-ceiling opening of the *ryokan*, a traditional Japanese retreat and spa. It was pure tranquility.

And it was insanely boring.

But he'd been told by the plastic surgeon many months, and several operations, ago that peace and relaxation were an essential part of a successful recuperation. So, he tried his best to stay awake and to appreciate the silence, beauty, and stillness before his weekly facial and full-body massage.

His name was Danny Cole, but he had a different name now, actually several of them, to go with his new face, which he still hadn't seen. He was a retired thirty-five-year-old thief and grifter, but he was running one final, elaborate con: trying to trick himself, and anyone who might still think he was alive, into believing that he was someone else.

Perhaps this would be the day, Danny thought, that he'd establish a deep, spiritual connection with nature, creating the necessary balance between his inner life and the outside world for him to be truly born anew.

And perhaps this would be the day that he finally looked at his reflection and, when he did, saw his face and not a mask that he could never remove. That was the true purpose of his doctor-prescribed tranquility.

The stillness of the bathhouse was shattered by the arrival of another man behind him. It wasn't the man's presence that did it. This was a communal bath, after all, and others were expected to regularly come and go. They were also expected to slowly emerge, showered and naked, from the changing room with a practiced, quiet grace and slip carefully into the bath, creating as few ripples as possible on the surface.

But this guy strode in like a Neanderthal, his heavy bare feet slapping loudly against the wet stone floor, and then plunked himself down hard in the bath beside Danny, sending water sloshing all around. It had to be a tourist.

Irritated, Danny turned and saw a man wearing a cowboy hat and flashing a friendly grin that hit him like a gut punch.

"Yikes, this is hot," the cowboy said. "I may never have a kid again."

Danny knew him. His name was Andrew Walker. They were both Americans, and about the same age and build, but they were *inyo*, as the Japanese would call it, two opposing, yet necessary, forces in nature. The last time Danny saw the lawman was nearly two years ago, in the middle of a massive wildfire in the Santa Monica Mountains.

"You're committing a cultural faux pas," Danny said.

"A what?"

"You're supposed to be naked."

"I am," Walker said.

"You're wearing a cowboy hat."

"It wouldn't fit in the tiny wicker cubby they have in the changing room."

"You could have left it there. Nobody will steal it. The Japanese are very law abiding."

"Then you're never going to fit in here, Danny."

There wasn't any hesitance or doubt in Walker's voice about who he was speaking to.

So much for the massive plastic surgery and the weeks of recuperation in this sanctuary, Danny thought.

He looked back out at the mountains, trying to see the beauty and feel the tranquility again, but it was just a bunch of trees. The dripping of the *suikinkutsu* wasn't soothing anymore, it was water torture.

Did Walker come alone, or were there dozens of police officers surrounding the *ryokan* now? Danny didn't see anyone moving through the trees on the hillside, but he'd know soon enough.

Danny looked at him with disdain. "You're confirming every cliché about the ugly American."

"Except that I'm stunningly handsome." Walker gave Danny a careful and unabashed once-over. "You don't look too bad yourself, especially for a guy who burned to death. But I don't see the point of changing your face if you're going to leave the rest of your body the same."

"I don't walk around naked and there aren't many people who'd recognize my body anyway."

"I know one who would," Walker said. "Your criminal defense attorney, Karen Tennant. You've been friends with benefits since college, even though the one time she represented you, she lost and you went to prison."

So, there it is, my mistake, Danny thought. *Or was it arrogance?*

"You've been watching her."

Walker nodded. "I figured you'd need a lot of legal help to create a solid new identity or two that could hold up to international scrutiny. She came out here alone on vacation a few months ago. I got my hands

3

on the Tokyo hotel's security video. I recognized you the instant you walked into the lobby in your Tom Ford suit. You may have a new face, but the way you move is unmistakable."

"How do I move?"

"Like a panther."

Karen didn't say anything about his walk, but she'd told him that the way he touched her was unmistakable. That hadn't worried him, since there wasn't anybody else from his old life that he'd be sleeping with again. But he should have realized there were some things about himself that plastic surgery, colored contact lenses, and dialect coaches couldn't change.

"I need to work on a limp," Danny said.

"You were also wearing one of the watches that Roland Slezak lost when his house burned down in the wildfire that you ignited."

"The Franck Muller Aeternitas Mega is a common watch."

"Only among people who have $2 million in pocket change to spend on jewelry," Walker said.

"It would be a crime to own a watch like that and not wear it."

"The crime was stealing it. Wearing it afterwards was chutzpah." Walker gestured to Danny's left shoulder. "The plastic surgeon couldn't do anything about that scar?"

It was a souvenir from being shot by a drug lord's assassin.

"It gives me character," Danny said, then glanced at the nicks and tiny puckered scars all over Walker's back. "What happened to you?"

"My wife has very long nails," Walker said. "But some of it is shotgun pellets, a souvenir from my marshaling days. The rest happened a few months ago, when I turned my back on a house that exploded."

"You're still an arson investigator with the Los Angeles County Sheriff's Department? I didn't think that would last."

"Generally speaking, it's safer than my old job chasing fugitives like you for the US Marshals Service," Walker said. "I'm usually home for dinner every night with my wife and two-year-old son."

It had to be hell for Walker, Danny thought, giving up a job he loved to be with his family instead. He admired the man's sacrifice, even if he couldn't imagine making it himself.

But it occurred to Danny now that he'd also walked away from doing what he'd loved. He'd made the snap decision after pulling off the biggest score of his life, a massive heist in the middle of a catastrophic wildfire that he thought he could control.

He'd made his sacrifice for himself, to assure his own freedom.

Freedom to do what? Sit stewing in a hot spring, smelling fruit boil, and listening to water drip in some ancient pot?

Not that it mattered now. It was over, and all for nothing. Walker had caught him again.

"You're a long way from home, Walker. You're going to miss your family dinner."

"My wife understands that I still have professional obligations that take me away from time to time. Nothing dangerous," Walker said. "For instance, right now I'm attending a four-day arson investigation seminar in Green Bay, Wisconsin."

"I hate to break it to you," Danny said, "but you got on the wrong flight."

"I'm heading home tomorrow, but don't worry, you're not coming with me. Everybody thinks you're dead and it's better for all concerned if you stay that way."

Danny had often wondered why the heist had never made the news and why he'd been portrayed in the press instead as an ex-convict firefighter who gave his life to help Walker and his partner, Walter Sharpe, rescue two lost hikers trapped in the wildfire.

Now he had part of the answer: Walker and Sharpe didn't tell anybody what they'd caught him doing. For some mysterious reason, they'd let him and the survivors of his crew get away with the crime and the spoils.

The *suikinkutsu* wasn't so painful for Danny to hear anymore. The air was somehow getting still again.

He looked at Walker. "So why track me down now?"

"Because you didn't finish the job."

Danny was surprised Walker knew that the Malibu fire was more than just the cover for a heist, that he was primarily avenging the death of Arnie Soloway, one of the members of the convict firefighting crew Danny had joined to do his time outdoors instead of in prison.

During another, earlier Malibu wildfire, a rich, loathsome guy named Roland Slezak used his political influence to force firefighters to devote their limited resources, and the efforts of Danny's convict firefighting crew, to protect his gaudy mega-mansion instead of a mobile home park in the lowlands that could be saved with far less risk.

Slezak's house survived unscathed, but the mobile home park was decimated, Arnie was killed by a helicopter water-drop gone wrong, and the convict's grieving family didn't get a penny in death benefits.

And it was all Slezak's fault.

So Danny spent the remaining years of his sentence devising a daring heist of Slezak's riches, and those of his equally entitled neighbors, that would leave the mega-mansions in ashes and cover up any evidence that the thefts had even occurred. And when he got out, he pulled it off with help from some of his fellow ex-convict firefighters and his old heist crew. It had worked just like he'd planned almost until the end, when everything went horribly, fatally wrong.

But not entirely.

"Arnie Soloway's widow and children will never have to worry about money," Danny said.

"Neither will you and your crew, at least the few who survived," Walker said. "But you didn't actually get revenge, which I thought was the point. You really fucked that up."

"Slezak lost his precious house and his valuables."

"So what? He was insured. He hasn't suffered at all," Walker said. "In fact, he's alive and well and even wealthier than before. The asshole bought a five-hundred-year-old castle in France just so he could dismantle it, ship the stones to Malibu, and rebuild it there. What did you really accomplish besides enriching yourselves? Nothing. Slezak should be destitute and in prison. You need to go back and make it right."

Danny knew a con when he heard one. "You aren't here to get justice for a convict's death and the desecration of France's cultural heritage. You've got something personal at stake."

Walker took off his hat and set it down on the floor behind him. "Do you know how Slezak got rich?"

"He buys pharmaceutical companies that make specialty drugs and then dramatically increases the prices of their products," Danny said. "The patients either have to pay or suffer."

"My son has epilepsy. His seizures are horrible. I can't stand to see him suffering and I'm powerless to stop it. There's only one anti-seizure drug that works for him, Xylaphram, and it's a godsend, but there's no generic equivalent. The cost for the medication before Slezak bought the company that makes it was $10,000 a year. Now it's $150,000."

"There's no law against greed."

"Slezak refuses to lower the price, despite pleas from patients, doctors, politicians, the media, even his own employees," Walker said. "Our insurance company won't cover Xylaphram and we can't afford to pay for it ourselves. We've already borrowed against our house."

"I'd be glad to pay for your son's medication."

"Hell no. I'm a cop. I can't take money from a crook," Walker said. "Besides, it won't solve the problem for everybody else on Xylaphram."

"Then what do you want from me?"

Walker looked him in the eye. "Destroy Slezak."

"How am I supposed to do that?"

"The way you do everything else. Just get it right this time. If he's out of the picture, the prices will drop on all of the specialty drugs that he owns. You owe it to Soloway and to me."

"What do I owe you for?"

Walker turned and put his hat back on. "Letting you go."

Danny knew there was a lot of truth to Walker's argument. Slezak's financial loss was ephemeral and his personal suffering was superficial and temporary. Their revenge was hardly adequate punishment for the selfishness and entitlement that led to Arnie Soloway's pointless death.

But that's not what struck a nerve with Danny. And it wasn't the plight of Walker's epileptic son, either.

It was the jolt of excitement he felt at even the fleeting thought of going after Slezak again, of finding a clever way to destroy him or, better yet, getting him to destroy himself.

It was like being shocked with defibrillator paddles.

Until that instant, he might as well have been actually dead, or at least comatose.

He was awake now and seeing the last year or so from a new perspective.

What was he doing seeking safety and tranquility?

What kind of freedom is that?

It isn't, he realized. Freedom is being who you are, doing what you love and what you are good at, enjoying the excitement that comes from constantly challenging yourself, from taking on the impossible and surviving, from proving your competence and skills with every breath you take.

Even if that means risking everything . . . and facing imprisonment or death.

Because if a man doesn't have anything at stake, he's just existing, like a lump of Jell-O, which was what he'd become.

For Danny, retirement was slow but certain suicide. Walker, without knowing it, had just saved his life.

Danny said, "It will take some time for me to plan and pull off. Maybe a few months. Can you hold on that long?"

Walker smiled. "Sure."

"And you'd better be ready if I need you."

"I'm always ready," Walker said, then studied Danny's face.

"What?" Danny asked, touching his own cheek, just to make sure it wasn't melting off.

"You look familiar."

"Because you already know me," Danny said. "It's an illusion."

Walker shook his head. "It's not that. Your face reminds me of someone else."

Danny knew who it was. "Chris Evans."

"Thor?"

"That's Chris *Hemsworth*," Danny said. "Chris *Evans* was Captain America. The plastic surgeon says I have the same facial bone structure as Evans, so he used him as his model."

"No, it's not him. It's a different actor." Walker snapped his fingers. "I know who it is."

"Who?"

"The guy from *Diner, Body Heat,* and *9½ Weeks.*"

"Mickey Rourke?"

"Yeah, him."

"He looks like whoever worked on his face did it blindfolded with a Weedwacker," Danny said.

"Exactly." Walker grinned, got up, and stepped out of the bath with all the grace of a rhino.

Danny turned away and didn't watch Walker leave. It wasn't just to avoid seeing the detective's naked ass. Instead, he watched the surface of the water intently, waiting for it to settle, so he could look at his own reflection in the glassy surface. Because now that he was alive again, a man reborn, Danny knew that whatever face he saw would truly be his own.

CHAPTER TWO

Reseda, California
September 4

Walker was asleep, dreaming that he stood in the dry, dusty street of a destitute Old West town, flies buzzing all around him in the oppressive heat, as he squinted at the three tobacco-chewing desperados standing in front of him. One of the desperados spit out his chew in a long, wet splurt and said: "You ready to die, Marshal?"

"Not until I've long forgotten whether I buried the three of you, or if I went to take a piss and left your scrawny bodies where they fell for the pigs and vultures."

They were all about to draw their guns when the *S.W.A.T.* theme, which Walker used as one of his ringtones, rudely interrupted the shoot-out before it could happen.

The music meant the call was from somebody at the Los Angeles County Sheriff's Department. Walker reached blindly in the dark for his iPhone on the nightstand, grabbed the device, and held it close to his eyes.

The time on the screen was 3:04 a.m. and the caller ID read DEPUTY SHARON CARTER. Walker rolled on his right side, his bare back to his wife, Carly, and put the phone to his left ear.

"Carter?" Walker whispered. He could feel the heat radiating off his wife's naked body.

"I'm really sorry to wake you, Detective," she said. "But it's urgent."

Carter was in her late twenties and a deputy in West Hollywood, where Walker and Sharpe had worked with her once to catch the arsonist behind a string of dumpster fires. Walker thought she could be overly conscientious, but she made up for it by having good instincts and not hesitating to act on them.

"What is it?" he asked.

"You've seen the apartment buildings here in West Hollywood. Many of them are built on top of open carports. Someone went around tonight torching cars under those buildings."

"Why are you calling me and not the duty officer in the arson and explosives unit?"

He could tell from Carly's breathing that she was awake now but he still kept his voice low so she could fall back to sleep.

"I did call him," Carter said. "Sergeant Gertz asked me what kind of damage was involved and if anyone was injured. I told him four buildings were hit, all within an hour and a few blocks of each other. Six cars were damaged, and one apartment was completely gutted by fire, but nobody was hurt. Gertz said the day crew could handle the investigation, there's no rush."

Gertz was a lazy-ass, counting the months until his retirement, but Walker thought he was right in this instance. The LASD's policy was to "triage" arson at night, when only a few investigators were available to cover all four thousand square miles of Los Angeles County. So the general rule was to immediately respond only to fires that involved death, major injuries, or property damage exceeding a half a million dollars. Car fires were not a high priority and were usually set by people trying to get out from under their loans. This one could be, too, the desperate lessee torching other cars to disguise his scheme. Walker had seen it happen before.

"It's the sergeant's decision to make," Walker whispered, and was about to say goodbye, when Carter quickly spoke up again.

"But those are just the car fires in West Hollywood. There are more. Out in Hollywood, cars at five more buildings were hit and so was a vehicle outside an unfinished apartment tower on Sunset."

"One right after the other?"

"Yeah, all within about two hours."

It was an arson spree. That was unusual, but with the exception of one gutted apartment, was it really much more than petty vandalism?

"What did Gertz say to that?"

"He said it's piddly shit and we don't care what burns in the city," Carter said. "Well, I do, Walker."

When Gertz mentioned "the city," Walker knew that he was referring to Los Angeles. West Hollywood was also a city, but it hired out its law enforcement to the sheriff's department and its firefighting to the county. Any crimes or fires outside WeHo's limits were problems for LA and, to the southwest, Beverly Hills. But the boundary lines were far from clear, and two sides of the same street could be in different cities. It often led to confusion and jurisdictional disputes, especially when a corpse was right on the line or in pieces scattered on both sides.

"The boundaries don't mean anything to the people on the street," Carter went on. "This is where I live and it's pure luck that nobody was killed tonight. Maybe next time somebody will be."

"What makes you think there will be a next time?"

"Instinct," she said.

Walker trusted her gut. But would putting off the investigation for a few more hours make any difference? He could go back to sleep and they could investigate the arsons when he arrived for his shift, fresh and rested.

Carter apparently guessed what he was thinking, because she said: "You can stay home, but Sharpe needs to get here before any more evidence is lost by firefighters doing their jobs. He's the one who counts."

That stung, but he knew she was right.

Sharpe was the arson expert. Walker was the manhunter. And Sharpe loved rooting around in ashes. "Text me the address of the first fire and we'll meet you there in an hour."

He ended the call and tried to slip quietly out of bed. But Carly rolled over and looked at him with heavy, sleepy eyes. "Where are you going?"

"A deputy tipped me off to a string of car fires in West Hollywood and the surrounding area." Walker opened the closet and started getting dressed in his tactical greens, the standard uniform for arson investigators and SWAT team members.

"It's not your shift."

"But the arsons will be waiting for us when we go into the office anyway, so we might as well get started on them now, while they are still hot."

Walker and Sharpe both kept gear bags, containing the necessary equipment and protective gear for gathering evidence at a fire, in their personal vehicles just in case they got called to a crime scene while they were off duty.

Carly yawned. "Aren't the duty officer and the arson detectives who are working the night shift going to be furious when they hear you're out there unassigned, investigating fires behind their backs?"

Yes, they would. Walker sat down on the edge of the bed to tie his boots. "I'll refer them to Sharpe."

"He's going to love that."

"I honestly think he will. Pissing them off is his favorite part of the job."

Sharpe was a brilliant arson investigator and he wasn't shy about letting everyone, particularly firefighters, know that. It wasn't endearing.

"You don't think any of their resentment for Sharpe will blow back on you?"

He stood up, reached for his Stetson on a side chair, and put it on. "I'm too lovable and I'm going to drive slowly so he gets there first."

"That's a very cunning plan. Do you manipulate me as adeptly?"

"I can't. You're a shrink, an expert in human behavior," he said. "And I don't know what 'adeptly' means."

She smiled at him. "Don't play dumb with me, cowboy."

"See? I can't put anything past you."

Except that he'd snuck off to Japan three months ago to talk a world-class con man and thief into committing a felony, which would make Walker an accomplice if Danny got caught. But the only cop who'd ever arrested Danny was Walker, and he wasn't entirely sure that the thief hadn't simply told him what he wanted to hear and then vanished, so he probably had nothing to worry about . . . besides going broke and his son being tormented with horrible seizures for the rest of his life.

Carly must have seen the worry on his face. "Are you okay?"

"Just shaking off a bad dream."

Walker leaned down, kissed her on the lips, and hurried off, calling Sharpe on his way out the door.

On a map, West Hollywood was shaped like a gun lying on a tabletop. The cocked hammer was up on Sunset Boulevard, the top of the barrel ran along Fountain Avenue, and the muzzle was La Brea Avenue. The grip was North Doheny Drive to the west, Beverly Boulevard to the south, and La Cienega Boulevard to the east. And the trigger was roughly at the corner of Waring Avenue and North Alfred Street, the location of the first carport fire.

The fire trucks were long gone when Walker arrived, but the street was slick with ash-blackened water and the smell of smoke still lingered in the warm night air. The neighborhood was a mix of charming little Spanish-style homes, bloated four-story condos ridiculously crammed onto tiny lots, and a handful of two-story midcentury-modern apartment buildings, their second floors perched on slim pillars over wide-open carports.

An LASD patrol car was parked in the driveway of one of those midcentury buildings, the torched remains of a BMW in the fire-blackened carport. There was some slight scorching along the front edge of the second floor where flames had licked the stucco.

Walker parked, put on his Stetson, and approached Carter, who leaned against the front grille of her patrol car and watched Sharpe, who was circling the BMW and taking pictures with his phone.

Walter Sharpe was in his fifties and had a slight bookkeeper's slouch, but his most distinctive feature was his craggy face. He'd never entirely lost his baby fat, which had sagged into folds and creases as he'd aged, making him appear perpetually weary. He knew this, of course, and shrewdly used it to his advantage with witnesses and suspects, who always underestimated him. Among the detectives and firefighters he worked with, his droopy features and dogged determination had earned him the nickname Shar-Pei, and not out of affection.

Carter glanced at Walker. "You took your time."

On purpose. Walker wanted Sharpe to get there first and finish the dirtiest aspects of the investigation before he arrived, sparing him some dry-cleaning costs.

"Traffic was terrible," he said.

"On the freeway at three in the morning?"

"In the drive-through line at McDonald's. I wanted to come here caffeinated. Where are the firefighters?"

"This was the first call Station 8 rolled on. They put the car fire out fast, then they saw a bigger fire raging on the next block and rolled on it. But that was only the beginning. They are now doing cleanup at the scene of their fifth fire of the night. It was one blaze after another."

Walker noticed some security cameras mounted on the edges of the building and an APT FOR RENT sign, with the manager's number, taped inside one of the two front windows on the second floor. "Anything on camera?"

"The manager's office is closed," she said. "I left a message. If I don't hear back by nine, I'll go there in person."

"What about the tenants? Did they see anything?"

"Two apartments are vacant and nobody seems to be home in the third."

"Then who reported the fire?"

"A neighbor across the street saw the flames at 12:58 and the firefighters were here in three minutes," she said. "The station is not even a block away."

That had probably saved the building, Walker thought.

He went over to Sharpe, who was crouched in front of the car, his open go-bag on the floor beside him. "What have you learned?"

Sharpe got to his feet. "God exists."

"How do you know?"

"Because a miracle occurred here tonight."

Walker looked around and didn't see anything miraculous or even particularly interesting. "What am I missing?"

"The firefighters didn't wash away all the evidence. The story is still here. So, given that, what can you tell me?"

Walker leaned over the car and sniffed.

"It smells like an outdoor grill. Maybe the accelerant was charcoal-lighting fluid."

"You're on the right track. Tell me what you see."

Walker circled the car, then squatted, careful not to let his pant legs touch the muck, and peered underneath the BMW. He saw a mound of mushy, brown slop. "I see a pile of dog shit under a burned car."

"The dog would have to be very limber to accomplish that."

"Another miracle." Walker straightened up. "God is great."

"It's not excrement."

"Is it puke?"

"It's the reconstituted remains of a Duraflame log." Sharpe took a clear evidence baggie from his pocket and held it up. The bag contained a scrap of yellow paper that was singed around the edges. "This is a portion of their trademark yellow wrapper."

"The log was *reconstituted?*" Walker said. "How does that happen?"

"The log burned up, but when the blazing car was sprayed with water, the waste congealed into a moist glob resembling undigested food and bile. But that's not what's significant."

"I think it is," Walker said and turned to Carter. "It reminds me of the shape-shifting liquid-metal guy in *Terminator 2.*"

"The one who looked like a cop at first," she said.

"Yeah, him. It's like that log is alive and might come back to kill us." Walker looked back at Sharpe. "That could be an arsonist sent here from the future."

Sharpe sighed, unamused. "What matters is that the flames generated by synthetic logs only rise about three to four inches and that isn't enough to reach the combustible plastics and spread the blaze throughout the car."

"So the arsonist used an accelerant," Walker said. "It's probably the lighter fluid that I smell."

"I don't know what the accelerant is." Sharpe reached down into his open go-bag, took out a tin evidence can and a garden trowel, and handed them to Walker. "Collect a sample so we can find out."

"Why don't you collect it?"

"My sciatica is acting up."

Walker knew that he'd been busted. He placed his cowboy hat on Carter's head, got down on the wet, mucky floor, and squirmed on his stomach under the car, the water soaking into his uniform.

Carter crouched beside the car and watched as Walker scraped some of the slop into the can and sealed the lid. "Why do the remains of the log look like vomit instead of a pile of black ash?"

Sharpe crouched next to her. "Synthetic logs are comprised of multiple materials, including kerosene, recycled cardboard, wax, fruit pits, sawdust, corn husks, and seeds that create a realistic wood-crackling sound when they're burning. That's why it looks like organic material that was hard to digest."

And it was all over Walker, who squirmed out from under the car, handed the can and trowel to Sharpe, and then stood up. "This arsonist isn't very bright. He could've left the log at home, doused the car with gasoline, tossed in a match, and got it burning a lot faster."

"You must still be half-asleep." Sharpe wrote something on the can with a pen and put it into his go-bag. "Think about what you just said."

Walker did that and then felt stupid. "The delay was the point. The log was a timing device."

"That's right," Sharpe said. "You might actually end up being a mediocre arson investigator someday."

"That's my dream," Walker said.

"I'm lost," Carter said. "Can someone please explain to me what you two just figured out?"

"It's called a Duraflame log for a reason," Sharpe said. "It's designed to endure, to burn steadily for three hours or more. The arsonist needed time to get to his next apartment building before this car was fully ablaze and attracted attention."

"It means your instincts were right, Carter," Walker said. "This was a premeditated spree, not a night of random vandalism, and it might not be over."

Sharpe nodded at her. "It was a smart move calling me."

"She didn't call you," Walker said. "I did."

Carter put the cowboy hat back on Walker's head. "Only because I didn't have his number."

Sharpe said: "Have your fellow deputies found any witnesses who can give us a description of the arsonist or his vehicle?"

"They haven't started asking."

"Are you saying that they aren't out there right now, canvassing the neighborhoods around the fires for witnesses?"

"That's right."

"Why the hell aren't they?"

"Because what little manpower we have at this hour is stretched to the limit just handling crowd and traffic control at all the fire scenes," Carter said. "In case you've forgotten, nobody has been officially assigned to investigate these arsons yet."

Sharpe scowled, an expression that somehow added even more lines and folds to his face. "I'm assigning us."

"You can do that?" she said.

Sharpe took out his notebook and pen. "Give me your watch commander's name and number."

"His name is Dolan," Carter said, and gave him the man's phone number. "You could use the radio instead of calling."

"I don't want what I have to say to him broadcast all over the county."

Sharpe made the call. He introduced himself by saying that he outranked the incompetent duty officer at the arson desk and that he was in charge of investigating the West Hollywood arson spree.

Carter whispered to Walker, "I thought Sharpe and Gertz were the same rank."

"If you're talking about shoulder stripes, yes, but they're not even close when it comes to experience and skill."

Sharpe told Dolan to immediately assign deputies to thoroughly canvass the neighborhoods struck by carport arsons, then said: "It's imperative to get it done before any witnesses go off to work in the morning. Call in deputies from other stations if that's what it takes."

Judging by the grimace on Sharpe's face as he listened to Dolan's response, Walker assumed that the watch commander was expressing some reluctance.

"What's the bigger risk? Quickly allocating all of your available resources to the investigation and getting your hand slapped later for overreacting," Sharpe said, "or being responsible for sabotaging a major serial arson case by wasting precious hours waiting for approval to act from a higher-up because you live in constant, quivering terror that someone might yell at you for actually doing your job."

Carter winced.

Walker whispered to her, "I think Sharpe just made another friend."

"Wise choice." Sharpe ended the call and looked at Carter. "Lead us to the next crime scene."

CHAPTER THREE

The next two carport-style apartment buildings torched in the spree fared much worse than the first one. Two cars were totally destroyed at the second place, while one car and the apartment above it were incinerated at the third. Sharpe found the remnants of synthetic logs at each of the scenes.

The last place in the string of West Hollywood arsons was unusual because it wasn't another carport apartment building. It was a ten-story unfinished condo tower, more of a shell of a building than anything else, that had stood abandoned for years at the corner of Roxbury and Sunset Boulevard, a half block west of the iconic Chateau Marmont hotel.

Sharpe, Walker, and Carter arrived at the scene at daybreak. The weedy property was surrounded by chain-link fencing, but the west-side gate on Roxbury was open and they walked through it, past a decayed, peeling billboard covered with graffiti. But under all the spray paint, Walker could still see the illustration of a shiny glass monolith called simply the Tower, "Sunset Boulevard's most prestigious address."

To his right, Walker saw the incinerated remains of a small car that was parked beside scorched, bent framing of what was once a twenty-two-foot camper trailer before it exploded. There were jagged, twisted, but recognizable pieces of the camper's ridged aluminum shell scattered everywhere, along with bits of burned particleboard and insulation. Walker assumed the camper had been the guard shack.

Straight ahead of them was the Tower itself. He saw vehicles from the Los Angeles County Fire Department, the Los Angeles Fire Department, and the Beverly Hills Fire Department parked around the building. Firefighters were still mopping up, dousing hot spots, and using a ladder truck to help a security guard come down from the fifth floor.

The only fire damage on the building that Walker could see was limited to the first and second floors, and it seemed more superficial than structural, but he wasn't an engineer. There was a big, smoking pile of burned and soggy debris—perhaps once stacks of leftover wood, PVC piping, and drywall—in the center of the lobby that the firefighters were now raking apart and spraying with water.

Walker turned to Carter. "What's the story on this place?"

"It was going to be a high-end condo tower, but inspectors discovered that it was leaning three inches to the west due to a flaw with the foundation," she said. "The construction work stopped, a shitstorm of lawsuits followed, and the Chinese developer fled to Guangzhou. Now it's a decrepit ruin, a shelter for tweakers, squatters, and prostitutes and a blank canvas for taggers."

Sharpe didn't seem to be listening. His attention was focused on the blackened husk of the incinerated car, which he was giving a thorough appraisal, walking around it slowly.

"It's tragic," he said.

"We've seen worse," Walker said.

"Those were just cars. This is a 1982 Special Service Mustang."

"How can you tell?"

Sharpe sighed, as if Walker's ignorance were exhausting. "Because of the distinctive Fox body frame, which Ford only used on the Mustang between 1979 and 1993."

"Right, of course, how could I have missed that? Everybody knows what a Fox body frame looks like." Walker glanced back at Carter, who shrugged. She didn't know what Sharpe was talking about, either.

Sharpe went on, ignoring Walker's sarcasm. "The square headlights, two on each side, and the pattern of what's left of the melted front plastic grille, indicate that it's an '82. And the driver's-side alley light is a dead giveaway that it's a Special Service model."

From where Walker stood on the passenger side, he hadn't noticed the armature of the melted spotlight, which was mounted on the windshield and could be pointed in various directions from inside the car. It was called an alley light because cops used it to light up dark alleys and alcoves as they cruised by.

"So it's an old cop car," Walker said. "Big deal."

"Not just any cop car," Sharpe said. "It's the first Mustang that Ford designed exclusively for law enforcement use. They weren't offered to the general public."

Walker said, "At least not until the Mustangs had a quarter of a million miles on them, were stripped by the police departments of their emblems, two-way radios, and light bars, and sold off for quick cash to suckers looking for a cheap ride."

Sharpe gave Walker a hard look. "My first car was a retired 1980 Plymouth Gran Fury Police Pursuit Vehicle with a fire-breathing V-8 that melted asphalt."

"How long did the old junker last?"

"I've still got it," Sharpe said.

That's when Walker saw two men he knew approaching from the Tower. They wore matching blue LAFD windbreakers and matching sour expressions that suggested they both had heartburn. It always amused him.

The man on the left, who had a pug nose that looked so wrong on his face that Walker often wondered if it was an organ transplant, spoke first. "What are you two doing here?"

Sharpe didn't look up from his examination of the Mustang. "Our jobs."

Walker turned to Carter and whispered: "That's Al Scruggs, LAFD."

The other man, who had shoulders like a boomerang and legs like twigs, said: "You're out of your jurisdiction, Shar-Pei."

Walker turned to Carter again. "That's Pete Caffrey, his partner."

Sharpe crouched beside the car. "This building is in Los Angeles County."

Scruggs pointed at the building. "Actually, the dividing line between West Hollywood and Hollywood runs right through the middle of this property."

Caffrey jumped in, as if he and Scruggs were singing a duet. "But the law enforcement jurisdiction in these situations is determined by where the front door and main driveway are, and they're on Roxbury Road. That's on our side of the line."

Sharpe stood up straight and looked at them now. "That was true of the previous building that was on this property. But it was torn down and the front door and driveway of this new building are on Sunset Boulevard, which is in West Hollywood."

"This building isn't finished yet," Caffrey said, "so who knows where the hell the front door and main driveway will be."

Carter marched over to the two men and got right in their faces. "When this building was tagged with graffiti from top to bottom, and people were screaming about what a rat-and-crackhead-infested eyesore it was, the LAPD announced that it wasn't their responsibility, that it was West Hollywood's, and that we weren't doing our jobs. *We* had to clear it out. Whenever some tweaker OD's inside and the smell of him rotting has people gagging around the pool at the Chateau, or some TikTok influencer asshole parachutes off the roof onto Sunset and causes a three-car pileup, or some stupid, horny tourist gets his dick bitten off by a whore in there, *we're* the ones who respond without any backup from you. *Now* you're saying it's your jurisdiction? What the actual fuck?"

Caffrey and Scruggs were startled, first because they hadn't noticed Carter was there, and second because they were flustered by the logic of her vehement tirade. She'd put them in a bureaucratic jam and they didn't know how to respond.

"Who are you?" Caffrey asked.

"Deputy Sharon Carter."

"We're LAFD," Scruggs said, pointing to the emblem on his windbreaker. "Not LAPD."

Sharpe snorted. "You're obviously firemen and not experienced law enforcement officers—you two have proven that repeatedly in the past and again today. You can both go home now. You're not needed here."

"Yes, they are," Walker said to Sharpe, then addressed Caffrey and Scruggs. "Look, guys, we're all chasing the same arsonist."

"We are?" asked Caffrey.

"Duraflame logs were the incendiary devices in your carport fires and ours," Walker said, then gestured to the Mustang. "And, I'm assuming, this one, too."

Scruggs nodded. "Yeah, there was a log under there. Except this time, he also cut the line on the trailer's propane tank so the car fire would blow it up."

"There you go. Same guy," Walker said. "And his technique is already evolving into something more dangerous. We need to catch him before he strikes again and causes worse damage or even kills somebody. We have a better shot at doing that if we stop squabbling over jurisdiction and combine our resources in a joint investigation."

Sharpe said, "That I will lead."

"Why you?" Caffrey asked.

"Because I'm older, smarter, and more experienced."

That was true, but also offensive. Walker spoke up quickly before the insult stung Caffrey and Scruggs too deep. "Because the county is the big gorilla, better able than the LAFD to cut through the interagency bureaucracy to marshal resources and get things done fast. You two will handle press relations and be the faces of the investigation."

Meaning they'd get all the attention and glory, which Walker figured was what they really wanted anyway.

"Why them?" Sharpe asked, but Walker knew his objection was an act. Sharpe avoided the media at all costs. He wanted Caffrey and Scruggs to think that talking to the press was important to him, which would be an added incentive for them to settle for the arrangement.

Caffrey said, "Because we're younger, better looking, and we won't antagonize the media."

"And the camera loves us," Scruggs added.

"The cameras aren't here yet," Sharpe snapped at him, "so you can start by documenting the scene and securing it until the crime scene unit gets here to collect the physical evidence."

"There were actually two fires here," Caffrey said. "There's this one at the guardhouse and there's the fire on the ground floor of the tower, where they kept all the used rags, canisters of paint, solvents, and other stuff they used to clean up the graffiti. The arsonist didn't need a fire log for that one, just some matches."

"Were there any witnesses?" Walker asked.

"There was a security guard up in the tower when it happened," Scruggs said. "A young guy, maybe in his twenties. His name is Kenneth Dodes. He inhaled some smoke and was crying hysterically when the firefighters got here, so the paramedics are checking him out. They asked us to back off while they gave him oxygen and cookies. We were just about to talk with him when you two showed up."

"We'll do it," Sharpe said, then glanced at Carter. "We're going to need a conference room at West Hollywood as our command center. Can you set that up?"

"Sure," she said.

"We'll all meet there at noon," Sharpe said. "You'll be our go-between with the officers on the street. I want to see whatever surveillance footage and witness statements that our deputies, and the LAPD's officers, have gathered by then."

"I'm on it," Carter said.

Sharpe and Walker walked away, heading toward the Tower and a paramedic unit that was parked amid the scrum of fire engines. When they were out of earshot of Caffrey and Scruggs, Walker asked: "How do you know where the front door of this building will be?"

Sharpe pointed to the deteriorating billboard that advertised the doomed condo tower. "It says 'Sunset Boulevard's most prestigious address,' not Roxbury's. I was going to point that out to Caffrey, the keenly observant detective, but then Carter made her speech, which I really enjoyed, and I didn't want to step on it."

"Okay, but why bother fighting with Caffrey and Scruggs? What difference does it make if they investigate this arson or we do?"

"This is the biggest fire in the spree and the only one that wasn't an apartment building with an open carport."

"So?"

"It could mean something and, if it does, those two idiots won't figure it out," Sharpe said. "Why'd you have to suggest a joint investigation?"

"Because we've already got three arson scenes to deal with and taking this one on, too, is a lot more work. But by bringing them in, they can do most of the drudgery while we do the high-level detecting."

"I like the way you think," Sharpe said, "when you're actually thinking."

"You have to stop showering me with compliments or it will go to my head."

They found Kenneth Dodes sitting on the bumper of the paramedic unit, wrapped in a blanket that looked like aluminum foil and eating cookies from a package of Oreos. He was a pear shape and had a greenish pallor, which Walker attributed to shock or smoke inhalation.

But one paramedic was a few yards away, talking to someone on his phone, and his partner was busy nearby, wrapping a bandage on a firefighter's hand, so Walker figured if the medical professionals weren't concerned about Dodes' health, he shouldn't be, either.

"Kenneth Dodes? I'm Andrew Walker and this is Walter Sharpe. We're LA County arson investigators. How are you feeling?"

Dodes had pulled himself together from his crying jag, but his eyes were puffy and his nose still ran a bit. "Fine. The Oreos help."

"They can cure anything," Walker said. "They're better than penicillin."

Sharpe gestured toward Roxbury. "Was that your car back there?"

Dodes nodded.

"Is it an actual Pursuit Pony?"

The question made tears well up in the young man's bloodshot eyes. "One of the original 406 Special Service Mustangs ordered by the California Highway Patrol. I have the paperwork to prove it. Not that it means anything now."

He started to cry, and Walker realized that it wasn't the fire that had made him hysterical. It was losing his car.

Sharpe squatted in front of Dodes. "It means something to me, Kenneth. That car was a classic. It's a terrible loss. Where did you find it?"

"The car belonged to an ex-cop in Fontana who kept it in his garage for decades. I bought it for $200 at his estate sale. It was a rat's nest. I spent six years restoring it." Dodes wiped his nose with the blanket. "It's like a part of me burned today."

"I know how you feel," Sharpe said. "I've been restoring an '86 Pursuit Pony for a while now."

That was news to Walker.

"Five-speed stick or automatic?" Dodes asked.

"The stick."

"That's a legend. It was clocked by the Montana State Police hitting 137 miles per hour on the test track."

"That's the one." Sharpe stood up again, his knees popping. "But I'd be happy if I could just get mine running again."

Walker said, "Sounds like you're really into cops, Kenny. How come you aren't one?"

If Dodes was offended by the question, he didn't show it. "I didn't meet the height requirement, or the weight, and I have a GED instead of a high school diploma, not that there's any difference. My application was rejected."

"So you became a security guard and made your own cop car."

"When you put it like that, it sounds sad," Dodes said. "And a little crazy."

"I don't think so." Sharpe gave Walker a scolding glance before returning his attention to Dodes. "I've been collecting cop cars all of my life. How long have you been a security guard?"

"Five years, but I've only been working here for a few months, ever since the politicians caved into the pressure and forced the bank that owns a piece of this ruin to hire full-time security."

"Pressure from who?"

Dodes pointed to the Chateau Marmont behind them. "That's where all the out-of-town celebrities and influencers stay for the Grammys and the Oscars and they like to take selfies with their view. An unfinished ten-story building populated by crackhead squatters and covered in graffiti, a lot of it dicks and gang signs, doesn't make a pretty picture."

"Unless you're the taggers," Walker said. "They take selfies, too."

"They sure do. This ruin is a magnet for them," Dodes said. "You guys ran everybody out of here in March, right before the Oscars. It was chaos. Then a crew hired by the bank hosed out all the shit and needles, painted over all the graffiti, built a fence around the property, and hired the security company I work for. Our job is to keep the squatters out and the taggers from doing it again, at least until the Emmys."

The award show was only two weeks away and would be held downtown at the Peacock Theater, which was formerly the Nokia Theatre, which was formerly the Microsoft Theater, and Walker figured would be "formerly the Peacock" as soon as someone wrote a bigger check for the naming rights.

"How's that going for you?" Walker asked.

"Hit and miss," Dodes said. "The one guard on duty each shift can't be everywhere at once, so the bank has a paint crew that comes out each week to cover up whatever tagging we can't prevent. But when there's a flash mob of taggers, swarming in here all at once like flesh-eating zombies, we call the cops and they chase them out. That happened to me two weeks ago. It was ugly, man."

"When did your shift start tonight?"

"Eleven p.m. I do one round every ninety minutes."

Sharpe said, "What is a round, exactly?"

"I go up to each floor, scan the transponder strip on the wall with my phone to show when I got there, and look for trespassers," Dodes said. "Then I go up to the next floor and do the same thing, until I reach the top, then I come back down. That takes an hour."

"That's a lot of stairs," Sharpe said.

"And I haven't lost a pound yet, which is cosmically unfair," Dodes said. "I did my first round, came back down, and was heating up some Hot Pockets for dinner when I heard the sirens and choppers."

Walker was sure he knew what happened next. "You got curious and started your next round early to take a look at what was happening from higher up."

Dodes nodded. "I saw fires all over West Hollywood. I thought maybe there was another riot, like what happened after the cops were acquitted for beating up Rodney King. I was so busy looking at that, I didn't notice my Mustang was on fire until the trailer blew up. I ran down the stairs, but I couldn't get out because the whole first floor was on fire. So I went up as high as I could go and called 911. The firefighters took forever to get here."

Walker could understand why. All the firefighters in the immediate area were tied up at other fires. It must have been chaos for the dispatchers, forcing them to call in help from Beverly Hills, Westwood, and other stations under their mutual-cooperation agreements.

"Did you see who set the fires?" Sharpe asked.

"I didn't see anybody until the firefighters finally showed up."

Walker and Sharpe thanked Dodes for his help and walked away. When they were out of earshot, Walker asked: "Do you really restore old cop cars or was that just a line to get him talking?"

"It's the truth."

Walker tipped his head back toward Dodes. "So you were that guy once."

"I was never that guy."

"The only reason you're not him is that you were a few inches taller, a few pounds lighter, and you graduated high school."

"And I'm a natural-born investigator," Sharpe said.

"Maybe he is, too, and got cheated out of his rightful destiny. He wouldn't be the only security guard who has felt that way."

"Far from it," Sharpe said. "I'm always suspicious of wannabe cops or first responders who are anywhere near an arson."

Because they were often the fire starters, especially in wilderness areas, where low-salaried first responders counted on the overtime pay from fighting wildfires to make a living. Or because they wanted the glory of stumbling on a blaze and extinguishing it. Or because they wanted to support the local economy, which was also dependent on serving meals and supplying equipment to the firefighters battling the flames.

"My first thought was that he's our guy and set this fire to rule himself out as a suspect on the others," Walker said. "But the timing doesn't work. We can confirm he was here, doing his rounds when those fires were set, by checking the transponder records, plus he was stuck in the building when the firefighters arrived."

"Unless he's figured out a brilliant way to fake his rounds, or he has an accomplice," Sharpe said. "Otherwise, Dodes has an airtight alibi for all of the fires."

"Except for this one," Walker said as they reached the debris field from the trailer explosion. "Maybe that's why this fire doesn't exactly fit the others. He wanted some attention, saw a chance at the spotlight, and took it."

Sharpe shook his head. "He'd never torch an '82 Pursuit Pony."

"Are you sure that's authentic and not the charred remains of an ordinary 1982 Mustang retrofitted to look like the real deal?"

Sharpe went over to the car, looked at the VIN plate on the dash, and snapped a picture of it with his phone.

"Can't be too careful," he said.

They'd both learned that the hard way.

"You run that VIN and supervise the evidence collection at the various arson scenes," Walker said. "I know that's what you love. I'll hit the street."

"What does that mean?"

On Walker's first day on the job, Sharpe told him that in an urban arson, the fires were almost always about revenge, making money, hiding a crime, or a combination of those motives.

"The arsonist didn't pick this neighborhood or his targets at random," Walker said. "There's got to be a motive and a common thread. I'm going to find them. I'll see you at noon."

It was a fair division of labor and they both knew it. Walker wasn't an expert in arson or forensics, but he was a relentless manhunter.

"Bring back some pizzas," Sharpe said.

Walker was good at that, too.

CHAPTER FOUR

Three Months Ago

Two days after Walker visited him at the *ryokan*, Danny Cole broke in his new identity and fake passport by flying first class on an Air New Zealand red-eye from Tokyo to Auckland, arriving at 9:30 a.m.

Danny checked into the five-star InterContinental hotel at Waitematā Harbour, practicing his limp for the cameras as he walked through the lobby, and stayed just long enough in his suite to shower and change into fresh clothes. He left the hotel, crossed Quay Street to the ferry terminal, and took a helicopter to Waiheke Island.

The helicopter cost ten times more than a ferry ticket, but it was faster and far less crowded than the boat. He shared his ride with an attractive, well-heeled young couple, the statuesque woman carrying a coveted $15,000 Hermès Birkin bag that would get her mugged within thirty seconds out in public in most major cities.

They crossed over the Hauraki Gulf, its sparkling water dotted with sailboats of all kinds, and out toward a string of islands known for their stunning beaches and breathtaking vistas. Twelve minutes later they reached the rolling hills of Waiheke Island, thirty-six square miles of rural country once populated by sheep, wineries, olive orchards, artists, and surfers that was now a retreat for the superrich christened the Hamptons of New Zealand by Auckland real estate agents.

The helicopter circled the vineyards of Chateau Le Roux, a winery and restaurant in the hills, and landed on the helipad behind the French chateau–style main house. Nobody on the property seemed impressed by their means of arrival, so Danny assumed it was a regular occurrence.

Danny helped the couple off the helicopter, then strode casually through a large potager garden and then along a path of lavender bushes and olive trees to the front terrace, which was dotted with umbrella-covered tables fashioned from wine barrels and wooden chairs aligned to face the spectacular view. The tables looked out over gentle slopes crisscrossed with grapevines and on to the Hauraki Gulf, the white sails on the water, and the distant skyline of Auckland.

He took a seat and ordered a glass of their pricey chardonnay and a charcuterie board from the stunning French waitress, and when she returned with everything, he asked for one more thing.

"Is the owner of the winery here today?"

"Oui," she said.

"Could you please tell him that the Saint is here to see him?"

It was the code name Danny had used for himself on his last heist. She nodded and went off to find her boss.

Danny sipped his wine, admired the view, and watched the couple he flew in with canoodling and drinking champagne at a nearby table.

After a few minutes, Sam Mertz showed up, a barrel-shaped man in his forties wearing an Aussie bush hat, an untucked khaki shirt, cargo shorts, and loafers over his bare feet. He held a bottle of the house chardonnay in one of his big hands and a wineglass in the other. He'd gained at least twenty pounds on his already huge frame since Danny had least seen him and his face was even ruddier.

Sam sat down heavily on the chair next to him and plucked the cork out of the bottle.

"Do I know you?"

"The last time you saw me was at the run-down farm in Paso Robles, where you, Tamiko, Alison, and I divvied up the score from the Malibu mansions we burgled and set on fire."

Sam must have recognized Danny's voice, but he was a cautious man. He poured himself a glass of wine. "That's a wild story and doesn't sound very saintly."

"I got the idea for the heist when we were convict firefighters together, fighting a blaze in Montecito. We were protecting a house with a huge art collection, including a Hockney. You said you weren't a Hockney fan. Do you remember what Arnie Soloway said?"

"Remind me."

"He said, 'Me neither, but I like it when they get into fights on the ice.'"

Only Sam, Danny, and Arnie, who died not long afterward, were in that conversation. Sam broke into a big smile and raised his glass to him.

"You got a new face."

"I had to," Danny said.

"I didn't."

"Because you weren't seen in that wildfire by anybody who is still alive or in law enforcement and you weren't presumed dead afterwards."

"Good point." Sam stole one of Danny's olives and popped it in his mouth. "What are you calling yourself now?"

"Brian Lockwood."

"It's an improvement, just like the face."

"Thanks," Danny said.

"Are you and Alison together?"

Danny shook his head. She was a civilian with a grudge of her own that he'd recruited onto their heist crew and he'd escaped the inferno with her. "She's living in Hawaii now."

"So you never . . . ?" Sam let his question trail off, the implication obvious.

"Strictly platonic. She took care of me after I got shot, and I taught her the finer points of being a fugitive from the law, not that anyone is chasing her. Nobody knows she was involved in the heist or that one even happened."

Except, perhaps, Walker and Sharpe, but Danny assumed they had their own reasons for keeping quiet about it.

"It's still a good idea for her to be careful."

"That's what I thought," Danny said. "How about you and Tamiko? Did you ever . . . ?"

"Hell no," Sam said. "She scares me."

"Me too."

"Besides, she wasn't interested in a fat old coot like me."

"You weren't so fat then."

Sam patted his belly with pride. "These are retirement pounds. It's what happens when you are happy and carefree. How is Logan?"

He was referring to another one of their convict firefighting crew, a car thief in his twenties, who'd also survived their Malibu fire heist.

"Living his dream. He's married, has two daughters, and is working as an LAFD firefighter. How's the wine business?"

"After all those years in prison, I love it out here in the country, with that amazing view. The wine is a huge success. So is the restaurant. We do a hundred weddings here a year." Sam gestured with his wineglass to the young couple. "Those two are coming up. I'm drowning in cash."

"You must have a hell of a safe."

"It's split between the bank and a wooden cask," Sam said and took another sip of his wine, savoring it. "One cask among many. Nobody knows which one but me."

"A cask isn't a very secure place for your money."

"Neither is a safe," Sam said.

"Only from you," Danny said.

"There are a lot of other top safecrackers and explosive experts out there, which makes me wonder what you are doing here. It's not for the wine and cheese or to check up on me."

"We didn't finish the job."

"We pulled off a heist for the ages and got away with tens of millions of dollars each and nobody knows the crime even happened. You don't finish better than that."

"That was the score," Danny said. "Not the job."

"Soloway's widow and his kids are set for life, too."

"But Roland Slezak, the man who got Arnie killed, is richer than ever before. We didn't truly avenge Arnie's death. Slezak still needs to pay."

Sam studied him for a moment. "Is that what you think about now when you look in the mirror and see a face you don't recognize: Was it worth it?"

"I'm still the same man inside."

"A softy. I got news for you. I didn't do the job for Arnie. I did it for the money, for this." Sam swept his arm out at the vineyard and the view in front of them. "I can look in the mirror without a problem. I could even if it wasn't my own face staring back at me."

"I don't like to leave things undone."

"What do you want to do about it? You're not going to kill him. That's not your style."

Danny had some of his wine and said: "I'll settle for destroying his life."

"Which involves a heist or you wouldn't be talking to me," Sam said. "Maybe you haven't noticed, but I'm retired and I certainly don't need the money."

"Good, because there isn't a dime in it for us."

"If I don't need the money, and I don't give a shit about revenge, why should I do it?"

Danny met his eye but said nothing, waiting for Sam's conscience to do its work.

"Shit." Sam finished his drink and refilled their glasses. "Are we visiting Tamiko next?"

"Do you know where she is?"

"I do, but it's a long trip," Sam said. "Can you fly commercial with that new face?"

"I did to get here, but that was only to test my new credit cards and passport. Otherwise, I prefer to fly private," Danny said. "It's more convenient and less complicated."

"But mostly you do it because you're insanely rich and it's a decadent, wonderful indulgence you used to only dream about."

Danny shrugged. "I do enjoy the finer things in life."

"If that were true, you'd be content just sitting here with me drinking a $1,500 bottle of wine and looking at that incredible view," Sam said. "You wouldn't be contemplating some outrageously risky, highly illegal heist, the kind of thing a brilliant criminal would do to be as wealthy as us. The truth is that pulling off an elaborate heist or a perfect con is your idea of the finer things in life."

Danny certainly couldn't argue with that. Instead, he took a slim leather wallet out of his pocket and set it on the table.

"Hermès," Sam said. "Nice."

"It's not mine." Danny tipped his head to the next table, where the man he flew in with was patting his pockets and looking frantically around for something while his girlfriend flushed with embarrassment and the waitress stood by, patiently holding her credit card reader.

Sam smiled mischievously at Danny. "You picked his pocket?"

"To find out if I was still in shape."

"You devil," Sam said.

"You can tell them that somebody found it near the helipad and gave it to a member of your staff." Danny thought this was one of the few places where somebody would actually return a wallet, especially one worth far more than the hundreds of dollars in cash that it contained.

"I can't believe you're giving it back."

"Consider it my wedding gift to that charming young couple."

"Screw them." Sam took the wallet and slipped it into a cargo pocket on his shorts.

"You just told me that you're drowning in money."

Sam shrugged and had some more wine. "I could use a new wallet and we don't have an Hermès store on the island."

"Not yet," Danny said.

"You also reminded me today of something important, spiritual, and dare I say, profound."

"What's that?"

"I'm a criminal," Sam said.

Five days later, Danny Cole and Sam Mertz were sitting together again, this time at a table set for three on the immaculate lawn behind a charming chalet in Walenstadt, a lakeside village nestled in Switzerland's Appenzell Alps. The men were sipping ice-cold Appenzeller Alpenbitter liqueur, smoking Partagás Serie E No. 2 Gran Reserva Cuban cigars, and admiring the dramatic view of the jagged Churfirsten peaks against the cobalt-blue skies. In the center of the table were a platter of sandwiches, an assortment of pastries, and a pair of high-powered Barska Gladiator Zoom binoculars.

Danny blew out some smoke and said, "How much longer until Tamiko gets here for lunch?"

Sam looked at his watch, a $2 million A. Lange & Söhne Grand Complication that was among those stolen from Roland Slezak. "Any minute." He picked up the binoculars and looked at the mountains. "There she is."

Danny didn't see or hear anything. "Is she arriving by chopper?"

"That would be too easy." Sam handed Danny the heavy binoculars. "Look up at the Hinterrugg."

Danny trained the binoculars on the sharpest, highest peak with the most jagged edges and flicked the zoom lever with his thumb. He was startled to see an enormous red flying squirrel on a rapid descent toward them.

But it wasn't a squirrel.

It was a person wearing what looked to Danny like an aerodynamic version of a ribbed air mattress flying horizontally downward at a high speed, swooping frighteningly close to the sheer cliff faces and spiky outcroppings of the stony foothills.

It was like watching Superman with a death wish.

Danny glanced at Sam, who seemed amused by his reaction. "That's Tamiko?"

"Yep," Sam said. "She made the four-hour hike up there before sunrise just so she could fly this line."

"Line?"

"The flight path down from the peak. They call this one the Trench Line because she has to fly through a very narrow, crooked ravine and then over the top of a tall forest."

"Wouldn't it be faster and safer to pick a route without so many obstructions?"

"The obstructions are what they want. The goal is to get as close to cliff faces, jagged outcroppings, treetops, rooftops, and anything else sticking out that you can slam into. It's called proximity flying. It heightens the sense of speed."

"She doesn't care about the speed," Danny said. "It's all about cheating death."

"You say that as if you've never met Tamiko before," Sam said. "Of course that's why she does it. But for the rest of the wingsuit fliers, it's also about shooting amazing GoPro videos, posting them on YouTube, getting a gazillion views, and scoring a corporate sponsorship so their hobby becomes their job."

Tamiko didn't need anybody to see her, except perhaps Danny right now, and she certainly didn't need the money. She was a Japanese American in her early thirties who'd been dishonorably discharged from the military, where he assumed she'd probably learned to parachute out of planes and maybe even jump off cliffs. She was both the muscle and the eye candy on Danny's jobs. She felt cheated if she didn't get to sleep with someone or taste some blood along the way. She usually got the sex, but not the violence. If she had a choice between the two, he was sure she'd pick the bloodshed.

She disappeared into the gorge and he waited for her to come out the other side.

"How dangerous is wingsuit flying?" Danny asked.

"Russian roulette is safer and you don't have to make a four-hour hike first to experience the thrill."

Tamiko shot out of the crack like a rocket and swept low over the treetops, missing them by mere inches. She was showing off.

Danny set the binoculars on the table and took a sip of his thirty-proof Appenzeller Alpenbitter. He didn't need the binoculars to see her now.

As soon as Tamiko cleared the forest, she pulled the chute and shot up into a vertical, rather than horizontal, fall and then expertly navigated herself to a perfect pinpoint landing right in front of their table.

It was an entrance that James Bond would envy.

"Nice of you to drop in," Danny said, as if her arrival was about as interesting as watching her open a door.

Tamiko studied the stranger in front of her and began unhitching her harness. "Do you know what happens when I pull the rip cord?"

"You thank God that the parachute actually opened?"

"I come," she said. "The climax is all consuming, stronger than anything I can achieve with a man or woman."

"Good for you," Danny said, and flicked the ashes of his cigar on the grass. "Personally, I'd rather stay in bed. If you fall off, you don't get killed."

She glanced at Sam. "How do you know this pretty boy is really Danny Cole?"

"You don't recognize his voice and that attitude?"

"He could be good at impressions."

"He proved himself to me," Sam said. "Make him prove it to you."

Tamiko unzipped herself from her suit and stepped out of it wearing a skintight yoga-style tank top and shorts.

"Istanbul," Tamiko said.

Danny set down his cigar, stood up, and kissed her as if he wanted to take her where she stood. She grabbed his ass and pulled him closer. When he finally broke off the kiss, she pushed him away and grinned.

"You're Danny Cole. No doubt about it."

He calmly sat down in his chair and picked up his cigar. His lust gone in an instant. It was entirely an act. Or at least that's how he wanted it to appear.

Sam said to her, "You could tell from one kiss?"

"I'd also recognize the feel of his tight ass with a blindfold on."

Sam looked quizzically at Danny. "I thought you two never . . ."

Tamiko answered before Danny could. "We haven't, not that I wouldn't, or that I have stopped trying."

She poured herself an Alpenbitter, drank it as a shot, and sat down sullenly in the empty chair at the table.

Danny had a rule that he never slept with any women in his crew before, during, or after a job, because it might cloud his judgment. He'd never shared that rule with Sam and wasn't going to now. Instead, he explained the kiss. "We were pulling off a jewel heist during an embassy party and we got caught somewhere we shouldn't have been."

"In a closet," Tamiko added. "Down the hall from the bedroom with the safe."

"We had to convince the guards that we were just two horny party guests who couldn't wait to rip each other's clothes off."

"Danny is a very good actor," Tamiko said, and picked out a sandwich from the platter. "I'm not. I still haven't forgiven him for leaving me that night with blue balls."

"You don't have balls," Sam said.

Danny gestured with his cigar to the wingsuit and parachute on the grass. "I guess you didn't see what she just did."

Sam said, "So it wasn't really his sloppy kiss or his flabby ass that convinced you, it's that nobody else was in that closet except the two of you. Only Danny would know to kiss you when you mentioned Istanbul."

Tamiko took a bite of her sandwich and, with food still in her mouth, said to Danny: "I'm in."

"I haven't even made my pitch."

She swallowed her food. "You don't have to."

"You could end up in prison if it goes wrong."

"Shut up before you make it sound so dull that I back out." She took another bite of her sandwich.

Sam sighed. "Spoken like someone who has never been in prison. Danny and I have."

She held up a finger, indicating that she intended to respond after she swallowed her food this time, and then she spoke.

"If our last heist went wrong, I faced having my appendages amputated by a drug cartel or being burned alive in a raging inferno. The risk of arrest is about as scary to me as the possibility of stubbing my toe."

"Well, it scares me," Sam said, then looked at Danny. "I'd like to know what we're stealing."

"The world's most valuable watch from the world's most impregnable museum."

"You have plenty of expensive watches from our last heist." Sam held up his arm to show off his A. Lange & Söhne Grand Complication. "We all do."

"It isn't for me," Danny said. "It's bait."

Tamiko poured herself another Alpenbitter. "Will I get to shoot anyone?"

"You might," Danny said.

She drank the shot and poured herself one more. "Do I get to sleep with anyone?"

"You just got done saying jumping off a cliff is the best climax ever."

"But I can't do that every day," she said.

Sam raised an eyebrow. "You have sex every day?"

"You eat every day, don't you?"

"It's not the same thing," Sam said.

"You poor man," she said, then faced Danny. "What's in this heist for us?"

Sam answered for him. "Nothing. We're doing it for Danny."

Who said: "Danny Cole is dead. It's Brian Lockwood now."

Sam held up his hands. "Excuse me, we're doing it for our old friend Brian. He's going after Roland Slezak again."

Tamiko appeared confused. "Didn't we already hit him?"

"Not hard enough," Danny said. "He's still standing."

"That's easy to fix," she said. "I'll kill him."

"I don't kill people."

"I do."

"I appreciate the offer," Danny said, "but I'd rather do it the hard way. Besides, it's more fun."

Sam took a puff of his cigar and blew out a stream of smoke. "The truth is, Brian misses the challenge of a big heist. Slezak is just an excuse."

"It doesn't feel like it to me," Danny said. "It feels like making up for a broken promise."

"That's the problem with having a conscience," Sam said.

Tamiko nodded in agreement. "It's going to be the death of you."

"Maybe it will be," Danny said, "but I'd rather go that way than jump off a cliff."

Sam said, "Where is this museum?"

"Deep inside a mountain on an island in Japan."

"Do you have a plan?"

"Not yet," Danny said and took a drag of his cigar. "But I'm sure I'll think of something."

Sam said, "I should have stayed in my vineyard."

Tamiko said, "I'm getting aroused."

"That just means you're awake," Sam said. "Have something more to eat, maybe it will go away."

Tamiko took another bite of her sandwich and unabashedly studied Danny as she chewed. "It's so weird hearing your voice coming out of a different face. It's like watching a foreign movie that's been dubbed into English."

"Imagine how it feels for me," he said.

"I got new boobs," she said.

He'd noticed. "That's different."

"Not if you're a woman," she said. "More men talk to my boobs than to my face."

CHAPTER FIVE

September 4

Walker called the property manager of the North Alfred Street apartment building, the first one targeted in the carport arson spree, and asked the woman who answered about reviewing the security camera video. She told him the cameras were dead, and had been for some time. He wanted to know why, but she said he'd have to ask the owner, a man named Bert Garant, who was at the building now. So Walker went to see him.

Garant was up on a ladder in loose-fitting painter's overalls, rolling white paint over the scorch marks on the front of the building, when Walker arrived in his Ford F-150, parked in the driveway, and got out.

"Mr. Garant?"

"That's me," Garant said, running his roller through the paint tray resting on top of his ladder. He was tall and thin and maybe in his forties, with a gray mustache that matched his wild Albert Einstein hair. "You must be the arson cop. My secretary told me you were coming."

"You're moving fast to clean the place up."

"I've got two empty apartments and I can't rent them if the place looks like a freeway overpass, so I keep plenty of paint around to cover up the graffiti, but it's like Whac-A-Mole."

"Then why'd you turn your cameras off?"

"They don't scare the taggers away and just get me into more trouble."

Walker didn't see what trouble that could be, but it begged another question. "Then why are the cameras still up?"

"It impresses the new tenants," Garant said. "It makes them feel secure, except for the ones who want to make out in the driveway."

"I don't understand."

Garant set the brush down in the tray and stepped carefully down the ladder.

"A year or so back, an old couple walking their dog saw one of my tenants giving her boyfriend a blow job in his parked car and complained to me," he said. "So I confronted her with the porno video and evicted her. She sued me, for invasion of privacy among other things, and my spineless insurance company settled with her, over my objections."

"Does she hold a grudge?"

"I do. I'm the one who's got huge premiums now and a massive deductible. It'd make more sense if I went to her place and burned her car, which is probably a new Mercedes, thanks to the settlement she got. It's why I can't afford to have empty units."

"Have you evicted anybody else lately who didn't take it well?"

"I haven't evicted anyone since the lawsuit," Garant said.

"How about before?"

"There have been some," he said, "even a few deadbeats that the deputies had to drag out of here."

"I'd like a list of your past and present tenants," Walker said.

"Only if you show me a warrant," Garant said. "I don't want to get sued again for violating anybody's privacy."

That was fair enough, Walker thought. The guy had lawsuit PTSD. Besides, Walker could get a list from the West Hollywood station of the tenants that the deputies had to forcibly evict. That would be a start.

Walker gestured to the torched BMW. "What can you tell me about the tenant who owns the car?"

Garant hesitated, so Walker added: "I know his name is Jack Monty. I got it off his license plate. I'd like to talk with him, that's all."

"Jack is an actor, shooting a science fiction TV series up in Vancouver right now," Garant said. "But I don't think this has anything to do with him."

"Why not?"

"He's a super-nice guy. Volunteers at soup kitchens, that kind of thing. Sometimes one of his fans will show up here, painted purple, wanting to speak to him in Umgluck, but they're harmless."

"Umgluck?"

"Or Gluckum, something like that," Garant said. "I don't watch the show. I called Jack this morning and told him what happened."

"Did he sound frightened or concerned?"

"Just pissed about his car. He called me back ten minutes later and said his insurance adjuster will get his ass here quick and remove the wreck so I can start showing the empty units as soon as possible. See? Super-nice guy."

"Have any gangs threatened you for covering up their graffiti?"

"Why bother? They've got a billboard across the street," Garant said, nodding to the apartment building directly across from his own. "The old coots who live there gave up painting over the shit years ago."

Walker looked across the street. He'd seen the building last night, when Carter had gestured to it, but now, in the daylight, he noticed the graffiti on the curbside wall. It wasn't the usual spray-painted gang tagging. It was a caricature of a well-known politician nuzzling the breasts of the Statue of Liberty while she blew out her torch. The politician and Lady Liberty were ridiculously rounded, like overinflated dolls. Walker didn't understand the message, if there was one.

"Show some pride of ownership, for God's sake," Garant continued, "or at least some selfish interest in neighborhood property values. But they're sure quick to complain when they see consenting adults having sex in their personal vehicle."

"Or when they see a fire," Walker said. "The old coots were the ones who called it in. If it wasn't for them, this might have been a lot worse. Is that the same graffiti that was on your place?"

"Yeah," Garant said. "That shit is everywhere."

Walker thanked Garant for his help, walked across the street, and took a picture of the graffiti in case it was some new kind of turf tagging that someone in the gang unit might be able to identify.

Over the next few hours, he visited each of the apartment buildings again and spoke to the other landlords and property managers. No motives or patterns had emerged for him by noon, when he picked up some pizzas and went to the West Hollywood sheriff's station at the corner of Santa Monica and San Vicente Boulevards.

The station was a low-rise, redbrick bunker that would have looked far less squalid, miserable, and governmental if it weren't literally in the shadow of the Pacific Design Center, a monstrously large, irregularly shaped blue glass building, derisively known as the Blue Whale, that was flanked by two other gigantic, garishly colorful siblings, one green, the other bright red.

Walker went inside carrying four large pizzas and found his way to the windowless conference room set aside for them. Sharpe, Carter, Caffrey, and Scruggs were busy taping and pinning papers and photographs to the walls to document the investigation so far. He saw a desktop computer on a table and a TV set in one corner that were probably old enough to be sent to the Smithsonian for display.

He set the pizzas down on the long, chipped, and scratched table and then browsed the redecorated walls. There were pictures of the apartment buildings, the burned cars, and the Tower. There was a map of West Hollywood and Hollywood with pins marking the locations of each fire. And there were screenshot printouts of a guy wearing a baseball cap and gray hoodie, a black surgical mask over his nose and mouth. The guy was carrying a black backpack, the kind used by students, not campers.

Walker tapped the screen grab with a knuckle as Sharpe approached him. "Is that our suspect?"

Sharpe nodded. "I'll fill everybody in while we eat."

Walker lowered his voice so nobody but Sharpe could hear him. "Have you heard from the boss?"

He was referring to the lieutenant in charge of the arson and explosives unit.

"Gertz filed a formal complaint against us for undertaking an investigation on his watch without his knowledge or approval. Norris and Baumgarten, the lead investigators on the night shift, informally complained, saying we're making them look like dipshits."

"Are you worried about that?"

"They *are* dipshits," Sharpe said. "We spend half our days going back to their crime scenes and finding obvious clues they overlooked, though to be fair to them, that wasn't the case last night."

Sharpe was never fair to those two, Walker thought. Norris and Baumgarten were capable, earnest, hardworking detectives—they just weren't brilliant, like Sharpe. Few people were. But Walker wasn't going to argue about it now.

"I meant about the formal complaint."

"Gertz isn't the only one counting the days until his retirement. So is the lieutenant. If we're reprimanded, it won't be very harsh."

Sharpe told everyone to grab some lunch and sit down. Carter brought in some paper plates and soft drinks, and while everyone ate, Sharpe went over the timeline of the fires, the number of properties hit in both jurisdictions, and that they were all started with Duraflame logs augmented with a flame booster.

"We have security camera footage from two apartment buildings showing a man dressed in a plain gray hoodie, wearing a baseball cap under his hood, and carrying a book bag–style backpack," Sharpe said. "We don't see him setting any fires, just walking into the carports from out of frame. Unfortunately, he's tilting his head so the visor of his baseball cap completely hides his face from the cameras."

Walker didn't think it was luck. "He already knew where the cameras were."

Caffrey said, "You think he cased these places before tonight."

Walker shrugged. "Or he was already familiar with them for another reason. Maybe he's the mailman, or the cable TV installer, or the guy who checks the gas meter."

Sharpe pointed to pictures of a white Camry and a white panel van on the wall. "These vehicles were captured by security cameras in the area. It could be residents or Uber drivers, or it might be the arsonist's vehicle."

Scruggs said, "Maybe he's someone who lived at those places or got evicted from them."

"I haven't got all the tenant lists yet—one owner is making me get a warrant—but so far I haven't come across any names in common among the properties that got hit."

Carter added, "The same goes for people the sheriff's department forcibly evicted over the last five years. I checked that out after I got your call, Walker. The buildings don't have common owners or operators, either. I checked that, too."

"Good work," Walker said, appreciating her initiative. He hadn't asked her to check into the owners. "Thanks to you, now we know these arsons aren't about a grudge against a particular landlord or property management company."

Sharpe grimaced. "We've got to be missing something. This is urban arson, so we know the fires have got to be about revenge, money, or hiding a crime."

"Okay," Scruggs said. "But why last night? What set him off?"

"And what was he trying to accomplish?" Caffrey asked.

Sharpe said, "I think I have the answer to your question, Caffrey, and it was the first thing I noticed when I got to the scene."

"The torched Mustang?" Walker asked.

"The firefighters from all the different stations and departments." Sharpe went to the map that was marked with pins. "Setting so many fires in such close proximity over such a short period of time occupied all of the fire stations in the immediate area. Ordinarily, with Hollywood Station 41 right there on Sunset and West Hollywood Station 8 just a couple of miles south on Santa Monica, firefighters would have been at the Tower in five minutes. Hollywood Fire Station 27 and West Hollywood Station 7 could also have responded quickly. Instead, with all those other fires going, they were all occupied and the dispatcher had to pull in firefighters from much further away in Beverly Hills, Westwood, and La Brea."

Walker said, "You think the arsonist's goal was to make sure the Tower burned down."

"Makes sense," Caffrey said. "Maybe the developer hired the arsonist to get out from under his legal problems with the property."

"How about the bank?" Scruggs said. "They have a lot of money tied up in that land. Burning the place down could be one way of getting it back. Or maybe the hotel did it because they don't want that eyesore in front of their place anymore."

"I've got another theory," Carter offered tentatively, "but I don't know how it applies to the Tower."

"Go ahead," Sharpe said, "let's hear it."

"Nearly 50 percent of the people who live in West Hollywood identify as LGBTQ, and more than half of those are gay men. I'd say at least 90 percent of tenants in the buildings that were hit are gay."

Scruggs smirked. "You asked them all about their sexual orientation?"

"No, of course I didn't." Carter hesitated, as if unsure whether she wanted to go on. But she seemed to make a decision, took a deep breath, and said: "I don't want to sound like I'm profiling, especially as a queer woman myself, but it was obvious to me that the people I spoke to were gay."

"I can't tell you're gay," Caffrey said.

Scruggs turned to him. "Maybe you could if she wasn't wearing the uniform."

Carter said, "What does *that* mean?"

"She may be onto something," Walker said. "While I was waiting for the pizzas, I googled Jack Monty, the owner of the first car that was torched. He's gay, a self-proclaimed LGBTQ activist, and plays a nonbinary alien on *Beyond the Beyond* that can mate with any living entity."

"Science Officer Glorp," Scruggs said. "A purple Umgluck, an amoeba-like glob that doesn't have to consider anatomical differences."

"You watch the show?" Caffrey said, clearly surprised.

"The special effects are amazing. The ship's counselor is a woman with mechanical breasts."

Now Caffrey was intrigued. "What do the breasts do?"

"Getting back to the gay motive," Carter said, "the bank that financed the Tower is based in West Hollywood and was founded by one of the richest gay men in America."

Caffrey turned to her. "You think we're dealing with a psychotic homophobe?"

Scruggs said. "Maybe he's got a hard-on against all the gays because they're overrunning his community and getting the best apartments."

Carter said, "A hard-on."

"It's a figure of speech," Scruggs said. "It means a grudge, and yeah, I was being cute, but now that I think about it, maybe the arsonist is sexually conflicted himself, and that's where his rage is coming from, so he's cleansing it with fire. I've heard about this kind of thing before."

"Where?"

"One of Glorp's mechanical breasts," Scruggs said.

"They talk?" Carter said.

Something was troubling Walker about the Tower being the arsonist's target but he was having a hard time pinning down exactly what it was. He looked at Sharpe. "Did you run that VIN?"

Caffrey said, "What VIN?"

"On the security guard's Mustang, the car that burned at the Tower," Walker said.

"I did," Sharpe said. "Dodes told us the truth. His car was an original 1982 Special Service Mustang."

Scruggs frowned. "Is that supposed to mean something?"

"It means the security guard isn't a suspect," Sharpe said. "He loved that car."

Now Walker understood what was nagging him. "And his love would have shown. I bet that car sparkled, even at night."

Scruggs turned to Walker. "What's your point?"

"If the arsonist's goal was for the Tower to burn, why waste time hitting the security trailer and the guard's car first?"

"That's easy," Caffrey said. "To distract the guard from the real fire while it was being set."

Walker shook his head. "I don't think so. It feels personal to me. He hit something the security guard loved."

Scruggs snapped his fingers. "What if we're looking at this from the wrong angle? Maybe it's not about the *buildings*, it's about the *cars*."

Sharpe stared at Scruggs in astonishment. "My God, you could be right."

"You don't have to sound so damn shocked," Scruggs said.

"You and Caffrey work that angle. Get a list of all the makes and models of the torched cars and see if there's any kind of pattern. And while you're at it, check out the drivers, too, and see if they have any traffic accidents or altercations in common, like a drunk driving citation or running a bicyclist off the road. Let's also chase the forensics. The arsonist used Duraflame logs and seems familiar with this neighborhood and its fire stations." Sharpe pointed at Carter. "You and your deputies check every local grocery store, hardware store, or sporting goods shop and see if anybody bought a carton or two of Duraflame logs lately."

Carter nodded. "I'll also get a list from the DMV of white panel vans and Camrys registered to people in the area."

Scruggs looked pointedly at Sharpe. "What are you and Walker going to do? Take a nap?"

"We're going to focus on the Tower fire and reinterview the security guard."

Walker said, "I'm also going to check back with the landlords and property managers to see if they share the same rejected rental applicant."

Scruggs snapped his fingers again. "That could be our psychotic homophobe."

"With the hard-on," Carter added.

Sharpe checked his watch. "Unless someone makes a break in the case, we'll meet back here at 8:00 a.m. tomorrow and compare notes again."

Everyone stood up, Scruggs snatching another slice of pizza for the road.

Caffrey said to Sharpe: "What do we tell the press in the meantime? They've already started calling public information officers at the fire department."

"Here too," Carter added.

"Tell them it's an active investigation and that we have nothing to share at this time," Sharpe said, and he hurried out of the conference room with Walker.

Once they were in the parking lot, Walker led them to his truck and they got inside.

As soon as the door was closed, Sharpe said: "I hope Scruggs isn't right about the cars."

"Why?"

"It'll mean I missed something simple and obvious, a sure sign that I'm suffering from diminished mental capacity."

Walker started the engine. "Don't exaggerate. You're just tired. We all are."

Sharpe shook his head. "The day one of those idiots spots something that I don't is the day I retire."

CHAPTER SIX

Kenneth Dodes lived in a small 1950s-era tract home in Simi Valley. The front lawn was dead, just like those of most of the other homes in the neighborhood. It was the same in Walker's neighborhood. Everybody had capped their sprinklers after years of drought and water rationing in Southern California. The drought had ended, but most people hadn't bothered to replant and weren't eager to begin paying gardeners and big water bills again. That included Walker, who was trying to save money for his son's medication.

As Walker and Sharpe drove up to the house, a local TV news van was leaving. Walker was glad they were in his personal pickup truck rather than an official vehicle or the reporters might have stopped and tried to get a quote out of them, too.

"This is just the beginning," Walker said. "I'll bet Dodes is on every newscast tonight. Are we sure he's not the arsonist?"

"I'm sure," Sharpe said.

Walker parked his pickup at the curb. They walked up to the front door and Sharpe rang the bell.

Dodes called out from inside: "Go away! I have no comment!"

Walker looked at Sharpe. "Well, that's a surprise."

Sharpe raised his voice. "It's Detective Sharpe and Detective Walker. We just want a quick word."

Dodes rushed up to the door and they could hear him sliding open several dead bolts and a chain before he opened the door. "I'm so sorry, I thought you were more reporters. Come in."

He motioned them inside, closed the door, and led them into his living room. He was barefoot and had changed out of his uniform and into a T-shirt and sweatpants.

The house was immaculate and the few pieces of furniture clearly belonged to an old person. The tables, couches, and armchairs weren't collectible antiques but dated pieces from another era, the kind Walker saw the elderly bring with them when they moved into "active senior living" apartments. He figured Dodes had inherited them from his grandparents, perhaps along with the house, because they weren't living there anymore. There wasn't any artwork on the walls or a lifetime of knickknacks. There was just a big-screen TV, a PlayStation 2, and a stack of gaming magazines.

Walker asked, "Why don't you want to talk with the press?"

"And tell them what? That I was stuck in the building, crying over my car, and had to be rescued by firefighters? Not a very heroic picture."

Sharpe went to the couch, moving aside a gaming controller and a TV remote, and sat down. "You could leave the crying part out and just tell them the rest. You have nothing to be ashamed of."

"Talking about it just makes it worse." Dodes sat down in one of the matching tall-backed armchairs that faced the couch. "It's like seeing your dog run over by a truck again and again and knowing you couldn't do anything to save him."

Walker remained standing, taking a spot by the TV. "We aren't going to make you relive what happened last night. We're interested in what might have happened before that."

"I don't understand," Dodes said.

"Have you made any enemies on the job?"

"Oh, so *that's* what this is about. I had nothing to do with it. The security company's lawyers told me I'm totally in the clear. It was an accident."

"What was?"

"I already mentioned it to you," Dodes said. "A few weeks ago a mob of taggers, more than I could handle, hit the building all at once, so I called the police. As soon as the taggers heard the sirens, they scattered like cockroaches. One of them fell down two flights of stairs, but the rest got away."

Sharpe said, "Do you think the injured tagger might hold a grudge?"

"I'm not sure he can hold a thought," Dodes said. "He cracked his skull open like a melon. Last I heard, he was in a coma."

Aha, Walker thought. *Now we're getting somewhere.*

Sharpe said, "Have you had any blowback from the other taggers?"

"No, nothing," Dodes said, then a thought occurred to him. "Do you think they're the ones who torched my car? That they were coming after me for what happened to their friend?"

I do, Walker thought. But what he said was: "We're exploring every possibility."

Sharpe stood up. "Thanks again for your help."

"Anytime." Dodes got up, too, and led them back to the door. "In fact, if you ever need a second pair of hands when you're working on your '86 Pursuit Pony, give me a call."

Sharpe smiled. "I'll do that."

They left the house. Walker pulled out his phone and dialed on his way to the truck.

"Who are you calling?" Sharpe asked.

"Cedars-Sinai Hospital. That's probably where they took the injured tagger."

Walker got on the line, identified himself, asked about the injured tagger, and was transferred to the duty nurse in the intensive care unit. He identified himself again and asked if the tagger was there and if he was still in a coma.

"That would be Mateo Bonilla," the nurse said. "But he's no longer here."

"When was he released?"

"He died yesterday afternoon," she said.

Walker thanked her, disconnected the call, and turned to Sharpe. "I know what sparked the arson spree last night."

Forty minutes later, Walker and Sharpe sat across a desk from Annette Minty, a Cedars-Sinai administrator in charge of something—the two detectives didn't know her full title. But her cramped office, barely wide enough to hold her desk, file cabinet, two desk chairs, and a potted plant in hospice care, suggested to Walker that she wasn't a woman who wielded enormous power.

She opened a thin file on her desk and peered at the single page through reading glasses that had a beaded strap to keep them from falling off her wide, flat nose and into her deep cleavage, where she'd stored some Kleenex tissues and, Walker thought, perhaps some acorns for the winter.

"Mateo Bonilla, age thirty-three, was brought in by paramedics two weeks ago. He was unaccompanied by friends or family, so all we know about him was obtained from the California driver's license in his wallet. There was no insurance card."

Walker said, "That must have been a disappointment."

She lifted her head and removed her glasses, letting them drop to her grand bosom so she could glower at Walker without any filter on the intensity of her disdain.

"We are required by law to immediately provide emergency treatment regardless of whether the individual can pay for service. It's also our moral and ethical responsibility as physicians."

"But you keep a running tab," Walker said. "Did he have a credit or debit card?"

"A debit card from Wells Fargo," Minty said. "We did try to use the information we had to contact Mateo Bonilla's family, friends, or coworkers."

"You mean anyone who might be able to pay."

"I mean anyone who might be concerned that their loved one or colleague was in a coma in intensive care," Minty said in a stern tone that implied both a correction and a reprimand. "Unfortunately, we were unable to locate anyone, but we did learn that Mr. Bonilla lived in Hollywood and was self-employed as a graphic artist."

Sharpe asked for Bonilla's address, which Minty gave to him and he wrote down. It was in West Hollywood. "Did anybody come to see him?"

"His boyfriend, or so he said he was. His name was Toniel Novar. He wasn't helpful in our inquiries regarding the patient's family, or whether Mr. Bonilla had given anybody a durable power of attorney or a copy of his advance-care directives."

Walker said, "In case you wanted to pull the plug and free up the bed for a paying customer."

"In case Mr. Bonilla didn't want us to take extreme measures to prolong his life if it meant that he'd remain in a vegetative state. Or if, after his passing, he wished to donate his healthy organs to save someone else's life. Surely you've given some thought to such directives yourself, Detective, considering your profession. If not, I recommend that you do."

"I'm having my body frozen so I can be defrosted in a hundred years and hunt down the descendants of whoever killed me."

And from the way Minty was glaring at him, Walker thought they could be her great-grandchildren.

"Getting back to Mateo Bonilla," Sharpe said. "Was Toniel Novar at his bedside when he died?"

"He held Mr. Bonilla's hand as he gently passed," Minty said. "It was very sad, but also quite touching."

Walker half expected her to take a tissue out of her cleavage and dab the nonexistent tears from her eyes. "You were there?"

"No, of course not," Minty said. "I heard about it from the nurses. I went to the ICU immediately, though, to ask Mr. Novar about his wishes regarding the disposition of the body, but he practically shoved me out of the way as he ran out of the hospital."

"You didn't chase after him?"

"Why would I do that? He was heartbroken."

"Because you're stuck with Bonilla's body and a few hundred grand in medical-care costs and Novar was your only lead to unloading all of that," Walker said. "Or have you found someone else?"

"As I told you before, Detective, we haven't located any loved ones. But it's only been twenty-four hours. I'm hoping you might be able to provide us with some information as your inquiries progress."

Walker smiled and got up. "You'll be our top priority."

Sharpe thanked her for her help, left her his card, and they walked out.

For Walker, it felt like he was escaping from a stalled elevator, though it didn't prevent him from heading straight for an actual elevator. At least Annette Minty wouldn't be in it.

Sharpe said, "Why were you so hostile to that administrator?"

"They all pretend like they want to help people, but they just want to bleed you for your money. Only millionaires can afford to pay the outrageous cost of medical care and prescription medication."

"It's why we have insurance," Sharpe said.

Walker punched the elevator call button. "It doesn't cover everything, believe me."

"Is something wrong? Are you and your family okay?"

"We're fine," Walker said, punching the button again. "I'm just tired and irritable."

"You hide it well."

"Let's go to Mateo Bonilla's place," Walker said.

"We'll need a search warrant to go inside and we don't have the grounds to get one yet."

"That's okay," Walker said. "I just want to knock loudly on the front door, look around outside, and press my face against the windows to see what I can see."

"What will that accomplish?"

"Maybe Novar will be there and make a break for it and I can tackle him," Walker said. "I haven't tackled anybody in months."

"Because you have a bum knee." The elevator arrived and Sharpe stepped inside. "I'll call for a patrol car to meet us there for backup."

"Don't," Walker said, following him in.

"Why not?"

"They might get there before we do and scare him off." Walker punched the button for the lobby. "That's my job."

Mateo Bonilla lived in a 1950s-era single-story, Spanish-style courtyard apartment building in the same neighborhood as the arson spree. The apartment row, with a red-tiled, gabled rooftop, was shaped into a horseshoe around a garden with an old fountain in the center that was filled with fake flowers.

The two detectives walked into the courtyard and knocked on Bonilla's door. There was no answer, and the blinds were drawn on the windows. So by unspoken agreement, they went back to the street, walked down to the nearest corner, and entered the alley behind the building.

Graffiti covered most of the back walls, fences, and dumpsters. But the spray paint on Bonilla's building looked more like a mural than gang tagging. It was full of globular people of different ethnicities dancing, some of them luridly, while Los Angeles burned around them.

"I've seen that person's work before," Walker said.

"Where?"

"On the wall of an apartment building on North Alfred Street, across from the first crime scene." Walker pulled up the photo of the mural on his phone and showed it to Sharpe.

"You're right, it's the same."

"It's more than that," Walker said, and took a picture of the mural. "I think last night Novar went around torching places that painted over Bonilla's art."

"Thank God," Sharpe said.

"What for?"

"That the tagging is the common thread in the arsons and not the cars that were hit. I can keep my badge and my dignity."

"Neither one was ever in jeopardy." Walker took another picture of the wall. "I'll text these pictures to Carter and have her show them to the landlords to confirm my hunch."

"You don't know what it's like to have your reputation as an investigative genius at risk." Sharpe pulled a pair of latex gloves out of his pocket and put them on. "Imagine if a parking-meter cop started wearing a cowboy hat and looked better in it than you."

"You think my entire identity is wrapped up in my hat?" Walker said, looking at his phone as he sent Carter the photos and composed a message to go with them.

"What else are you known for?" Sharpe went over to the nearest dumpster, which Bonilla had tagged with a bunch of bulbous chicks in a nest, their open mouths pointed up to the lid.

Walker heard the whoosh confirming that the text had been sent, then noticed Sharpe climbing up on the dumpster. "What are you doing?"

"What you usually do when we visit a suspect's home or place of business without a warrant—looking at his trash. You don't need a warrant for that."

"I'm glad you've learned something from me."

Sharpe lifted the lid and looked inside. "Novar definitely lived with Bonilla and we won't have any problem getting a search warrant for their apartment."

"Why? Is his body in there?"

Sharpe got down and peeled off his gloves. "Nope."

Walker hauled himself up and leaned over the open dumpster. He saw two flattened boxes for Duraflame logs amid the trash.

That's it, he thought. *Case closed.* All they had to do now was find Toniel Novar and slap the cuffs on him.

Walker could do that in his sleep. In fact, he might have to. He was exhausted.

"We're going to make Caffrey and Scruggs look very good."

"Don't blame me. You're the one who picked them as the faces of the investigation."

"At least you get to keep your dignity." Walker dropped back down on his feet. "What am I getting out of this?"

"Dinner with your family tonight and a chance to read a bedtime story to your kid."

He'd gladly settle for that. "If I go home, what are you going to do?"

"I'll stay and secure this dumpster until CSU gets here to process the evidence, then I'll have a deputy take me back to the station and call it a day," Sharpe said. "You and I will come back here together in the morning with a search warrant."

"What if Novar returns tonight?"

"That would be nice but I don't think he will," Sharpe said. "If he has friends in the building, they've already warned him that cops have been here. But I'll park some deputies in unmarked vehicles at each corner to keep an eye on the place just in case he decides to make our lives easier."

"It should be me parked out front," Walker said.

"You'll fall asleep," Sharpe said. "You can barely keep your eyes open as it is."

"Good point," Walker said.

He stuck around until the two patrol cars arrived, just so Sharpe wouldn't be alone in an alley waiting for the crime scene unit, and then drove home.

It was a good day at the office.

CHAPTER SEVEN

Walker pulled up to his small ranch-style home in Reseda, in the flats of the San Fernando Valley, and was surprised to see his wife's 3 Series BMW parked on the street instead of in the garage. He was even more surprised when he saw a FOR SALE BY OWNER placard resting on the dashboard with her email address written on it.

He parked in the garage, locked his weapons in the vehicle's gun safe, then entered the laundry room, his residential decontamination chamber, where he stripped off his filthy uniform and stuffed it into a hamper. He washed his hands in the sink, then changed into fresh sweats so he wouldn't track ashes, grime, and deadly chemicals into a house with a toddler toddling around who put everything in his mouth. More or less clean now, Walker slipped his Stetson back on and opened the door into the house.

His son, Cody, was waiting for him, wearing a onesie and a cowboy hat of his own and holding his arms out for a hug. "Daddy's home!"

Walker scooped Cody up in his arms and nuzzled his neck, making him giggle. "How's my little cowboy?"

"Trade hats?"

"Absolutely," Walker said. It was all part of their nightly ritual.

He set Cody down and took off his hat. So did Cody, who held up his hat to his dad. Walker put Cody's tiny hat on his head, making his son laugh, then stuck his hat on Cody, completely covering the toddler's head. Cody stumbled around, bumped into a wall, and then fell on his diapered butt and couldn't stop giggling.

Carly joined them from the kitchen, a big smile on her face, and gave Walker a kiss. "He never gets tired of that."

Neither did Walker.

Cody stood up, took off Walker's hat, set it upside down in front of him, and sat in it, toppling over. And then he did it again. And again.

"He's breaking it in for me," Walker said. "I just hope his diaper holds."

"You're home early. Does this mean you've caught the serial arsonist?"

"We're close. We know who did it and why. All that's left is finding him and slapping on the cuffs."

"That's your specialty," she said. "There was a time you wouldn't come home until the chase was over."

"My priorities have changed." Walker took off his son's little hat and put it on Carly's head. "I'll catch him tomorrow."

"I appreciate that new attitude, but we could use the overtime pay." Carly went back to the kitchen and Walker trailed after her. She got a big pot out of the cupboard and took it to the sink.

"Well, that explains the 'For Sale' sign on your BMW." Walker opened the pantry and plucked a package of spaghetti from a shelf. "We aren't so bad off that we have to sell the car."

Carly filled the pot with water and set it on the stove. "We aren't? Where are we going to get the money for Cody's meds next year? And the year after that? Selling the car buys us a few months before we have to think about taking a second loan on the house, or putting it on the market."

Walker wanted to tell her that it wouldn't come to that, that he was working on a solution. But he hadn't heard from Danny Cole in months and couldn't be sure the convicted con man would come through for him . . . or that ruining Slezak would guarantee a drop in the price of the drug. So, the truth was, he had no alternatives to offer.

Carly shook some salt into the water, then turned the heat on under the pot. "Maybe by then the insurance company will change their minds about covering Cody's meds or he'll outgrow the epilepsy. Some children do."

"How are you going to get to work without a car?"

She opened the refrigerator and took out two cans of Kona Big Wave beer. It was as close as they'd get to Hawaii for the foreseeable future. It made him feel guilty about spending the money to sneak off to Japan.

Carly opened a can and handed it to him, then opened one for herself.

"Taking Uber every day will cost a lot less than the car payment and we'll save on auto insurance, too. Besides, I mostly just go back and forth to the office," she said, referring to her psychiatric practice. "But if it becomes a problem, we can find a cheap used car."

"There is no such thing anymore, not if you want one that runs and isn't older than you," Walker said, but he thought if it came to that, he could borrow Sharpe's old cop car and give her his truck.

"We'll manage," she said. "Nobody needs a $60,000 German luxury car. I'm almost ashamed to have it now."

Walker dropped some noodles into the boiling pot of water. "Why be ashamed? You've earned it."

"Do you realize how privileged we are? We both have good-paying jobs with benefits. We own this house outright and have hundreds of thousands of dollars in equity we can tap. How many people can say that? Giving up that car isn't a big sacrifice. We don't know what sacrifice is . . . at least not yet."

"I think I do," he said, and took another sip of his beer.

She set down her can and slipped her arm around his waist. "Oh God, I'm sorry. I'm such a bitch."

"No, you're not."

"I made you give up the US Marshals job you loved because I wanted you to spend more time with us . . . and then what do I do?

I criticize you for coming home and not working overtime. You must hate me."

"Of course not," he said. "You're just a mother who is worried about her son. I'm worried, too."

"It's a lot of pressure."

"I know," Walker said.

"I feel tight all over."

"I can fix that."

She turned her back to him. "A shoulder rub?"

He began kneading her shoulders. They were very tight. "That's a start."

"A foot rub?"

"And everywhere in between."

"You know what sounds even better?"

"Tell me," he said, feeling her shoulder muscles relaxing in his hands.

"We have dinner, then you give Cody a bath, get him into his jammies, and read him his bedtime story."

"And then you want me to give you your foot rub."

"That won't be necessary," she said, leaning back against him now. "You taking care of Cody is all the foreplay I need."

He whispered into her ear, "What happens if I tuck him in, and then I do a quick load of laundry?"

"You might find me wild with lust, grinding myself against the bedpost."

"Hmm," he said. "I might have to do two loads."

September 5

At 1:45 a.m., Walker was awakened by the opening guitar licks of "Burning Down the House" and knew immediately that it was

Sharpe calling. He grabbed the iPhone off the nightstand and sat up in bed.

"Did Novar show up?"

"In a manner of speaking," Sharpe said. "We've got another arson spree."

"Where and how many?"

"So far, two in West Hollywood, two in Hollywood, and one directly over the hill in Studio City," Sharpe said. "I'm at the first scene in West Hollywood now, two blocks over from where he struck last night. He used a Duraflame log again, but he must have liked the way the security trailer exploded at the Tower, because he's also using mini Coleman propane tanks."

"That's risky." Walker went to his closet, putting the phone on speaker, and pulled on a pair of jeans. His only clean uniform was in his locker at sheriff's department headquarters in East Los Angeles, so street clothes would have to do. "If the guy's not careful, he'll blow himself up. Has anybody been hurt?"

"Not so far," Sharpe said.

Walker yanked a black shirt off a hanger. "I'll meet you there."

"No, meet me at Bonilla's place. I've already got the search warrant. Caffrey, Scruggs, and the LASD night-shift arson detectives can handle the evidence collection and documenting of the fire scenes. You and I need to find Novar."

Walker was still half-asleep, so it took a moment for him to fully register the implications of what Sharpe had just said. "You had a hunch this would happen. You sent me home but you always intended to spend the night at the WeHo station. After CSU showed up at the dumpster, you went back and killed time by writing up the search warrant and finding a judge you could wake up who'd approve it."

"I called the judge while I was waiting for CSU to arrive and got it approved over the phone. I was leaving the station for home when the fires started."

Walker didn't believe him and was angry with himself for letting Sharpe talk him into going home. He should have stayed on the job, too, running a deep-dive background check into Bonilla and Novar. What he found might have led him to Novar before he could start another arson spree.

"I'll be there in thirty minutes." He put the phone in his pants pocket, picked up his shoes and socks, then sat on the edge of the bed to put them on. His back was to Carly, who was wide awake and sitting up in bed now. She'd overheard everything.

"I know what you're thinking," she said.

"I'm going to get the overtime after all."

"You think these fires are your fault, that you would've caught him if you didn't give up the chase to come home."

That's right, he thought. But he didn't want her sharing his guilt, so what he said was: "I didn't give up. I took a short break for a few hours while Sharpe stayed and moved things along. We didn't lose momentum."

"But he's not the manhunter. You are. That's how the partnership works."

"It wasn't a chase yet. It is now. And I got the rest I need so I can track him without losing my stamina." Walker tied his shoes and then looked over his shoulder at her. "I see the shrinky thing that you did there."

Carly smiled, which somehow lit up the dark bedroom.

"The best way for me to help someone is to get them to argue themselves out of their negative thoughts." She gave him a kiss on the cheek. "Now go get the bastard."

Walker arrived at Bonilla's courtyard apartment building to see a patrol car, two deputies, and Sharpe waiting out front for him. He got out of his truck and approached Sharpe.

"Any new developments?"

"This is Toniel Novar." Sharpe held up his phone to show Walker a picture of a lanky, oval-faced man in his twenties with shaggy black hair, deep-set eyes, a narrow nose, and prominent cheekbones. "I got his picture from the DMV. He doesn't own a vehicle but Bonilla does."

"Let me guess," Walker said. "It's the Camry or that panel van we caught on video."

"The van, a 2018 Ford Transit. I've put out an APB. Every patrol car in Los Angeles County has their eye out for it."

"And they will see hundreds of them. It's the most common van on the road. And if Novar is smart, or has ever watched *Law & Order*, he's already switched the plates. What else do we know about him?"

"He's a twenty-seven-year-old Grubhub delivery driver and he's originally from Fresno. He's been arrested twice for vandalizing buildings with graffiti, but since he wasn't in a gang and marking territory, the judges let him swap imprisonment for community service, mostly scraping off or painting over tagging."

"That must have been painful for him," Walker said.

"Less painful than ten years in jail and a $50,000 fine," Sharpe said, "which was what he was facing if he stuck around the Tower and got arrested after his boyfriend, Mateo, fell down the stairs."

"Is the owner or manager meeting us here?"

"The landlord lives in apartment number two," Sharpe said. "Her name is Loretta Hadley."

"Let's go wake her up."

They went to the door, but she must have been awake already and waiting for them to come her way, because she opened her door as they approached.

Loretta Hadley was a middle-aged woman in a pink bathrobe and furry slippers who Walker guessed had spent so much of her life scowling that it had become her default expression.

Sharpe identified himself and Walker and said: "We have a search warrant for apartment six, Mateo Bonilla's residence. You can give us a key or we can break down the door. It's up to you."

Hadley sighed heavily, as if getting the key would require extraordinary physical, mental, and emotional effort. Walker figured that was also her default reaction to anything, whether she was asked to pass the salt or split an atom.

"Okay, give me a minute to find it."

It took her less than that. She scrounged in a bowl of keys in her entry hall, found what she was looking for, and stepped out into the courtyard, leaving her door ajar behind her.

"The poor man is dead," she said, leading them to Bonilla's apartment. "I don't see the point of going after him now. He's beyond your reach."

Walker said, "How do you know that he's dead?"

"A private investigator from the hospital came by yesterday, wanting to know if I had any information about his relatives."

"Do you?"

"No, and I told Magnum the same thing."

"How about on his boyfriend, Toniel Novar?"

"All I know is that Tony is a sweet, very talented young man with a bright future who was blossoming as an artist under Mateo's loving tutelage," she said. "They were both perfect tenants."

Sharpe said, "Are you aware that they've tagged the back of your building?"

Hadley stopped on Bonilla's stoop and somehow managed to deepen her scowl for Sharpe's benefit.

"It's a beautiful gift that I will cherish," she said. "Mateo could've been the next Banksy. He still could be, once his brilliant work is widely discovered and appreciated. His epic work on the Tower would have done that. Now it will just take more time."

Hadley unlocked the door and then stepped out of their way with a grandiose bow, like a game-show host showing off the prize behind the curtain. Walker thought it was a bizarre gesture, but it made sense once they went inside.

The walls and ceilings were covered with wild, garishly colorful scenes featuring Bonilla's rounded characters in a world where every animal, plant, and object was outrageously rounded, too. All of it was set against many different locales and landscapes, most of which Walker recognized as being in California or the Southwest.

Walker looked back at the landlord. "I guess Bonilla didn't care about getting his security deposit back."

"I will be keeping this as is," she said. "Someday, it could be a tourist attraction, like the Gaudí houses in Barcelona."

Sharpe said, "It's definitely gaudy."

"That's not the 'gaudy' she's talking about." Walker set his iPhone camera to Pano mode and swiveled in place to get pictures that captured the full story of the walls.

"There are different kinds?"

"Antoni Gaudí," Hadley said. "The architect whose signature style put Barcelona on the map. His Basílica de la Sagrada Família, the Park Güell, and the homes he designed are architectural treasures that draw tourists from around the world."

Walker did a Pano of the ceiling, too. He thought if Bonilla's vivid scenes depicted places the couple had visited, or that were meaningful to them, the murals could contain clues about where Novar was hiding or where he might run.

The living room was full of mismatched furniture that suggested to Walker that Bonilla and Tovar liked flea markets and rummage sales, but other than that possible insight into hobbies, there wasn't anything that grabbed his attention.

They wandered down the short hall to the bedroom, which Walker assumed was the master, though not so much because of the four-poster bed and basket of sex toys at the foot. The giveaway was a mirror painted on the ceiling above the bed that showed the reflection of rounded, naked caricatures of Tovar and Bonilla curled up together asleep. The rest of the walls were covered with cartoonishly muscular naked men coupling amid all kinds of implied and explicitly phallic imagery.

Hadley stared, slack-jawed, at these images, which she apparently hadn't seen before. Walker couldn't tell if she was offended or just surprised by them.

"When you open the museum," Sharpe said, "this room might require a separate ticket for adults only."

"You're being flippant," she said. "But I like that idea."

Walker took pictures of the walls and ceilings in this room, too, just in case the images contained clues, but was already thinking about how he'd explain them to his wife if she ever stumbled upon his camera roll.

They moved on to the second bedroom. The walls were bare but paint spattered, because the room had been converted into a studio and storage area. It was filled with paint cans, spray paint, ladders, brushes, rags, paint thinner, and other art supplies. There was also a drafting board, a desk covered with papers, and a desktop computer with a large screen.

"This is a firetrap," Sharpe said.

Hadley said, "Is that why you're here? Looking for safety violations?"

Walker spotted a closet and headed over to it. "We're looking for anything that might point us to where Novar is now or where he might strike next."

Hadley put her hands on her hips. "Strike? What are you talking about? He's a grieving artist, not a criminal."

"Novar is on an arson spree." Sharpe went to the desk and turned on the computer. While he waited for it to boot up, he began sorting through the papers. "He's seeking revenge on property owners who painted over his dead lover's graffiti."

"It's *art*, not graffiti, and they're fucking philistines," Hadley said, enjoying the alliteration by emphasizing the *f*s just a little too much. "They'll regret what they've done."

"I think that's Novar's point."

Walker opened the closet, which was stuffed with winter coats, adjustable walking sticks, an old Coleman lantern, a bag of tent spikes, a cooler, a sleeping bag, a tackle box, mud-caked hiking boots, fishing poles, and other stuff for spending time outdoors.

He looked back at Sharpe. "They liked to camp."

"That would explain why Novar's go-to fire starters are Duraflame logs, charcoal lighter fluid, and Coleman mini propane tanks." Sharpe glanced up at the computer screen, which now showed an empty password field against a black backdrop.

Walker joined Sharpe at the desk. "Find anything helpful?"

Sharpe shook his head. "I was hoping to find his password on a sticky note."

"Not all of us practice your rigorous security protocols."

"All I'm finding are a lot of invoices for website design, logos, and other graphic-art work."

Hadley said, "It's what Mateo had to do to support his art. It's like Michelangelo or Rembrandt taking portrait commissions so they had the freedom to pursue their personal artistic visions."

"They weren't defacing buildings," Sharpe said.

"The Tower is blight, what Mateo did is *art*," Hadley said. "He beautified everything his spray paint touched. The Tower was Mateo's Sistine Chapel."

"Maybe Bonilla felt the same way about his work," Walker said. "If he did, he might have kept track of what he was doing. We need to sort through all of his papers, and get into his computer, to see if he kept some sort of map or photographic record of all the places he tagged so we can find them all."

"Absolutely," Hadley said. "It will be essential for the historical preservation of his work."

What Walker had in mind was finding the places where the art had already been painted over so they could anticipate where Novar might strike next . . . and set a trap for him. But he smiled and said: "The tour bus operators will need it, too."

Hadley wasn't amused. Her hands went back on her hips. "You're mocking me, but I will have the last laugh."

"I hope so," Walker said.

She left the room in a huff but paused for a moment outside the other bedroom door for another peek at the decor on her way out of the apartment.

"I've got Bonilla's credit card statements here," Sharpe said. "That might help us pinpoint Novar's location. Maybe he's still using the cards for food and gas."

"Or, if he's smart enough not to be, at least where he bought the Duraflame logs," Walker said.

Sharpe's cell phone rang. He took it out of his pocket, answered the call, listened for a moment, and got a grim expression on his face. "Thanks for the heads-up."

"What's wrong?" Walker asked.

Sharpe put the phone in his pocket. "That was Carter. As if an arson spree isn't bad enough for one night, an I-10 overpass downtown is on fire."

Walker knew it was potentially catastrophic news. Interstate 10, known locally as the Santa Monica Freeway, cut across the center of Los Angeles on its way from the Pacific Ocean all the way to the Atlantic, and was one of the city's busiest and most important arteries, moving over three hundred thousand vehicles a day.

The two detectives hurried to Bonilla's living room and turned on the TV, where the fire was breaking news on every local channel, not that there was much else to see at that hour besides infomercials. They settled on a channel that was showing the view from a helicopter circling over the Santa Monica Freeway, a quarter mile west of the Harbor Freeway interchange. An overpass was consumed by the massive fire raging underneath it between Toberman Street and West Washington Boulevard, the enormous flames wrapping the ten-lane interstate in a roiling fireball that filled the night sky, totally obscuring the downtown Los Angeles high-rises in the background.

The newscaster speaking over the live shot said that the blaze had forced the shutdown of the I-10 and the Harbor Freeway interchange for miles in all directions, creating a traffic jam domino effect that was already snarling traffic on freeways throughout the region.

And it was only 3:00 a.m.

Walker knew the nightmare would be far worse at daybreak, when the morning rush hour began, even if the LAFD managed to put the fire out that fast, which he didn't think was likely. The fire was a raging monster that was a long way from being contained.

Walker looked at Sharpe. "I'm glad that's the LAFD's problem and not ours."

"It will be," he said.

"Do you think Novar has something to do with this?"

"No, but I hope he's done setting fires, because containing and investigating that freeway disaster is going to be the city's top priority now. It will suck up every available resource."

"So we'll lose Caffrey and Scruggs. Big deal. We're at the endgame anyway. Are you really going to miss them?"

"Good point." Sharpe turned off the TV. "But where will we ever find a face for our investigation?"

"Deputy Carter's isn't hard to look at," Walker said.

"We're saved," Sharpe said.

CHAPTER EIGHT

The Seto Inland Sea, Japan
Eleven Weeks Earlier

Three days after Danny Cole, Sam Mertz, and Tamiko Harada met for lunch in Switzerland, they were together again, riding on a crowded passenger ferry from Hiroshima to Surudoikiba Island, one of the three thousand mountainous isles in the Geiyo archipelago that cluttered the Seto Inland Sea, Japan's central waterway.

From the ninth to sixteenth centuries, Danny told Sam and Tamiko, the Geiyo was the domain of pirates whose business model gradually evolved from looting and pillaging into a massive protection racket, extorting tolls from seafaring traders, fishermen, and merchants to assure their safe passage to Osaka.

Now Surudoikiba Island was owned by billionaire Tadashi Mikitani, who was something of a pirate himself, making his fortune by mounting hostile takeovers of companies and stripping them of their assets.

His island got its name, which roughly translated to "sharp fangs" in English, from its imposing central peak and the high, craggy cliffs along its entire shoreline and not, contrary to popular opinion, from Mikitani's brutal business practices. But Danny figured it was probably one reason why the billionaire chose Surudoikiba as the home for his Gallery of Curiosities, one of the largest, and certainly most eclectic, private museums in Asia.

Only adults were allowed into the museum but there were still some families with kids among the one hundred passengers on Mikitani's private ferry, one of two that made the trip six times daily. That was because one of the government's conditions for allowing Mikitani to purchase the island for his museum was that he set aside the rest of the land as a public park, open to anyone willing to pay for a ferry ticket.

There weren't any beaches and was very little flatland for sunbathing or casual recreation, but the island was a magnet for hikers, who were drawn by the spectacular views of the inland sea from Surudoikiba's signature peak. The hikers were easy to pick out from the museumgoers on the ferry by their boots, walking sticks, and backpacks.

Upon arrival at the island's only dock, there were two ways for the passengers to scale the cliff to reach the museum and the hiking trails. They could go on foot, taking a steep, winding concrete staircase to the top, an ascent that was time consuming and exhausting. Or they could ride in one of the two glass elevators, which quickly shot up a ten-story tubular tower that was linked to the cliff top by two glass-bottomed suspension bridges that created the illusion of walking on air.

A family of four in the elevator with Danny, Sam, and Tamiko arrived at the top and, when the doors slid open, took one look at the seemingly free-floating bridge in front of them and decided to go back down to the bottom and take the stairs instead.

Tamiko shook her head in disgust as the family scrambled back into the elevator. "I don't know how people like that survive in this world."

"Like what?" Sam asked, following her and a dozen others across the bridge.

"People who think that not seeing something makes it go away. If the bridge wasn't transparent, revealing the drop below that everybody already knows is there, they wouldn't be scared."

"That's not what it is," Sam said. "It's the fear of walking on fragile—"

That's when they all heard an ominous crackle and looked down to see the glass shattering beneath their feet. Tamiko and Danny froze, while Sam and many others scrambled in terror to clutch the railings on either side of the bridge.

It took Tamiko barely a second to realize she was safe, but in that second, Danny was surprised not to see the slightest hint of fear on her face. She almost seemed excited by the possibility that she might plunge to her death. Or perhaps she noticed the total lack of fear from Danny and sensed a con at work.

Several people began wailing and screaming, while just as many others broke into gales of laughter and began jumping on the glass, creating more cracks.

The laughing people already knew, like Danny did long before their trip, that the expanding spiderweb of cracks was a special effect and that the sound of shattering glass was piped in over hidden speakers.

Tamiko smiled. "I think I'm going to like this place."

Sam let go of the railing, his face red with anger and embarrassment, and surveyed the other people clutching the rails. Many of them still weren't convinced the breaking glass was fake. "I wonder how many people have had heart attacks or pissed themselves just so an arrogant billionaire could laugh at them."

"Which reaction did you have?" Tamiko said.

Sam ignored her comment and continued walking, but he still seemed to do so a little gingerly, even though he knew the cracking glass was an illusion.

"I don't believe it has anything to do with arrogance," Danny said. "I think this bridge, which is essentially an interactive art piece, is his way of shattering the pomposity, elitism, and formality that surrounds most museums and art galleries. He wants us to let go and have some fun."

At the end of the bridge, two paths bisected a grassy field dotted with sculptures and other outdoor art. One route was made of gravel and weaved through the field before branching off into several trails that went up into the hills and to the peak beyond. The other path, made of cobblestones, led to the Gallery of Curiosities, an overturned glass pyramid that seemed to defy gravity while also acting as an arrow, pointing to the bulk of the museum, which, Danny explained to Sam and Tamiko, was deep underground and could double as a nuclear bomb shelter.

Sam said, "That's one way of making a museum impregnable."

"There's no such thing," Danny said. Or at least he hoped not, or he was out of business.

The inverted pyramid was between two single-story buildings that each resembled a row of children's building blocks. Beyond that, Danny could see a field of high-tech windmills, a massive greenhouse complex, and a fenced-off industrial area of brightly colored pipes, fans, and assorted machinery that he assumed handled the museum's energy, water, and air-conditioning.

They walked into the overturned pyramid, the grand lobby of the museum, where Japanese staff members in matching red blazers used handheld devices to scan the QR codes on everyone's prepurchased tickets, which people presented to them either on paper or on their phones.

After that, all the guests were directed through an airport security–style checkpoint, where their bags were x-rayed and where each person had to walk through a full-body scanner, though Danny knew it wasn't the first time they'd been electronically probed since their arrival. The elevators, escalators, bridges, and corridors in most museums, just like those in casinos and airports, didn't just exist to get people where they had to go but also served to funnel them past a hidden array of scanning devices for security and data-capturing purposes.

Every guest of the Gallery of Curiosities was required to check their coats, umbrellas, and large bags, but they were encouraged to carry their phones so they could download the free app that allowed them to chart their own course through the museum, access in-depth information on every display, and save it all so they could virtually relive their Gallery of Curiosities experience at home whenever they wanted. And also, of course, so the staff could track their every move . . . not just in the museum, but also everywhere else, whenever *they* wanted.

People who didn't have phones were given tablets loaded with the same application, but the electronic surveillance was restricted to the museum. Naturally, Danny, Sam, and Tamiko chose the tablets.

The buildings to either side of the pyramid contained restrooms, the gift shop, the coffee shop, and, Danny presumed, various offices. In the center of the glass lobby was a vast ragged hole cut into the rock below, a glass elevator and wide industrial-style steel staircase going down into the actual museum space.

As Danny, Tamiko, and Sam neared the opening, the home screen on their tablets came alive with a short message, available in text or audio, and in a multitude of languages, from Tadashi Mikitani:

"Welcome to my Gallery of Curiosities, which you are on your own to explore. There are no tour guides, no paths to follow, and no signs telling you what you are seeing or how to interpret it. If you want more details on anything, it's all on the app. Just click the rabbit icon to go down the hole. What you will find here will be profane and offensive to some, exciting and inspiring for others. Either way, I hope you leave here provoked."

At the rim of the hole, Danny peered over the edge and saw a staircase that seemed to spiral endlessly into the depths. But as he started walking down the first flight, he saw much more. The flights of the stairs wound between a myriad of crisscrossing staircases, some upside down and sideways, populated by people who were defying all the laws of gravity as they went up and down the steps.

It took a moment for Danny to realize those other staircases were fake, populated by holographic people who were heading up or down or sideways to corridors and staircases that were projections, paintings, or dioramas. Even so, the complex illusion gave him vertigo and he found himself, like everyone except Tamiko, holding the handrail as he went down to the gallery's first subterranean level.

The vast space's naked stone walls, dim lighting, and discreetly positioned red-suited Japanese staff immediately gave Danny the impression that he'd wandered into the secret underground lair of a supervillain from a Sean Connery or Roger Moore Bond film. He half expected Tadashi Mikitani to emerge from the darkness in a mandarin coat, greet him with a smirk, and say: "Welcome to Spectre, Mr. Cole. We've been expecting you."

But there was no way Mikitani could know that he was Danny Cole, or what he'd come here to steal. And even if Mikitani did know, the billionaire would undoubtedly feel smugly secure in the certainty that it was impossible for Danny to get away with it.

The first exhibition they wandered into seemed to be a history of human executions, expressed with pictures, paintings, videos, sculptures, and life-size dioramas of people being shot, beheaded, boiled, crucified, electrocuted, hung, incinerated, poisoned, gassed, and the like, along with the actual implements of death through the ages, from guillotines and cauldrons to electric chairs and gas chambers, ending with the bullet-riddled corpse of a naked man, preserved in liquid in an enormous jar.

Danny thought it was almost as if Mikitani was trying to warn him, or any other prospective thieves, what would happen if they tried to take anything from this place.

The other collections and displays on the first floor were far less grim, at least the ones that Danny, Sam, and Tamiko strayed into.

They saw a Frankenstein car made up of pieces from dozens of other automobiles and an airplane made the same way.

They saw a churning mass of goo in a suspended glass box that somehow formed into faces and other objects, including the faces of the people watching the display. Danny was so unfamiliar with his own face that he didn't recognize it at first when it emerged from the goop.

Finally, they passed through a long corridor, the black walls on either side lined with a hundred white plaster casts of men's penises, some erect and some not.

Tamiko said, "I'd like to do this in my place. I've been looking for something to decorate the hall to my bedroom."

"What a great idea," Sam said. "Maybe offer guys a tape measure to really get them in the mood."

"I wouldn't bring home any man who'd be intimidated by this."

Danny asked, "Would you make the plaster casts before or after sex?"

Tamiko shrugged. "Maybe during."

Sam said, "There's nothing a man likes more than having his junk slathered with plaster."

"Men like *any* attention from me down there," Tamiko said. "So do women. I could do plaster penises on one wall and vaginas on another." She stopped and examined one of the penises. "That one looks familiar."

After that, Danny cut short their tour of the first floor, ignoring a gallery of Rembrandts, Picassos, Warhols, and obscure artists nobody had ever heard of, and took the dizzying staircase down to the second level, where they walked through a room full of graffiti from around the world, including slabs of the Berlin Wall and an entire public restroom stall from Central Park.

That led to an immersive multimedia display of banned art, books, and photographs, while prohibited music played on speakers and scenes from forbidden movies were projected all around them. Some of the banned material was sexual, violent, or political, but Danny found most shockingly mundane.

Another exhibit displayed a toilet made of solid gold and an identical one made of chocolate, a urinal made of pages from the Bible and another from pornography, a shower that sprayed oil and another that sprayed champagne, and a bidet with goldfish in the bowl and another with snakes.

They saw a display of surgical tools and torture devices through the ages, not that it was really possible for Danny to clearly discern one from the other, which he assumed was the point.

And they walked through a zoo of living, deformed animals of all kinds . . . into a giant brain where thoughts and images whizzed past as electric bolts that somehow contained images, sounds, and smells.

Danny saw all he wanted to see of this level, ignoring an exhibit of rare Egyptian antiquities in an actual tomb (deconstructed in Egypt and rebuilt in the gallery, stone by stone), and led Sam and Tamiko down the staircase to the bottom floor, where the exhibit that mattered most to him was located.

He was anxious to see it, but he'd controlled his impatience. He hadn't gone directly to it as soon as they'd arrived at the museum because their every move was being tracked and logged by their tablets. He didn't want their path to be flagged later by some algorithm as unusually direct, matched to their body and facial scans, and sent to security for further analysis. The digital tracks they left on their tablets had to indicate nothing unusual. They were just a typical group of tourists, randomly ambling through the gallery, seeing the average percentage of what the museum had to offer.

The first exhibit they walked through appeared, initially, to be an indoor zoo of common animals. But then he noticed they were truly uncommon—two-headed cows, snakes, turtles, dogs, fish, cats—and then, to his astonishment, conjoined twin women, seemingly in their twenties, joined at their midsections, sitting naked and bored on a couch. One of them read a book, while the other listened to something on a pair of headphones. They shared a bowl of popcorn and ignored the guests staring at them. A sign in front of them read: No Photos or Videos Allowed. Do Not Feed.

Danny checked his tablet for more information and learned the women were from New Zealand and were hired to "perform" for six months out of the year. They'd also been paid a "substantial sum" to bequeath their bodies to Mikitani upon their deaths. Danny wondered if their dead bodies would be preserved in a jar like the executed corpse upstairs.

From there, Danny, Sam, and Tamiko wandered through a staggering collection of weapons of all kinds, from the Stone Age to the present, that were displayed in no sort of chronological, technological, or narrative order. There were prehistoric clubs and AK-47s. Slingshots and ballistic missiles. Hand grenades and cannonballs. A giant wooden medieval catapult and a genuine World War II–era artillery gun in a concrete German emplacement. Samurai swords and battle-axes. A fifteenth-century war hammer and an array of ninja *shuriken* throwing stars.

Most of the weaponry, with the exception of small items like knives and *shuriken*, weren't in display cases and were separated from the guests only by a simple wire line that would set off an alarm if it was stepped over or touched.

The final weapon on display was a 25-ton, 26-foot-long Soviet AN602 Cold War–era hydrogen bomb, a steel butt plug with fins, capable of delivering a 50-megaton blast. Although it was inactive, people walked past it cautiously, as if it might blow at any moment.

This exhibit led directly into a space of total darkness, a black hole with only a pinprick of light in the distance. They walked toward the light, which somehow exploded into a whirling tunnel of colors that reminded Danny of the warp-speed effect in a *Star Trek* movie. A cacophony of ticking, an orchestra of individual clocks creating a strange music, came from hidden speakers accompanied by laser streaks of light, all of it creating a sense of motion and the passing of time.

It felt as if they weren't just walking somewhere but traveling a great distance, twisting both time and space, to arrive at their destination, which turned out to be an alien world, someplace that seemed both unnatural and yet clearly organic, the walls and ceilings covered in plantlike, glowing orbs.

And as Danny got closer to them, he could see that each transparent orb was atop a slender stalk and contained a timepiece—a wristwatch, pocket watch, or small clock. The timepieces were vintage, historical, or rarities worth anywhere from hundreds of thousands of dollars to tens of millions.

Many of the timepieces had extraordinarily intricate and complex mechanisms, or were lavishly bejeweled with diamonds, sapphires, crystals, and rubies, and had parts made of the highest-quality gold, silver, and titanium. They came from Patek Philippe, Abraham-Louis Breguet, George Daniels, Richard Mille, and many other legends of horology.

There were also timepieces that were simple, and mass-produced in their day, but were valuable because of who owned them, people like Winston Churchill, Benito Mussolini, Ernest Shackleton, John F. Kennedy, Elvis Presley, Adolf Hitler, Abraham Lincoln, and Marie Antoinette.

The main attraction, in an orb the size of a basketball atop a slender, almost tentacle-like stem, was the Infinitum, a one-of-a-kind masterpiece by Josiah Barer, the greatest living watchmaker, who'd spent twenty-seven years making it entirely by hand in his tiny workshop in Scotland.

Danny didn't need to read the tablet to know the Infinitum was commissioned by Steve Jobs, who not only wanted a watch with every known complication but wanted to be able to see its mechanisms at work.

The Infinitum was an engineering marvel encased in transparent sapphire, the gold-and-silver mechanism floating in the center of the watch suspended by nearly microscopic strands of titanium.

But Jobs didn't live to see it, dying a decade before its completion. The watch was put on the auction block, with the proceeds going to a nonprofit dedicated to feeding starving children.

Mikitani won the Infinitum for $40 million, the highest amount ever paid at auction for a watch.

And Danny Cole was going to steal it.

CHAPTER NINE

But he wouldn't be taking the watch today. He was casing the joint, a phrase Danny couldn't even think of without hearing Jimmy Cagney or Edward G. Robinson saying it, though he wasn't sure if they ever did.

He admired the Infinitum for a few minutes, all of its tiny and complex mechanisms moving to track time, and he imagined how it might have fascinated, entertained, and inspired Steve Jobs to gaze at that on his wrist while he contemplated his next innovations.

Danny looked around until he spotted a red-jacketed male staffer standing a discreet distance away, beside the emergency exit door.

He took out his phone and eagerly approached the staffer. "Could you take a picture of me and my friends with the Infinitum?"

"Of course," the staffer said.

Danny gestured to Sam and Tamiko to stand beside him with the Infinitum in the background in its otherworldly glowing orb.

The souvenir Danny wanted wasn't the picture of the watch. It was the unique RFID signal from the staffer's ID card that would be captured by an app on Danny's phone.

The staffer took the picture and offered the device back to Danny. "I took a bunch."

"Thank you," Danny said. "It's a souvenir I will treasure."

He pocketed his phone and returned to his friends. Sam gestured to the orb and whispered, "I assume that's the prize in this box of Cracker Jacks."

"Yes, it is."

Tamiko looked at him. "What are Cracker Jacks?"

"God, I feel old," Sam said.

Danny said: "It's a box of caramel-coated popcorn and roasted peanuts with a prize buried inside, like decoder rings, toy cars, stickers, that kind of thing."

She frowned with disgust. "I try to avoid foods that have foreign objects inside."

"It's for kids," Sam said.

"Even worse. Why not put a rat in there and really make it fun?"

The final exhibit, which all of the guests were ultimately led through, was an elaborate network of pipes filled with either some kind of sludge or strange fluids, pushed along by elaborate machinery that generated a horrible smell.

Danny checked his tablet and learned that they were walking through the industrial entrails of a mechanized digestive system that was reprocessing all the solid waste from the facilities' restrooms into fertilizer for the museum's gardens and greenhouses, which provided all the fruit and vegetables served at the coffee shop, and all the liquid waste into drinking water for the fountains throughout the gallery.

They emerged at the base of the staircases and the glass elevator tower, where staffers waited with free samples of the gallery's bottled water for the guests.

Danny, Sam, and Tamiko declined the freebies and took the glass elevator up through the tangle of infinite staircases rather than make the climb.

Tamiko said, "All of this stuff we just saw is from Mikitani's personal collection of oddities?"

"That's how it started," Danny said, "but some of it, like that sewage treatment plant we walked through, was created or commissioned especially for this museum."

Tamiko craned her head to follow one of the twisted staircases they passed. "It's like we're traveling through his mind and learning how he sees the world around him."

"We certainly are," Sam said. "Having us walk out of the museum through an asshole tells you a lot about the guy who created this place and what he thinks about people stupid enough to buy a ticket to see this shit."

Tamiko said, "This is the best museum that I've ever visited."

Danny said, "You visit museums?"

They stepped out of the elevator before Tamiko quietly answered: "Only the ones we've broken into."

And those were among the best in the world, so Danny considered her opinion an informed one.

Sam looked down the hole they'd just emerged from, then up and around the inverted glass pyramid that they were standing in, and shook his head. "I don't see how we're going to do that here."

Danny tipped his head toward the coffee shop. "Let's think about it over lunch."

"Good idea," Tamiko said. "I'm starving."

She and Danny started across the lobby.

Sam followed along, but he wasn't happy about it.

"I'm only eating meat," he said. "And I'm not drinking anything that doesn't come out of a bottle with a brand name on it."

The coffee shop took orders at the front counter, then gave customers a flag to take back to their tables so their food could be delivered.

Danny lucked out in the line to place his order. There were two security guards standing right in front of him. What set these red-jacketed staffers apart from all the others were the earpieces they wore, their muscular statures, and their general stony attitudes, which were the direct opposite of the friendly, eager-to-please, smiley persona that the rest of the staff displayed. He assumed their RFID codes would get through just about any door in the building. By law, private security personnel in Japan weren't allowed to carry guns, which made Danny feel very secure.

Danny, Sam, and Tamiko ordered their food and Danny took their numbered flag back to a table near the floor-to-ceiling windows, which offered them incredible views of the steep cliffs below, the inland sea, and a few islands in the distance. As soon as they sat down, Sam gestured to Danny's phone on the table.

"Let me guess," he said. "That has an app on it that captures the signals or whatever else is emitted from the staff's IDs so you can clone the badges or track the movements of whoever is wearing them."

Danny smiled. "You've been keeping up on the latest tech. I thought you gave up crime for the wine business."

"Force of habit," Sam said.

Tamiko leaned forward and spoke in a low voice so only Danny and Sam could hear her.

"Okay, so you want the $40 million Infinitum watch, but I'm sure the transparent ball it's encased in is bulletproof, bombproof, and can't be cracked open without using some kind of industrial laser, which you couldn't sneak in here, even if it was stuffed up your butt."

Sam said, "That could be the museum's next exhibit and light show."

Tamiko ignored the comment and went on. "Everyone who comes in here has to go through a full-body scan and has to check their bags, so you can't hide anything on yourself. The only devices they let you carry are phones and cameras."

"Or their tablets," Danny said.

"Which they use to track your every move, while also watching you from a thousand hidden security cameras and probably infrared sensors, too," she said. "But let's say you have some brilliant way of getting the watch out of its unbreakable case—"

"I have a simple one," Danny interjected.

"That was quick," she said, her surprise registering on her face.

Sam waved his hand, like he was brushing something away. "I wouldn't get too excited. Whatever his way is, you're forgetting that we still have to break in here to snatch it and then get away."

That's when a young Japanese waitress approached the table, carrying a tray with their orders.

"Here's your lunch," she said, announcing each dish as she laid plates down in front of them, her breath smelling like an ashtray. "Salad and Diet Coke?"

"That's for me." Danny picked up his phone to make room for his plate and drink, and as she leaned down to place them in front of him, he made sure to pass his phone close enough to her to pick up her RFID code. Her entire body reeked of cigarette smoke, which nearly killed his appetite. He wondered if the odor was just on her uniform or was also coming out of her pores.

"Sushi platter and plum wine?" she asked.

Tamiko gave her a little wave. "That's mine."

That left a plate of skewered grilled meats and a bottle of beer, which the woman placed in front of Sam. He examined the bottle warily. "This beer is imported, right?"

She picked up the flag. "Sapporo is a Japanese beer."

"What I mean is, it's brought to the island," he said. "You don't make it here out of everyone's recycled pee."

The waitress gave him a look. "How would we do that?"

Sam shrugged. "Is that a yes or a no?"

"Have a nice lunch," she said and walked away.

Sam scowled at her, then gestured to Danny's salad. "I don't know how you can eat that knowing it was grown here using sewage."

"How do you think it's grown everywhere else?" Danny said. "All farmers use fertilizer to nourish their crops."

"I'd rather jump off this cliff with Tamiko than eat any of that poop salad."

Danny looked out the window. It was a big drop. But the thought gave him a tingle of inspiration.

Sam twisted the cap off his beer and said: "There's probably no way we can get to this island undetected, even under cover of darkness. But let's say we can, for the sake of argument. You know that both the interior and exterior of this building have got to have every alarm and surveillance system that exists—cameras, lasers, motion detectors, pressure plates, thermal imaging, radar, jingle bells, snake pits, punji traps, vats of acid, vicious two-headed Dobermans, and probably stuff we've never heard of."

"Definitely," Danny said, and dug into his salad. "But it's those damn jingle bells that have me worried."

"It's also deep inside a mountain," Sam continued. "And if you think I can blow a hole in it, you're wrong."

"I don't. It took a decade to blast, dig, and drill this museum out of the rock."

Tamiko said, "Maybe we could borrow one of Mikitani's bombs. He's got a big selection right here."

Danny felt another tingle. A plan was taking shape.

"The problem isn't just getting in," Tamiko continued. "It's getting out. Once the system detects we have the watch, and it will, it'll lock us in down there."

Sam nodded in agreement. "Face it, Danny—"

"It's *Brian*," Danny interrupted. "Brian Lockwood. Since you brought up faces."

"You can't avoid the facts," Sam went on, ignoring the correction. "It's impossible to break into this place, or to bust the Infinitum out of its globe, or to escape without being seen."

"So, we won't," Danny said.

Sam did an exaggerated double take, worthy of a cartoon character. "You're calling it off?"

"No, I'm telling you how we'll do it."

Tamiko stared at him. "By not breaking in, removing the watch, or escaping."

"That's right," Danny said with a smile. "It's simple when you think about it that way."

"It is?" Sam said.

"It's like martial arts," he said. "We are going to use our opponent's strengths against him."

"I don't get it," Sam said.

"I don't entirely get it yet, either," Danny said. "But I will."

They finished their lunch and then Danny said he wanted to visit the gift shop. There was a book on the making of the museum, another on the collection itself, and an assortment of souvenirs, including bars of soap, key chains, can openers, pillows shaped like penises, two-headed plushy toys of various animals, and a replica of the Infinitum watch.

Danny bought the two books and a replica watch. Tamiko bought some penis soaps. They were walking out of the gift shop when Danny's phone vibrated.

He took it out and glanced at his RFID-capture app. "We need to go."

Danny led them quickly out of the pyramid and into the park, where he called up another feature of the app. His screen showed a map of the island with a blinking dot tracking a particular RFID code.

Tamiko peered over his shoulder. "Who is that?"

"The waitress."

"Why are you watching her?"

"Because she reeks of cigarettes," Danny said.

"You find that attractive?"

"Today I do," Danny said. "Twenty percent of the Japanese population smokes. I assume that percentage is matched by the employee population of this museum."

Sam grinned and jerked a thumb back at the pyramid. "And Mikitani isn't going to let them light up in there."

Using the app as their guide, they walked through the park and around to the side of the museum that faced the peak, and there they spotted the waitress standing outside with a half dozen other red-jacketed smokers. The door to the museum was propped open with a rock.

Danny shared a grin with Sam and Tamiko. "The thing about airtight security is that it's inconvenient. And people will always be people."

Danny, Sam, and Tamiko found a spot to sit on the grass and surreptitiously watch the smoking area for another hour.

Sam napped on the grass while Tamiko looked through the books that Danny bought.

Danny shifted his attention between the fake Infinitum he bought, reading the details on the box, and watching the ebb and flow of employees coming out for a smoke. He learned that the watch was made in Shantou in the Guangdong Province of China by a company that, a quick Google search revealed, specialized in replicating expensive products as cheap, but convincing, costume jewelry for people who couldn't afford the real thing. Most of the time, though, the company made the replicas without licensing the right to do so. It meant they were primarily bootleggers, and that this officially licensed copy of the Infinitum was an outlier for a company that ordinarily operated outside of trademark law. That was good to know.

The last employee remaining in the smoking area tossed his cigarette stub in a trash can, kicked the rock aside from the door, and went inside the museum, the door clicking shut behind him. In the hour that Danny had watched the smoking area, nobody had pressed their ID card to the sensor by the door to get back inside. Security was the responsibility of the last person to go through the door.

Danny nudged Sam and got up. "Let's take a hike."

Sam groaned. "You're kidding."

"It would be a waste to come here and not see the view."

They followed the trail up the peak. It was steep, and they had to stop a couple of times to rest, but they reached the top in three hours. The view was well worth the journey. They could see clear across the water to the next island, only a few miles away, and on out to the countless others dotting the inland sea.

Tamiko was the only one who wasn't out of breath and soaked with sweat when they got there. The hike was a casual jaunt for her. There was a time, only a few years ago, when it would have been for Danny and Sam, too.

Back then, they were both convict firefighters, and they climbed a lot of terrain more difficult than this, on trails they cut themselves with twenty-pound chain saws, while wearing face shields, goggles, and bright-orange Nomex suits and carrying fifty-pound packs full of tools and water on their backs, and all while inching through a raging firestorm of smoke, cinders, and flames. They still had the calluses on their hands to show for it, but otherwise, they weren't the same men anymore. Danny didn't even have the same face.

He glanced at Sam, who was breathing hard and studying his own calloused hands, and Danny realized his friend was having the same thoughts that he was. But it was more than that for Sam—he could see it in his eyes.

"You're right," Sam said. "We didn't finish the job. You have to figure out a way to do this."

The emotion in Sam's voice got Tamiko's attention, and she studied both men, but then she fixed her gaze on Danny, cocked her head, and smiled.

"You've cracked it, haven't you."

Danny nodded. "I think so."

Tamiko broke into a big smile. "When do we do it?"

That was a good question. Danny gave it some more thought. After a moment or two, he said: "There's some significant preparation involved. I'm guessing a month, maybe two. The timing depends on some things that are out of my control."

"That's the fallacy of a heist," Sam said.

"Fallacy?" Danny asked.

"It's a mistaken belief."

"I know what the word means, Sam. It's just not one I've ever heard you use before."

"This is only my second opportunity," he said.

"What was the first?"

"Our last heist," Sam said, "when you thought you could spark and control a wildfire."

"I didn't hear you say it then."

"I didn't want to undermine your confidence."

Tamiko swatted Sam, a little too hard, on the shoulder. "But you do now? He's broken into dozens of museums without getting caught."

"Not one buried in a mountain on an island."

Danny understood it was a challenge but still didn't understand Sam's point. "What's the fallacy?"

"You said you're waiting on some things that you can't control."

"That's true."

"No, the truth is, you can't control *anything*," Sam said. "You may have a great plan, but there's no guarantee the universe is going to follow it. You know the old saying . . ."

Danny nodded. "To succeed, planning alone isn't enough. You have to improvise as well."

"You're good at that," Tamiko said. "I've seen you do it a dozen times."

"Thank you," Danny said.

"That's not the saying I was referring to," Sam said. "It's *Der mensch tracht, un Gott lacht*. It's Yiddish for: 'Man plans, God laughs.'"

"I'm glad he has a sense of humor. It'll give me an edge."

Danny started back down the trail. He wanted to catch the next ferry back to Hiroshima and then the first Shinkansen high-speed train back to Tokyo. They had a lot of work to do.

Tamiko clapped Sam on the back again and pointed at Danny. "He's already planning to con God. That's how good he is."

"Or how crazy," Sam said, and the two of them followed Danny down the hill.

CHAPTER TEN

Los Angeles
September 6

The overpass fire on Interstate 10, also known as the Santa Monica Freeway on its path through Los Angeles, burned for nearly twelve hours before firefighters from the city and county were able to put it out. The flames were so intense that windows on some nearby buildings melted.

Even before the smoke had cleared, the mayor, the governor, and even the US secretary of transportation wanted to know if the disaster was an accident or arson, and whether the fire started at a homeless encampment or at one of the businesses under the overpass. Or was some sort of vehicle collision responsible?

But Sharpe and Walker were only vaguely aware of all that. What little they knew they gleaned from listening to the news and from what Caffrey and Scruggs, who hadn't yet been pulled from the arson spree investigation, had heard from their coworkers in the LAFD.

Instead, the detectives focused their efforts on building a case against Toniel Novar and tracking him down.

There had been no activity on either Mateo Bonilla's or Novar's credit cards or any cash withdrawals from their bank accounts at ATMs. Also Novar wasn't using his cell phone, nor his boyfriend's, so he couldn't be tracked that way, either.

The white panel van Novar was driving was an old model without any internet connectivity, an "analog vehicle" as Walker liked to call them, so the only way to track it was with the license plate readers on passing patrol cars or from those hidden at state and municipal parking lots and on freeways. But if Novar had swapped license plates, that wasn't going to be much help.

Caffrey and Scruggs showed pictures of Bonilla's artwork to the owners of the torched apartment buildings. The owners immediately recognized the style from tagging they'd painted over or sandblasted away on their buildings, which supported Sharpe and Walker's theory of the motive behind the arsons.

That meant that either Novar remembered every wall in Los Angeles that Bonilla had ever tagged, or he had a list of the locations on him, perhaps in a notebook or written on a map. The search of Bonilla's apartment hadn't turned up anything like that, and none of the sheriff's computer experts had been able yet to crack the code on Bonilla's desktop. So Sharpe sought a search warrant to access Bonilla's cloud drive and any photos of his tagging that he might have backed up, which could give them clues about where Novar might strike next.

Meanwhile, Carter found clerks at a Ralph's grocery store in West Hollywood who recognized Novar's pictures and remembered that he'd purchased a box of Duraflame logs the day of the first arson spree. Not only that, but he'd come back the next day and bought two more cartons and several mini Coleman propane tanks. Carter pulled the security camera footage and was rewarded with clear shots of Novar making the purchases while wearing the same hoodie and cap he was seen wearing at the arson scene.

By the end of the day, there was no doubt among the detectives that Toniel Novar was their serial arsonist.

But where was he . . . and would he strike again that night?

To exert more pressure on Novar, and perhaps prevent another arson spree, Sharpe and Walker decided to release his picture to the media along with a description of his van, giving Caffrey and Scruggs their first, and possibly last, big TV moment as the faces of the investigation.

That night, the West Hollywood watch commander put dozens of deputies out on the street. Walker and Sharpe were out there with them, patrolling West Hollywood neighborhoods in Walker's pickup.

But there were no more fires. And no sign of Novar, though West Hollywood sheriff's station operators logged dozens of calls about white panel vans. Those that had plates all checked out as legitimate. None of them were mismatches, suggesting stolen plates, and none matched Bonilla's registration.

◆ ◆ ◆

September 7

At daybreak, Sharpe and Walker returned to the West Hollywood station, exhausted after more than twenty-four hours without sleep. But there was no way they could go back home to shower and get rested, not with the traffic in Los Angeles snarled because of the I-10 closure downtown, and the rerouting of hundreds of thousands of cars to surrounding freeways and surface streets.

So Sharpe took the single cot in the station's "sleep room," while Walker stretched out in the bed of his pickup truck, and they both slept until the alarm apps on their iPhones woke them at noon. They met in the snack room, picked up vending machine coffees and donuts, and trudged into the conference room to continue their investigation.

Carter was waiting for them and passed along two messages. One was from ADA Rebecca Burnside, who said that a judge refused to grant a search warrant for Bonilla's cloud backups, so she would need more evidence before taking a second swing at it. The second message was from Scruggs and Caffrey, who told her that they were on a road trip to Fresno, Novar's hometown, to see if their suspect had contacted family or friends there or might be hiding out with them.

"Damn them," Walker said, his back and bad knee aching from the night in his truck. "I was going to do that today."

"You just wanted an excuse to avoid the traffic nightmare in LA," Sharpe said, "and all the paperwork we haven't done."

"My talents are best used on the streets," Walker said, "not at a desk."

But with no new leads to follow, Walker was stuck at the station, where he worried they were losing vital momentum. His instincts told him that Novar had fled.

Carter left them to fill out reports at her desk, leaving Sharpe and Walker alone in the conference room.

Sharpe sat down at the computer and began handling the mountain of reports and other paperwork that got set aside in the chaos of the arson spree but that would be necessary to complete to get more warrants and to prosecute the case once Novar was caught.

Walker spread out a map of California on the conference table and scrutinized the photos he'd taken of the murals in Bonilla's apartment and those he'd seen in the city, looking for clues in the graffiti about where Novar might be hiding.

Over the next hour or so, Walker compiled a list of about a dozen locations he recognized. Most were places in the city, but others were in Ventura, Palm Springs, Big Sur, Yosemite, and Lake Tahoe.

While Sharpe and Walker silently worked, the local news played on the TV in a corner of the conference room. There were no new developments, at least not any that were made public. The big question, outside of how the fire was started, was whether the overpass would have to be demolished or if it could be repaired. Either way, the governor vowed to have the freeway opened in weeks, not months.

Sharpe frowned and shook his head as he typed his report into a computer. "The investigation is doomed."

Walker looked up, bleary-eyed from lack of sleep and from squinting at the photos on his phone and the maps spread out around him.

"Jeez, have some faith in me. I'm an ex–US marshal who spent eleven years chasing fugitives. I'll catch Novar. It might just take a few days."

"I'm not talking about our case. I'm talking about that one." He gestured to the TV.

Walker glanced back at the TV to see a helicopter view of the catastrophic gridlock on Southland freeways caused by the partial shutdown of the I-10. "It's the worst traffic jam in Los Angeles history. The city and state are going to throw everything they have at it."

"You say that like you think it means something."

"It doesn't?"

"Here's what's going to happen." Sharpe set aside his laptop and turned in his chair to face Walker. "The LAFD fought the fire, but they'll refuse to investigate it."

"Well, that explains why Scruggs and Caffrey haven't been pulled off this investigation and ran off to Fresno, those bastards," Walker said. "But how can LAFD do that? The fire was smack in the middle of Los Angeles."

"Because, technically, the fire wasn't in their jurisdiction," Sharpe said. "The overpass, and the land below it, belongs to the state, which means the investigation will fall to the California Department of Forestry and Fire Protection."

"They've certainly got experience investigating fires."

"In forests, mountains, and grasslands, not in big cities," Sharpe said. "They won't touch this. So, it'll be tossed to the California state fire marshal's office."

Walker had never dealt with the state fire marshals, but he'd only been an arson investigator for a short time. "Is that a bad thing?"

"They are a four-person unit that primarily oversees pyrotechnic safety at concerts, fireworks shows, amusement parks, and on movie sets. They couldn't figure out how the candles were burned out on a birthday cake. They'll guess at a solution and leave it at that."

"You're very cynical," Walker said. "Has anybody ever told you that?"

"It comes from experience."

"I'm glad to hear you say that," a voice boomed out behind them, with the same authority and tenor as a TV anchorman. But the comment hadn't come from the television.

Sharpe and Walker turned to see Richard Lansing, the Los Angeles County sheriff, standing ramrod straight in the doorway in full uniform, every crease pressed and starched, his badge gleaming. He was in his late fifties, with a touch of gray in his short hair, and the son of a preacher, so even when he ordered a cup of coffee at a Starbucks, it sounded like the beginning of a sermon.

"You obviously see this whole situation with absolute clarity, Sharpe," Lansing said as he stepped into the room. "It's going to make what I've come to say a lot easier. Our department has stepped up and volunteered to take on the investigation, and I'm putting you two in charge."

Sharpe waved an arm at the mess of papers on the conference table and all the photos on the wall documenting the carport arsons case. "We're busy investigating an arson spree involving nearly two dozen fires, maybe more if the guy isn't caught right away."

"You know who did it, how, and why. The case is basically closed, your expertise is not needed anymore," Lansing said. "The LAFD will take it from here."

Walker noticed that Lansing didn't say "could," he'd said "will." The decision was already made.

But Sharpe missed the distinction or refused to acknowledge it. He said, "The guy could strike again tonight."

"Yes, he could," Lansing said. "But it won't be your problem."

Walker spoke up, hoping to cut off Sharpe from arguing any further with the sheriff.

"We're coming into this two days after the fire and I assume some legwork has already been done. What background can you give us?"

Lansing sighed. "The land below the overpass, where the inferno started, is leased by the state to Southland Premier Properties, which subleased parcels to many small businesses, including a car salvage operation, a painting company, and storage lots for resellers of old tires and pallets."

"Is that all?" Sharpe said, his voice dripping with sarcasm. "No open barrels of gasoline or vats of linseed oil? How about a meth lab or a moonshine operation? It was so flammable under there a sparkling personality could've ignited the place."

"Which is why the fire was so intense," Lansing said, "and took ten hours to contain. It's a miracle nobody got killed, especially with a huge homeless encampment under there, too."

"Another firetrap full of half-assed electrical hookups, propane gas grills, and addicts freebasing smack," Sharpe said, making Walker wince. The sheriff was a politician, after all, and probably wouldn't appreciate Sharpe's heartless embrace of every negative stereotype involving the unhoused.

Lansing stiffened with disapproval, in his expression rather than his body, since he was already standing as straight as a flagpole. "There's no shortage of possible causes for this catastrophe and none of them look good for the city. I wouldn't want to be the mayor now."

"But maybe next year," Sharpe said.

Lansing smiled, and glanced at Walker. "You're right, he's very cynical."

If Lansing didn't need Sharpe so badly, Walker thought, he might've fired him. And Sharpe probably knew he had the edge, which was why he didn't keep his opinion to himself.

Walker said, "What kind of resources will we have, sir?"

"The LAFD, CAL FIRE, and the Office of the State Fire Marshal will help in any way they can."

Sharpe snorted. "Which they've already shown by running away screaming from this whole mess as fast as they could."

"You'll also get whatever you need from our department, whether it's manpower, equipment, or forensics. No restrictions," Lansing said. "Assistant Sheriff Molly Luft will be your point person. ADA Rebecca

Burnside will be on call 24/7 to prepare search warrants and get them granted as quickly as possible. You're off leash. Run with it. Figure out what happened and do it fast."

Sharpe sighed, giving in. This was a done deal—it had just taken him five minutes longer than Walker to accept it. "Who is in charge of the reconstruction project?"

"George Petroni. He's the contractor who has overseen emergency overpass repairs before here and in Pittsburgh and Milwaukee," Lansing said. "He's easily the most experienced man for the job. The mayor and the governor want the Santa Monica Freeway open before the Emmy Awards show."

The Emmys were being held in a theater a few blocks northwest of the Santa Monica Freeway / Harbor Freeway interchange. If the overpass on the Santa Monica Freeway, less than a half mile west of the interchange, was still shut down, it would be a nightmare getting celebrities and press to and from the event.

"That's less than two weeks away," Walker said.

"It's a big swing," Lansing agreed, "but if Petroni pulls it off, his company gets a $4 million bonus. He's earned them before."

"What's our incentive?"

"The satisfaction of a job well done and a certificate of appreciation, signed by me, and suitable for framing," Lansing said. "Keep me informed."

The sheriff walked out before Sharpe could raise any more objections. Walker looked across the conference table at his partner.

"Why were you arguing with him? I figured you'd jump at the chance to investigate a major catastrophic fire like this and prove how smart you are."

"I know how smart I am," Sharpe said.

"So you should be flattered that Lansing does, too."

Sharpe laughed. "Don't kid yourself, Walker. He didn't give us this case because he thinks we're brilliant detectives. He's sacrificing us on the altar of his own political ambition."

Walker got up and went to the door to make sure Lansing was gone, or at least out of earshot. There was nobody in the hall.

Sharpe said, "I'm not worried about him hearing me."

"I am. I like my job." Walker closed the door. "Now, what are you talking about?"

"This is an act of pure, naked desperation, a Hail Mary shot to restore his reputation so he can run for mayor. Do I have to remind you about the jail beatings, the deputy gangs, the Malibu sniper cover-up, or what happened out in Hidden Hills, all under Lansing's watch?"

No, he didn't.

All those scandals, except the jail beating, came to light because of Eve Ronin, a deputy whom Lansing had promoted to homicide detective, the youngest in the department's history, as a distraction from incessant negative press. It backfired. Political pundits put his chances of becoming mayor at zero while Ronin grabbed positive headlines with her exploits and now had a fictional cop show about her airing on a streaming service.

"You think Lansing wants us to find out what caused the fire and created a history-making Carmageddon in Los Angeles so he can blame it on the mayor's incompetence and negligence."

"Why stop with the mayor?" Sharpe said. "Depending on what we find, regardless of whether it's an accident or arson, he can blame the governor for it, too. He'll be a political hero, even if the mayor and governor manage to get the freeway rebuilt in record time."

"Don't be so sure," Walker said. "All people in LA really care about is not being stuck in traffic."

"You're right. But, if you and I don't screw up, Lansing will be the crusader who stepped in to discover why it happened when the state and local agencies, controlled by the mayor and governor, wouldn't do it," he said. "Why did the agencies refuse? Because the governor and the mayor told them to. They wanted to hide their roles in creating the circumstances that allowed this traffic nightmare to happen. What's next? Lansing has a shot at the big desk at city hall or maybe the capitol."

Walker sat down. This conversation was exhausting him. Or maybe it was trying to survive on only six hours sleep over two days. "How is any of that bad for us?"

"Because we'll be seen as Lansing's lackeys," Sharpe said.

"Technically, we already are. He's the sheriff and we work for him."

"We'll be the stooges who did the black bag work that got him into the race."

"This isn't Watergate," Walker said. "We're doing our jobs, investigating fires, not planting bugs or breaking into campaign offices."

Sharpe waved off the objection. "And if Lansing loses, which is very likely, we'll go down with him. The governor and the mayor will put our heads on spikes."

"What if Lansing wins?"

"Every fire agency in the city and state will hate us for making them look bad."

"Well, shit." Walker laughed. "That'll happen with or without our involvement, and it's something you'll be proud of."

"Okay, that's true. I just hate being used to help Lansing's personal ambition."

Walker wagged a finger at him. "But you love solving mysterious fires and I love catching bad guys. Let's do that and not worry about the politics."

Sharpe nodded, giving in, not that he really had a choice. "You just want that certificate of appreciation from the sheriff on your wall."

Which reminded Walker of the wall of photos in the conference room, tracking the moves in the carport arson case, and he glanced over at them. "Now it will be up to Scruggs and Caffrey to catch Toniel Novar and close this case."

Sharpe followed his gaze to the wall. "That's the easy part. We've done all the work for them. They won't just be the faces of the investigation now. They will *be* the investigation. We won't be mentioned at all."

"But we'll always know that we were the ones who solved it and so will they."

"It's still going to give me acid reflux," Sharpe said.

The door opened and Carter came in, looking confused. "I saw the sheriff come and talk to you. What was he doing here?"

"Reassigning us," Walker said. "We're investigating the Interstate 10 fire now and so are you. Sheriff's orders."

Walker glanced at Sharpe, who nodded his consent.

Carter grinned, glad to be taking on this added high-profile assignment. "He knows who I am?"

"Of course not," Sharpe said. "Contact Assistant Sheriff Molly Luft at HQ. Tell her we need a list of all the businesses that were located under the overpass and the names, addresses, and phone numbers of the owners and any records of building code violations or fire inspection citations."

Carter took out her notepad and quickly wrote down her instructions. "Will do."

Walker gestured to her notebook. "We also want all the videos captured by any residential, business, or traffic cameras around the scene in the hour or so leading up to the fire and in the hour that followed. I'm assuming some of it's already been collected. If not, we'll have to get it ourselves. ADA Rebecca Burnside can help you with warrants, if necessary."

Carter made the note and nodded. "Got it."

"Get us all TV news footage of the fire, too," Sharpe said. "And tell Luft that I want tech services to edit it together chronologically, from multiple angles, as fast as possible."

Carter paused mid-note, uneasy, and looked up at Sharpe. "You want me, a mere deputy, to tell an assistant sheriff what to do."

Walker said, "He means you should ask her politely and respectfully."

"No, I don't," Sharpe said.

Now Carter looked *very* uneasy.

"Relax, Sharon," Walker said. "It's not going to be awkward. Luft is waiting for our call. She won't fight you on any of our asks."

"Demands," Sharpe said.

Carter shook her notebook, as if gauging its heft. "This is a big to-do list you've given me. We're going to need a lot more manpower."

"Tell Luft what you need and she'll get it," Sharpe said. Walker mouthed the word "ask" behind his back. "You'll be working out of the arson and explosives unit at LASD headquarters for the duration of this investigation. It's much closer to the crime scene."

Sharpe turned to Walker. "Speaking of which, we'd better get moving. It's going to take us two hours to get to the overpass in this gridlock, even with lights and siren."

Walker got up with a groan, his back aching, and put on his cowboy hat. "Screw that. We're taking a chopper."

"We can't order air support to ferry us around the city."

"Of course we can," Walker said. "You heard Lansing. He said no restrictions, no leashes. I'm holding him to it."

"Hell, why not? Let's get our stuff and go." Sharpe got up and went out the door to get his kit from his car. Walker started to go, too, but Carter tugged his sleeve.

She gave him a grin. "I like the way you two roll."

"Buckle up," Walker said. "We're just getting started."

CHAPTER ELEVEN

Sharpe and Walker were belted into the two passenger seats in the back of the Airbus H125 and were dressed in their tactical greens, boots, gloves, and hard hats. Their investigation kits were between their feet. The only things they weren't wearing yet were their goggles and gas masks, but they would be necessary. The scene of the fire was likely highly toxic given the nature of all the vehicles, chemicals, and materials that burned on the ground and within the freeway structure during the ten-hour blaze.

The two detectives sat behind the helmeted tactical flight officer to their left and the pilot on their right and were wearing headsets so they could talk over the sound of the rotors.

Behind the pilot, and at Walker's knees, was a mounted gun rack holding an Aero Precision AR15 pointed upright. Walker knew that the weapon was loaded with a seated magazine but without a round in the chamber on the extremely remote chance some kind of bizarre accident could occur, causing a shot to fire into the rotor system or main blades above, which could down the aircraft.

There was a toggle switch on the headset microphones that allowed Sharpe and Walker to choose whether to have a private conversation or to communicate with the tactical officer and the pilot and hear all the radio chatter.

Sharpe flipped the switch now to speak to the crew. "Can you circle the overpass, please, when we get there? We want a full picture of what we're dealing with."

"Roger that," the pilot said.

The fire occurred under the Santa Monica Freeway, near the intersection of Toberman Street and West Washington Boulevard, just as it fed into the massive three-level clover-leaf interchange with the Harbor Freeway at the southwest corner of downtown Los Angeles.

The I-10 was completely closed between Normandie Avenue, two miles west from the scene of the fire, and the Harbor Freeway interchange. Police vehicles and concrete K-rails on Santa Monica Freeway, and its exits and on-ramps, at Normandie and the interchange formed the barricades. Cars were backed up for miles east and west as police detoured traffic onto clogged surface streets.

But the impact on traffic went even further, causing congestion on freeways all around the Los Angeles Basin, from the Ventura Freeway to the north, the San Diego Freeway to the west, and especially the Harbor Freeway to the east. Commuters felt the pain all the way down to Orange County.

The first thing Walker noticed as they flew over the scene of the blaze was that calling it an "overpass fire" was a monumental understatement. From the sky, he could see that it wasn't a single overpass impacted by the fire but actually *six* of them, including the transition loops to the Harbor Freeway.

All six spans, which seemed to merge into one swath of concrete, crossed over the intersection of Toberman Street, a north-south thoroughfare, and Washington Boulevard, a major boulevard running from east to west across the city. The I-10 then crossed Oak Street, below the Seventeenth Street intersection.

The edges of the six parallel overpasses, at the narrow gaps between each individual one, were scorched from the flames that had licked out from below, the railings mangled by the intense heat.

Under the freeway, there was a large block of fenced-in state-owned land that remained in perpetual shadow, bordered to the west by Toberman Street, to the south by West Washington, to the east by Oak Street, and to the north by Seventeenth Street, that had been leased by the California transportation authority, commonly referred to in the state as Caltrans, for parking lots, storage facilities, and some businesses. The property, along with the vehicles and homeless encampments on the streets underneath the freeway, supplied the fuel for the inferno. That was where Sharpe and Walker would be conducting their investigation.

The four streets that emerged from under the freeway were blackened with soot and runoff from the fires.

Sharpe saw the same thing. "Firefighters doused that inferno for ten hours with a million gallons of water, washing most of our evidence into the drains. But the damage to the freeway structure, and the charred rubble and ashes left behind, might still tell us the story. Ashes never lie."

It was Sharpe's usual rant, one Walker could have repeated himself, word for word. It was at the heart of Sharpe's animosity toward firefighters. Walker saw firefighters as well-meaning colleagues, not adversaries. Their priorities were different, that's all. Firemen put out fires and saved lives. Securing a crime scene and maintaining evidence was a minor consideration, especially in the true heat of the moment. What happened after the flames were put out wasn't their concern.

The freeway was right on the dividing line between two economically depressed majority-Latino neighborhoods, Pico-Union to the north and University Park to the south. Homes and schools within two miles of the freeway in both neighborhoods were evacuated during the blaze and in the immediate aftermath because of the toxic fumes, and only now were people being allowed back into the area.

On the Pico-Union side of the freeway, the streets appeared largely residential to Walker, with a park, a recreation center, a school, and some older homes mixed with apartments, office buildings, and warehouses.

On the University Park side, the streets looked more industrial and gritty to him, with lots of warehouses and several storage yards close to the freeway. He also noticed a large warehouse, perhaps some kind of distribution center, with over two dozen loading docks for big rigs, strategically located near one of the now-closed freeway's on-ramps. It gave Walker a thought that he tucked away in his mind to explore later.

The pilot's voice came over their headsets. "I'm going to set us down in Toberman Park, north of the freeway."

"That's fine," Sharpe said.

The park had a large baseball field, several fenced-in sports courts and playgrounds, and a recreation center with a banner out front that read RED CROSS SHELTER & DISASTER RELIEF CENTER.

As they landed in the field, Sharpe turned to Walker. "We'll scope out the situation, then get every available arson investigator we have out here to document the scene and collect the evidence. Between all of the businesses that were under the freeway and the homeless encampment along the streets, it's going to be a huge job."

"I can't wait."

This was Walker's least favorite aspect of the job and yet it took up the majority of his time now. He loved the hunt, not the forensics. It was the opposite for Sharpe. But Walker reluctantly accepted that this case would be an invaluable training opportunity. After nearly two years on the job, he was still learning, and he'd never tackled a fire investigation of this scope before.

They picked up their bags and climbed out of the chopper, carrying their equipment, and dashed out of range of the rotors toward the street.

"Don't forget where we parked," Walker said to Sharpe.

When they hit Toberman Street, they turned to their right and headed for the fire-blackened freeway.

What they saw brought Sharpe to a sudden stop.

On one side of the street, several construction trailers were set up in a stack, like Lego blocks, and tall, portable floodlights were positioned everywhere for night work, which was to be expected.

Underneath the freeway, all the rubble was gone, exposing the damaged, crumbling pillars and the savaged underbelly of the overpass, where the blaze had violently clawed at the concrete like a ferocious animal, exposing the rebar and pebbly aggregates, the bones and sinew of the structure. Walker was amazed that the freeway was still standing.

But it wasn't the fear of being crushed that stopped them.

There were no traces of the businesses that had been on the property under the freeway or of the homeless encampment that had lined the streets. All the charred, melted, and destroyed tires, pallets, cars, tents, trucks, campers, barrels, shipping containers, and other structures had vanished.

The ground was cleared of everything that existed before. It was now filled with an army of hard-hatted workers, dozens of construction vehicles, and piles of fresh wood and girders for shoring up the freeway.

Sharpe just stared at it all in quiet fury.

Walker knew exactly what he was thinking.

Our crime scene is destroyed. We're fucked before we've even started.

"You must be Sharpe and Walker," a boisterous voice said behind them. They turned to see a stocky, ruddy-skinned man in a hard hat who would have been instantly identifiable to Walker as a construction worker even if he'd seen him naked on a beach, nowhere near a bulldozer and a stack of lumber. There was just something about the man's body and his manner that screamed that he'd been hammering and welding objects together since he'd emerged from the womb. "I was told you'd be coming. You make quite a goddamn entrance in that chopper. I feel like I should have had an orchestra here to greet you."

The man held out a meaty, calloused hand to them. "I'm George Petroni, the man in charge of this operation."

That was obvious.

Sharpe ignored his outstretched hand and said tightly: "You're lucky I'm not armed right now or I'd probably shoot you."

Petroni shifted his hand to Walker, who shook it out of social reflex. "What's his problem?"

"My partner, Walter Sharpe, is reacting to what you've done here, Mr. Petroni. To be honest, I'm not thrilled about it, either."

"Hey, it's only been two days," Petroni said. "We're moving as fast as we can. Even miracles take some time."

Sharpe said, "You've contaminated the crime scene."

"It was already contaminated," Petroni said. "While that inferno burned, thousands of people were told to hunker down in their homes or get the hell out of the area because of the toxic fumes. And once the fire was out, we couldn't get under there to safely assess the structural damage without clearing away all the rubble and the hazardous materials. We've cleaned and wiped the site as best we can, but even now, it'd probably be safer for the three of us to suck the tailpipe of a pickup truck than breathe the air here."

As if to underscore the point, Petroni took out an asthma inhaler and took a hit from it, a light flashing on the device. He held his breath for a moment, holding up a finger as he did so to indicate they should wait, then he exhaled.

"But my lungs are already shot," he continued. "I'll probably spend my golden years wheeling around my oxygen tank in Aruba."

Sharpe said, "You'll spend them in prison."

"What are you talking about?" Petroni's boisterous good nature was beginning to fade.

"In your greedy rush to earn your bonus, you bulldozed and cleansed a possible crime scene."

"Listen, buddy, the governor declared this a state emergency." Petroni swept his arm in front of him to encompass the entire scene they were facing. "My orders are to get traffic moving ASA-fucking-P. Every second counts. I saw in Pittsburgh and Milwaukee how long it takes you people to investigate an inferno and we don't have the time to waste. I immediately cleared away the junk."

"So you knowingly tampered with evidence, destroyed the scene, and obstructed justice. That's a felony." Sharpe turned to Walker. "Arrest this stupid son of a bitch."

Petroni clearly wasn't intimidated. Instead, he just shook his head at Sharpe with something akin to pity. "You really don't understand, do you? I don't give a shit how this fire started. Nobody does right now. My job is to fix the damage. You have a problem with that, get back in your impressive helicopter, go up to Sacramento, and arrest the governor. I did it on his authority."

Walker spoke up, taking a more measured, less confrontational tone than his partner, though he felt Sharpe's anger was more than justified. "You have a job to do, Mr. Petroni, and we appreciate that. We're just trying to do ours. Did you photograph the scene before you cleared away everything?"

"Not me. Maybe CalFire or the state fire marshal or Smokey the Fucking Bear did that," Petroni said. "My priority was determining the structural integrity of the freeway."

"What have you determined?"

"We got damn lucky. There are about a hundred damaged pillars, but only a few appear to be structurally unsound. The rest range from moderately compromised to superficially scorched as you go further out from the middle, where the heat was the most sustained and intense."

Walker glanced at the freeway, which looked to him like a strong breeze could make it crumble. "So it isn't going to collapse while we're walking underneath it?"

"It'll hold. We are still waiting on some test results, but it looks like we won't have to demolish it and rebuild," Petroni said. "We can shore it up, make some surface repairs on the roadway, and get traffic moving again while we spend the next few months replacing and retrofitting columns."

"Where is everything you cleared away?"

"It's at the dump, I suppose. One of the state agencies handled it. Are you going to arrest me, or can I get back to work?" Petroni held out his arms to be cuffed.

"Let me have a word with my partner," Walker said, then gestured Sharpe to one side and whispered to him, his back to Petroni. "This isn't a fight we are going to win. The milk has been spilled and wiped up. Move on."

Sharpe didn't reply. Instead, he turned around to face Petroni. "We won't arrest you now."

Petroni lowered his arms and sighed theatrically. "Oh, wow, that's a big relief. I was terrified there for a minute."

"But you are on notice," Sharpe said, getting right in Petroni's face. "This is our investigation now. Do not get in our way."

Petroni didn't flinch. Instead, he smiled. "Have at it, gentlemen. If I can be of any help, don't hesitate to ask. My door is always open."

"You've done enough damage already," Sharpe said.

Petroni turned his back on them and walked to his trailer. Sharpe stared after him.

Walker said, "I know you're angry and frustrated. But he's a construction guy, not a cop. He's just doing his job to the best of his ability. You can't treat everyone we meet as an enemy."

"We are being set up to fail, Walker."

"No, we aren't. There is no grand conspiracy. Nobody but Lansing cares about us or our investigation. We don't exist. The politicians just want to get this freeway open as fast as possible."

"And cover their asses while they're at it."

"Fine, let them," Walker said. "But we're here right now, so let's just get on with our work."

"What work? The evidence is gone. We'll just be sightseeing."

"Look on the bright side," Walker said. "We don't have to wear gas masks and goggles."

◆ ◆ ◆

Once they were under the fire-damaged freeway, Sharpe couldn't help but go into investigator mode, examining the blackening and spalling of the concrete with obvious fascination.

"Spalling" was the technical term for the pitting, chipping, and disintegration of concrete caused by intense heat, which draws out the moisture in the aggregate, causing the sand and gravel mixture to crumble. The heat also made the rebar inside the columns expand, compromising the integrity of the concrete from within.

Walker had seen it before, just not to such an extreme degree or over such a wide area, but he grew quickly bored looking at it. He shifted his attention to what he could see of the neighborhood.

If the warehouses and businesses had security cameras, he figured they would be pointed at their own front doors and parking lots, not at the freeway. But even if they were pointed in that direction, they probably wouldn't catch a fire that started deep under an overpass, shrouded in the darkness of both the freeway above and the night itself.

He noticed some big rigs emerging from outside a huge warehouse south of the freeway and heading toward the detour that would lead them around the section of West Washington Boulevard that was blocked off. At the same moment, he noticed another big rig backing up into the loading bay that had just been vacated. The same thought he'd had in the helicopter came back to him now.

Sharpe spoke up, breaking into his thoughts. "I've never seen anything like this."

"What do you see?"

"Nothing."

"That's what I see," Walker said. "But you always see something else."

"The fire didn't leave any tracks we can follow."

"One of the first things you told me about arson investigation is that fire always leaves a trail."

"But this one burned so long and so hot, we don't have the scorch patterns and varying levels of damage that we'd normally be able to track to the exact origin of the blaze."

"Why is that?"

"Because there was so much fuel down here, between the tires, pallets, chemicals, and the trash, that the fire was intense and sustained everywhere," Sharpe said. "The blaze could have started in the middle of the lot and spread out from there, or on the periphery and then inside. The walls and columns don't tell us . . . ordinarily, we'd look to the rubble next, but it's all gone. So that's it. We're done."

"What do you mean 'done'?"

"It's over, Walker. Case closed."

"I'm not ready to give up yet," he said.

"The evidence is gone. There's nothing we can do."

"We'll just have to do this the old-fashioned way."

"What way is that?" Sharpe asked.

"We'll talk to people," Walker said, and started walking back up Toberman Street. Sharpe fell into step beside him. "It's how I investigated things before I met you. We can start with people from the encampment. The Red Cross has created an emergency shelter at the Toberman Park recreation center."

"Talk isn't worth anything if you can't back it up with evidence."

"It can lead you to evidence," Walker said.

"Not if all the evidence has been washed into the gutter or hauled away."

"I don't think it has. When we flew over, I noticed a logistics warehouse on Washington Boulevard. They are always strategically located near freeway interchanges to get goods moving in from the ports and out to their customers."

"So what?"

"That means they constantly have big rigs going back and forth under the overpass to get on and off the freeway," Walker said. "Those trucks have front-view video cameras for insurance purposes. The footage might show us where the fire began."

Sharpe looked at him as if noticing he was there for the first time that day. "That's actually a great idea."

"I'm capable of them sometimes."

"More often now, thanks to my expert tutelage," Sharpe said, his mood brightening. "While you start talking to the unhoused and unwashed, I'll call Burnside and get her working on warrants for those videos."

"Unhoused and unwashed?"

"Isn't that the politically correct way of talking about filthy, crazy hobos?"

"I'm glad I'm the one talking to them and not you," Walker said as they reached the front steps to the recreation center. "While you're on with Burnside, ask her to get video from any Ubers, Lyfts, or city buses that were traveling under this overpass about the time the fire started. They'll have video, too. Uber and Lyft are ride-sharing companies."

"I know what they are," Sharpe said.

Walker took off his hard hat, handed Sharpe his bag, and went inside.

The entire gymnasium was filled with dozens of army cots, about two-thirds of them claimed by street people of all ages who'd been left without anything by the fire. Along the back of the room, there were tables covered with packaged food, bottles of water, and piles of donated clothing, children's toys, and books.

Walker talked to a number of the encampment residents. Most of them, if they saw anything, only saw the fire as it was moving like a tidal wave through their highly flammable community. They barely outran the flames and now had nothing left but the blankets, pillows, and thrift store clothing the Red Cross was providing them. They admitted they'd used jerry-rigged electrical hookups and cooked over open fires, but they were all asleep when the fire happened, awakened by screams, the smoke, or explosions as things blew up under the overpass or within the encampment.

Finally, he came upon a woman who sat on her cot with her blanketed knees up against her chest, her arms wrapped around her legs. She was caked with dirt, her hair matted. She could have been in her twenties or her fifties, it was hard for Walker to tell, and she wore a new Hello Kitty pink tank top and gym shorts that were baggy on her emaciated frame. She said people called her Buttermilk.

Walker sat on the edge of the unclaimed cot beside hers and introduced himself. "I'm trying to find out how the fire started. I'd appreciate your help."

"This is all the rat-fucker's fault." Her voice was raspy and raw. He wondered if that was from the smoke or her lifestyle.

"Who is the rat-fucker?"

"The people on the other side of the fence we was up against," she said, picking at some dry skin on her bony knee. Her legs were covered with scabs. "They put razor wire on top, like we was gonna steal their shit, and that disrespected us, made us feel like we was in prison. We was just trying to get by. Live and let live, you know?"

"What did they have worth stealing?"

"Old tires. Oil drums. Pallets."

"What are those good for?"

She looked at him like he was stupid. "You can sit on tires, you can cook over an oil drum fire, and pallets make good foundations and firewood."

And perfect fuel for an inferno, he thought.

She said, "They got them pallets and tires stacked all the way to the top. Rows and rows of them. How they know if any is gone? What do they care if some is? It was a junkyard over there."

"So they were right," he said. "Their stuff *was* being stolen by people in the encampment."

It wasn't exactly a Sherlockian deduction.

"I didn't say that. But sometimes the stacks would tip over and some of them tires and pallets would just fall on our side of the fence. They lucky we didn't sue." She waved him closer and whispered, "What we *did* take was electricity, which is a natural resource that belongs to everybody. Like water. We didn't need to climb their fence for that." Her breath smelled like a wet dishrag.

Buttermilk gestured across the room to a thin, trembling man curled up on a cot. "Charlie's an electrician. He'll hook your rig up to the line for a twenty, a hand job, or smack. Good thing I don't need a line in my crib."

"I'm sure he's very good at his work, but did his wiring ever start fires?"

"Not really," she said. "Just four, five, maybe six or ten times."

Walker nodded. "What about this time?"

"I told you," she said irritably, yanking a piece of dry skin off her knee and flicking it across the room. "It was the rat-fuckers."

Walker saw blood ooze up from the tear. "How do you know?"

"I got out of my crib to take a piss, and was squatting in the street to do my business, when I heard a boom, saw a fireball of oil drums and wood blast out from the junkyard and rain hellfire down on us. I ran up the street screaming 'Fire,' barefoot and bare-assed, my cooch out there for everybody to see. It was the beacon that led everybody to safety."

Walker took out his notebook and a pen. "Can you show me where your crib was?"

Buttermilk drew him a picture and seemed to really enjoy doing it, taking her time and biting on her low lip as she concentrated, totally oblivious to the blood rolling down her leg. She handed the notebook and pen back to him.

The map she drew was surprisingly well done. It looked like her crib, which appeared to be just a pallet, was on the sidewalk on the southwest side of the property, right in the middle of the portion of West Washington Boulevard that ran under the overpass. She'd also drawn the location of several other shelters, campers, and cars that were part of the encampment.

Looking at the map, and thinking about her story, it occurred to Walker that Buttermilk was a hero. She may have been the first one to actually see the fire, and quite possibly saved everybody's lives in the encampment with her warning, if the sound of the blast didn't do the job.

"This is very helpful, thank you," Walker said. "Could I get your full name for my report?"

"I don't want to be in no report."

"You're not in any trouble. It's so people know I didn't make up what you're telling me."

"People being the rat-fuckers." She shook her head vehemently. "I don't want the rat-fuckers coming after me."

"You lost everything you had," Walker said. "If I can prove the rat-fuckers are responsible, they may have to pay you back."

"What I lost was a pallet with a thrown-away mattress on top, the blankets I was under, a grocery cart of my clothes, and a hairbrush. What you think that's worth? Not enough for the risk." She turned her back on him.

Walker took a twenty-dollar bill out of his wallet, along with his card, and set them down on the cot. "That's for your help, and the card will tell you how to reach me if the rat-fuckers, or anybody else, ever comes after you."

He got up and went outside, where Sharpe was waiting for him with their bags on the steps. Walker immediately noticed the smell of barbecue in the air, which made his stomach growl. He hadn't eaten anything since his breakfast donut.

Sharpe got up as Walker came out. "What did you learn?"

Walker told him, while looking around for the source of the incredible aroma, and spotted Duke's BBQ up the street. There was a line out the door, mostly filled with construction workers in their reflective vests.

He took out his notebook and showed Sharpe the drawing.

Sharpe looked at the drawing, then said: "That doesn't mean anything. There were encampments on both sides of the property. The fire could have started in the other encampment and swept across the block. It's useless information."

"Only for the moment," Walker said. "A nail is useless until you have a hammer and a piece of wood."

"Very profound," Sharpe said. "So, what now?"

Walker nodded toward Duke's BBQ. "Looks like they are doing a booming business, no pun intended."

"It fits, though," Sharpe said. "Most of the people in line are construction workers who are here because of the explosive fire."

Yes, they were, and Walker thought it was meaningful. What if business had plummeted for local merchants because of the homeless encampment? Driving the homeless out with a fire might have been some struggling merchant's desperate effort to solve the problem. And now it had, far more successfully than they could have imagined.

"Maybe it's not a coincidence," Walker said. "Maybe it was intentional."

Sharpe gave him a glance. "Now who is being cynical?"

CHAPTER TWELVE

They headed over to the restaurant and moved past the crowd to go inside. Nobody objected since they were obviously police officers and, since they were in their tactical greens and lugging bags, seemed to be there on business, not to cut in line for lunch.

Customers ordered food from the cashiers at the front counter. Behind the cashiers was an open kitchen, where a big African American man and half a dozen others worked cutting meat and doling out the side dishes of corn bread, beans, and macaroni and cheese onto plates with a rhythm that almost seemed like a dance. A screen door at the back of the kitchen opened out to the smokers and grills outside the building, the smoke filling the restaurant with the smell of meat.

The tables and chairs in Duke's didn't match in age or style. The walls were covered with fake wood paneling and brick sheets. There were rolls of paper towels, bottles of barbecue sauce, and cups full of assorted plastic cutlery at every table.

It was Walker's kind of place.

The detectives introduced themselves to the cashier at the front counter and asked if they could speak to the owner. She said his name was Duke Dukesny and led them behind the counter and into the kitchen, where Duke was using a meat cleaver to chop slabs of barbecued ribs apart on the greasy butcher-board counter.

Duke was in his forties and hid his big, bald head under a filthy Dodgers baseball cap, his stained apron stretched taut across his huge belly. This was a chef, Walker thought, who definitely enjoyed eating his own food.

Duke used the edge of the cleaver to slide the ribs down the counter to the assistant beside him, who put them on a plate and brushed them with barbecue sauce, then sent the plate down the line for side dishes. Once an ice-cream scoop of mac 'n' cheese, a dipper of beans, and a square of corn bread were added, the plate was put on a tray and taken to the counter for the waiting customer.

Walker said, "Mr. Dukesny, we're sheriff's department arson investigators. Can we talk with you about the fire?"

"As long as we can do it while I work," Duke said. "This is peak time for us."

"Seems like that must be all day while that construction is going on."

Duke took another slab of ribs from a pile in an aluminum tray and started cleaving them apart. "Those men are working hard, day and night, to get that freeway open. The least we can do is see that they are fed and I'm grateful for the steady business. It's been a long time coming."

"Were you here when the fire started?"

"We closed at 9:00 p.m.," Duke said, moving through the ribs with the mindless, automatic precision of a machine on an assembly line. "But everybody knows how it happened."

Sharpe said, "That's funny, because we don't."

"It was the homeless camp," Duke said, glancing up at a greasy flat-screen TV mounted on the wall that listed all the lunch orders. "They did it. We're lucky the entire neighborhood didn't burn down."

"You're going to have to be more specific."

Duke paused in his chopping to take a slab of brisket from a drawer, pick up another knife, and begin slicing pieces onto a sheet of brown paper.

"They burn trash on the streets and wire up their appliances to the electric line with coat hangers, tinfoil, and chewing gum. There have been a dozen fires over there that the fire department had to put out. Check it out yourself. This disaster was inevitable. But I'm glad it happened."

"You are?" Sharpe said.

Duke passed the sliced meat to his assistant, put the slab back in the drawer, and returned to separating the ribs with his cleaver.

"You know what draws people here? The hickory smoke. Makes your mouth water and your stomach growl."

Walker self-consciously put his hand on his stomach. "Sorry about that."

"Don't apologize. It's instinct. The aroma is irresistible." Duke wagged a rib at him to make a point. "The only thing that can overpower that instinct is revulsion. Those filthy people dumped their buckets of shit and piss into the drains right in front of my place. The smell was repulsive. It drove away customers . . . but it drew swarms of flies during the day and hordes of rats at night. It damn near killed my business, though I was still doing better than every other restaurant around."

Sharpe said, "You know what this sounds like, right?"

"Like I had a motive to set the fire myself. I did," Duke said as he continued cutting meat and filling orders, "and so did everybody in the neighborhood. Talk to the owners of the grocery store, the beauty parlor, the flower shop, any business, and they'll tell you how the shoplifting, the vandalism, the garbage, the human waste, and the violent, foul-mouthed, naked, stoned crazy people outside their doors destroyed their sales. Talk to the people who live here and they'll tell you how the encampments destroyed the quality of life. How would you like to walk your kids to school through a gauntlet of crack addicts and whores? The fire was a biblical cleansing, driving the vermin out."

Walker said, "What about all those businesses under the overpass? Are they vermin, too?"

Duke grabbed a dirty rag draped on his apron tie, and dabbed some sweat from his face. "I feel terrible for them. They're hardworking, God-fearing, salt-of-the-earth family men, just trying to get by, abused by everybody. They're the only real victims of the fire, not the people whining about the horrible traffic."

"How were they being abused?"

"Ask them yourself." Duke waved his rag in the direction of the dining room. "They'll tell you. Bunch of 'em are in the back, corner booth."

Walker followed his gaze and saw three men crammed into one of the small restaurant's two booths. "What are they doing here?"

"Where else have they got to go? We're like their second home." Duke quickly cleaved three slabs of ribs and piled them into an aluminum pan. He put ten thin paper plates on top of the ribs, hefted the pan, and pressed it against Walker's chest. "Here, bring them this, and take some for yourselves. You'll find the soda machine on your way."

Walker fought the temptation to lick his lips. "How much do we owe you?"

"It's on the house, like it is for them until they get back on their feet, the poor souls."

Walker took the pan, Sharpe picked up their two bags, and they made their way around the counter and to the back booth of the dining room to the three men, who were clearly surprised to be served by two arson investigators.

"Compliments of the chef," Walker said, setting the pan down in the center of the table.

One of the men, a balding guy in his thirties, with a flat nose, big cheeks, and permanent bags under his eyes, said: "The barbecue sauce must be awfully hot today if it's got to be delivered by firefighters."

Walker dragged over a chair from a nearby table. "We're not firefighters, we're arson investigators with the sheriff's department. I'm Walker, he's Sharpe."

The man who'd spoken to Walker introduced himself as Frank Trikonis, and his friends as José Suarez and Farhad Madani.

José looked to Walker to be about the same age as Frank but was about ten pounds lighter, mostly in the face. Farhad seemed to be the youngest, thinnest, and hairiest of the trio and wore a Ralph Lauren knockoff polo with a logo that looked like a man riding a giraffe instead of a horse.

Sharpe found a chair, brought it over, and sat down beside José, who looked at him and said: "You think we started that fire? Burned down our own livelihoods?"

Sharpe shrugged. "Accidents happen."

Walker handed out the plates, then went to the nearby soda machine to get himself and Sharpe a couple of Cokes.

Farhad reached for a rib. "It wasn't an accident."

"What was it?"

José answered, "Evil and greed."

Frank shook his head and reached into the pan for two ribs. "It was desperation and stupidity."

Walker returned with the drinks and sat down. "What does that mean?"

José gestured behind him, presumably to the overpass. "You have to understand the way of life under there."

Walker picked out a rib for himself. "Educate me."

It was Farhad who began to as they all settled in to eat. As they finished a rib, they tossed the bone onto a plate in the center of the table and reached for another.

"There's about thirty of us, though businesses come and go," Farhad said. "Most of us have been under the freeway for ten years or more. Carpenters, house painters, rain-gutter fabricators, cleaning companies, you name it."

Frank added, "It's a community of craftsmen and entrepreneurs, working long, hard days, and barely scraping by."

Walker said, "What are your professions?"

José said, "I'm a mechanic, Farhad makes cabinets, and Frank is in the salvage business."

Sharpe looked at Frank. "What do you salvage?"

"Anything I can resell, whole or stripped for parts. Junked or overstock stuff. Electronics, restaurant grease, batteries, pallets, car parts, hand sanitizer, whatever has value."

Sharpe said, "You're talking about some highly toxic and flammable materials that require special permits for handling and storage."

"I'd show you my permits, boss, but I lost everything in the fire, including my ID." Frank glanced at Farhad, gestured to the plate of bones, and fake-whispered: "You think they can lift fingerprints from a spare rib bone?"

Frank was joking, but he was expressing a concern that Walker realized could end this conversation quickly. Walker spoke up before Sharpe's blunt inquiry made the men shut up.

"Don't worry, we aren't interested in permits or IDs or in anyone's immigration status. We just want to learn how the fire happened. Why did you gentlemen decide to do business under a freeway?"

José said, "Where else can you rent a workshop or storage space if you don't have a bank account, insurance, permits, licenses, or legal residency?"

"Or enough cash for a security deposit," Farhad added.

Frank reached for the paper towel roll, pulled off a few sheets, and wiped barbecue sauce off his face. "All our money got us was a patch of dirt. I started with a shipping container and grew from there."

José explained that the rest of them built either their workshops, sheds, or storage units between the columns for support and beneath the freeway's concrete belly for a roof. The biggest structure under there, and the only one that was a legitimate building, was a large, unstaffed documents storage facility for businesses like law firms and accountants. Rents ranged from $1,000 a month to ten times that depending on your square footage . . . probably twenty times that for the documents company. They had no garbage collection, mail delivery, running water, or utilities.

So no smoke alarms or fire sprinklers, Walker thought. "What did you use for power?"

José said, "Gas generators, diesel air compressors, batteries, and propane."

"And rats running on hamster wheels," Frank added.

"We couldn't afford hamsters," Farhad said, "but rats we could get for free. They swarmed in from the encampments. They were the only thing we could thank those bums for."

The three men laughed, but there was a bitter edge to it.

José said, "There's no sunshine under a freeway, so solar power wasn't an option."

Frank grimaced. "It was a shame, too, because I had a pile of old solar batteries I was trying to unload that still had some life in them."

Every time Frank opened his mouth and mentioned another flammable item he'd salvaged, Walker could see Sharpe grimacing, holding back the urge to say something.

Walker quickly changed the subject. "What did you do for sanitation?"

It was José who answered. "For years, it was camp toilets and tin cans, until Frank opened his Country Club."

Farhad nodded, smiling at the memory. "Ah, that was a glorious day."

Sharpe eyed Frank warily. "What was the 'Country Club'?"

"An old portable toilet shed I got from a bankrupt construction company," Frank said. "Only club members could use it. The monthly membership dues were a few dollars to have it emptied once a week or so by a sanitation company. As a courtesy, I supplied hand sanitizer and old newspapers for everybody's enlightenment and ablutions."

Farhad said, "I don't think I've ever abluted. It sounds awful."

Frank ignored the comment and said, "I was working on adding a little putting green before the fire."

"Let's get back to that," Sharpe said, and shifted his gaze to José. "You said the blaze was caused by evil and greed. What did you mean?"

"Rent is due in cash on the first of the month, no excuses, or the interest is 18 percent per day."

"And if you still can't pay?"

José hesitated, so Farhad answered for him.

"Big Mike will beat you up, trash your shop, and take whatever you have of value, and if you still don't pay, he'll torch your car, or your business, or both." He looked at both his friends, then back to Sharpe. "We've seen him do it."

"Is that what happened two nights ago?"

José shrugged. "There's a gardener who didn't pay up this month. Big Mike broke his arms, took his mowers, and said he'd torch his truck next if he didn't see some cash. I think that's what Big Mike did and accidentally burned us all out."

"That'd be the evil and greed," Walker said, but then saw Frank shaking his head. "But you don't buy that. You said the fire was caused by desperation and stupidity. What does that mean?"

"All of those desperate and stupid street people with their bonfires, charcoal grills, and half-assed power hookups."

That got Sharpe's attention. "*You* were concerned about the fire hazards?"

"Of course I was," Frank said. "Do you have any idea how flammable restaurant grease is? Or a pallet of hand sanitizer?"

"Vaguely."

"If a couple of drunks get in a fight and knock over one of those drums full of burning wood, or their tangle of power-line wiring shorts out and starts throwing sparks and my place explodes, you'll get exactly what happened two nights ago. I complained about it to the Caltrans inspector every time he showed up but he did nothing."

Walker and Sharpe shared a look, then Sharpe said: "There were property inspections?"

"Yeah, every few months, and we passed them all," Frank said. "But what good did that do if nobody was inspecting the encampments for hazards?"

Walker passed his notebook and pen over to José.

"We're going to get you gentlemen a big, ice-cold pitcher of beer, courtesy of the County of Los Angeles. While we do that, could you draw us a map that shows where each business was located on the property?"

Sharpe added, "And any stacks of pallets, tires, or anything else."

Farhad took a pen out of his pocket and tore a sheet of paper towel off the roll. "Throw in a second pitcher and I'll draw you a picture of Big Mike."

"Deal," Walker said.

◆ ◆ ◆

Walker and Sharpe stood in the baseball field, watching the chopper approach, their return ride back to the West Hollywood station.

Sharpe said, "It's astonishing to me the fire didn't happen a long time ago. There's no shortage of possible accidental causes for the blaze."

"And at least two criminal ones," Walker said. "The local merchants setting fire to the encampment or the landlord torching businesses that didn't pay up."

"It's also criminal that any of the businesses under the freeway passed a Caltrans or fire department inspection," he said. "There are a dozen ways that Frank's inventory alone could've blown up the place and I doubt he's the only one. He shouldn't have ever been allowed under there to start with."

"Why not?" The helicopter circled the park, preparing to come in for a landing. In a moment, they'd have to yell to be heard above the sound of the rotors and the wind they kicked up.

"State regulations prohibit Caltrans from renting property under freeways to businesses that manufacture, store, or utilize explosive, flammable, or hazardous materials. But they did it anyway."

"Actually, Southland Premier Properties did it," Walker said. "They were the ones who rented the land from Caltrans, then subleased it to José, Farhad, Frank, and everybody else."

"But the Caltrans inspector saw what was going on down there and let it go. So Caltrans had to know what was going on."

"Did they?" But whether the fire was the result of an electrical accident or arson by Southland's enforcer, Walker realized that Caltrans would still bear a lot of responsibility. He was beginning to see the political implications Sharpe was talking about after Lansing gave them this case. "We need to talk to that Caltrans inspector. Either he was incompetent, or he was paid off by Southland to ignore the violations."

"If I were him," Sharpe said, "I'd be in Mexico by now."

The helicopter landed. The two men picked up their bags, hurried to the chopper, and climbed in.

When they got back to the West Hollywood station, Sharpe and Walker finished up all their paperwork for the carport arson spree so Caffrey and Scruggs could carry on the investigation without them.

They were both exhausted and decided to start fresh in the morning, especially since it would likely take them hours to drive home in the midst of the city's epic gridlock.

Walker called Caffrey on his way home and learned that the two detectives had no luck getting any useful information out of Novar's family in Fresno. That didn't surprise Walker. He told them that he and Sharpe had been reassigned to the Santa Monica Freeway fire, so it was entirely their case now. Even so, he shared with them his gut feeling that the key to finding Novar would be hidden in Bonilla's murals on the walls of their apartment.

Caffrey didn't have much faith in Walker's gut but thanked him anyway and wished them luck on the freeway case, though he said it would likely end their careers. It was a perceptive comment, Walker thought, considering he hadn't told Caffrey that all the evidence was gone.

◆ ◆ ◆

September 8

Walker got his first full night of sleep in days and was up at 6:00 a.m., sitting by himself at the kitchen table, dressed in clean tactical greens, eating Raisin Bran, and mentally preparing himself for a long drive to LASD headquarters in East Los Angeles, when he got a call from Sharpe.

"You're in early," Walker whispered, not wanting to wake Carly and Cody.

"The office is a short trip south from South Pasadena on city streets and they aren't too badly impacted by the traffic nightmare."

"I wish I could say the same." He'd looked at a traffic app and it was going to be close to a three-hour drive for him. "I'm seriously considering commandeering a chopper from Lost Hills station."

"Don't bother doing either," Sharpe said. "You're actually better off where you are. I've tracked down the Caltrans inspector. His name is Monte Murphson."

"He's working in the valley today?"

"He lives in Agoura Hills. He's supposed to be out reinspecting the fourteen other lots that Southland Premier Properties leases under Los Angeles freeways. But, according to his office, he hasn't shown up for work since the fire."

"You might be right about him fleeing to Mexico."

"I checked last night with US Customs and Border Protection and he hasn't passed through the border in California, Arizona, or Texas."

At least not through the official border crossings, Walker thought.

"I'll stop by his place."

"Southland Premier Properties is in Woodland Hills," Sharpe said. "You can pay them a visit, too."

"Looks like you have my day all planned out," Walker said. "What are you going to be doing?"

"Going through all the video."

That would be a big, mind-numbing job and Walker preferred to be out on the streets anyway. Sharpe had done him a favor.

They agreed to stay in touch and ended their call. Walker put his bowl in the sink, picked up his cowboy hat, and slipped out of the house as quietly as he could.

◆ ◆ ◆

Agoura Hills was sixteen miles west of Reseda in the opposite direction of the cataclysmic traffic snarl and Walker was able to get to Murphson's home in twenty minutes. Murphson lived in a 1970s-era tract home on a tiny cul-de-sac visible from the freeway that abutted a huge warehouse and jutted into Lake Lindero, a sixteen-acre man-made water feature that looked to Walker, from the vantage point of his truck, like a catch basin for storm runoff and sewage.

There was a new Chevy pickup truck parked in Murphson's driveway. Three days of the *Los Angeles Times* and the weekly edition of *The Acorn* lay on the dead grass, yellowing in their plastic wrapping.

Walker took out his phone, called Deputy Carter, read her the license plate on the truck, and asked her to check the registration. A few seconds later, she confirmed it belonged to Murphson. He thanked her, got out of his own truck, and was immediately hit by a hot breeze of carbon monoxide kicked up from the cars passing on the freeway.

He didn't understand the appeal of living here. He supposed the six residents of the cul-de-sac sat in their backyards, enjoying the view of a lake and the hills to the north, and pretended they lived far away from the urban sprawl. But Walker knew he didn't have the imagination to ignore the sound of constant traffic, the squalidness of the lake, or the fact that his front yard faced a warehouse. And yet, the house was probably worth $2 million. How did Murphson afford that on a Caltrans inspector's salary?

He put on his cowboy hat, walked up to the front door, and knocked. There was no answer. The place felt still. No, it was more than that—it felt lifeless. He knocked again, but this time he said: "Mr. Murphson, I'm Andrew Walker, an arson investigator with the Los Angeles County Sheriff's Department. I'd like a word with you."

There was no response, not that he expected one. He leaned on the doorbell, hearing the ring echoing inside, and looked around for cameras or any sign of an alarm system on the house, but saw nothing.

Walker decided to take a walk around the property and crossed the driveway to get to the other side of the house. But as he passed the attached garage, he caught a whiff of something rotting and unmistakable.

It was death.

He figured that counted as exigent circumstances.

Walker went to his truck and reached behind the front seat for the crowbar he kept there.

He marched up to the front door, wedged his crowbar into the space between the door and the jamb, and pried it open, splintering the wood until all it took was a solid kick to break it in.

No alarms went off. No one came running.

The smell was even worse inside.

A short hallway adjacent to the foyer led to the garage. He walked down it, used the toe of his foot to open the door, which was ajar, and saw a man hanging from a rafter, a garden hose around his neck, his body bloated from decomposition.

Walker swore to himself, retraced his steps, and went outside into the middle of the cul-de-sac to call Sharpe. The polluted air on the street smelled fresh and sweet compared to the garage.

Sharpe answered after the first ring, and Walker said: "I found Murphson hanging around his house."

"What did he have to say for himself?"

"Nothing, unless he left a suicide note. He's swinging from a rafter in his garage."

"Shit," Sharpe said.

"He's ripe, so I'm guessing he hung himself shortly after learning about the freeway fire."

"He knew what we were going to find."

"I think a lot of people knew," Walker said. "Can you ask Burnside to get us a search warrant for Murphson's house, his truck, and his bank accounts?"

"Sure. That should be the easiest thing she's done all week. Have you notified Lost Hills yet about Murphson?"

Sharpe was referring to the Lost Hills sheriff's station, which handled law enforcement in the communities of Agoura Hills, Calabasas, Westlake Village, Hidden Hills, the Santa Monica Mountains, and all the way out to Malibu.

"I will as soon as we're done talking," Walker said.

"Was the house on fire?"

"Don't you think I would have brought that up if it was?"

"Then once the homicide detectives arrive, and you've answered all of their questions, you have no reason to be there," Sharpe said. "You investigate fires, not suicides or murders. So just walk away."

"Will do," Walker said.

"No, you won't," Sharpe said.

"Have some faith in me. I'm laser focused on finding out the cause of the freeway fire as quickly as possible. I won't let anything distract me from my mission."

Walker hung up and made another call, which was answered after two rings by Eve Ronin, the ridiculously young but relentless Lost Hills homicide detective he'd worked with once before.

"You're lucky I'm answering this call, Walker, and not sending you directly to voicemail."

"You're not still mad at me about the Wonder Woman thing, are you?"

Their last case had ended with her in a Wonder Woman costume and with a broken nose.

"I will always be mad at you for that," she said.

"You should be grateful to me for helping you star in another viral video. It probably scored you a second season of your TV series."

"That's one more reason to be mad at you."

"Yeah, I can see why you'd be pissed about that," he said. "It must be awful having another dump truck full of money show up at the door of your mansion in Calabasas."

He knew it was more complicated than that, that she now had to live up to an idealized version of herself on TV and battle the resentment of everybody in the department, with the exception of her partner, Duncan "Donuts" Pavone, two uniformed Lost Hills deputies, and Walker and Sharpe.

"What do you want, Walker?"

"Lansing ordered me and Sharpe to determine what caused the big fire on the I-10."

"Lansing doesn't care. You're being used for a political stunt," Eve said. "You're going to get burned, no pun intended."

"That's what Sharpe says, too. But what can we do? We work for Lansing, so we're stuck."

"What does any of that have to do with me?"

"The Caltrans inspector who visited the site before the disaster lives in Agoura Hills," Walker said. "I thought it would be a good idea for me to talk with him."

"You're a tough guy who loves taking down dangerous predators, so this inspector must be one insanely violent, vicious sociopath if you need me for backup."

"What I need is a coroner," Walker said.

"You killed him?"

"He was already dead when I got here. He's hanging from a rafter in his garage."

"Shit," Eve said.

"That was Sharpe's opinion of the situation, too."

"Give me the address and we'll be right there."

He did.

CHAPTER THIRTEEN

A Saturday in Late August

Danny rode the ferry to Surudoikiba Island on an exceptionally clear, sunny day, which he saw as a good omen. Only yesterday, it had been raining. It was his sixth visit to the island, but this would only be his second visit to the Gallery of Curiosities.

On Danny's previous visits, he'd spent most of each day sitting on a hillside with a pair of binoculars, watching the museum's smoking area, identifying the patterns and timing when it was most likely to be empty or full of employees. He'd also made the three-hour hike up the mountain again to look at the view, something Tamiko had done as well. In fact, she was already on the island now, having taken an earlier ferry.

Danny looked at the other passengers and was pleased to see that dozens of them were wearing replicas of the Infinitum watch. These passengers were among the two hundred or so who were approached on the streets of Hiroshima, by people he'd hired, and given free tickets to visit the museum today on the condition that they wear the replicas, which he'd also given away. It had taken Danny almost eight weeks to receive the watches, which he'd ordered directly from the manufacturer in China. He was wearing one now himself.

He wore a prosthetic nose and chin and a Broadway-quality fake goatee. He didn't want his face immediately matched to the one that the museum's facial-recognition sensors undoubtedly captured from various angles on his first visit weeks ago. He was wearing khaki slacks, a collared white shirt, and a navy-blue sport jacket with red lining.

On his arrival at the island, he took the elevator up to the sky bridge, made his way quickly past the visitors freaked out by the cracking-glass effect, and headed for the inverted pyramid lobby, where there was already a line of tourists going through the security checkpoint.

As Danny gathered his watch, phone, and belt from the X-ray conveyor, he saw a red-coated museum guard watching him as he strapped the Infinitum replica on his wrist.

The guard said, "Seems like everybody has one of those today. Where did you get yours?"

"At the gift shop here on my last visit," Danny said. "I can't afford the real one."

"Nobody but Mr. Mikitani can," the guard said good-naturedly in perfect English. "And he bought the only one in existence."

The guest in front of Danny, one of two loud, sunburned Australian men in colorful *kaiju* T-shirts that he'd spotted on the ferry, turned around and looked at him. This one was wearing Godzilla, breathing fire on Tokyo.

"You paid for yours, mate?" Godzilla said, then held up his arm to show off his Infinitum. "I got mine free with a ticket to this place to celebrate World Horology Day."

The other Australian, wearing a T-shirt depicting Ultraman battling a lobster creature, said: "What do whores have to do with a watch and this museum?"

"I don't know," Godzilla said, "but I heard they have a hallway of dongers."

Danny said, "Horology is the study of mechanical timepieces and the Infinitum is the most exceptional one in the world."

"Oh, that makes sense," Ultraman said. "I wonder what they give away on World Donger Day."

Danny laughed, declined the electronic tablet offered to him, and continued on, this time taking the glass elevator directly down to the third floor.

◆ ◆ ◆

The conversation between Danny, the guard, and the two Australians was observed in the museum's windowless security command center by Koicho Saito, the chief of security, and his younger second-in-command, Noriko Noda.

They were both looking over the shoulder of a seated staffer at his console, where the man was intensely monitoring activities at the security checkpoint from several flat screens, though he did so a lot less intently when his bosses weren't standing behind him, making him sweat. He was one of the dozen people manning similar consoles in the darkened room. They were the museum's eyes and ears, keeping watch over everything.

Saito straightened up and frowned at Noriko. "They're celebrating World Horology Day?"

"That's what they all say," she said.

"Are they all part of the same tour group or club?"

"They don't seem to be," Noriko said. "We've had guests today of all ages and nationalities, some arriving as families, others as couples or individuals, all wearing the Infinitum souvenirs. They were handed out in Hiroshima with the tickets."

"I wonder if this is a promotional stunt that the marketing department neglected to share with us beforehand."

"It wouldn't be the first time," Noriko said.

Even so, he didn't like it. Not one bit. "Find out."

Saito was a retired chief inspector with the Tokyo Metropolitan Police's major crimes unit. He'd learned to trust his instincts, which he believed hadn't dulled, not even after three years of commuting each day from Hiroshima out to this rock, where the only major crimes were guests who hung their hats on the plaster penises, vomited on the infinity stairs, or urinated in the Bible toilet.

Noriko lowered her head in an apologetic bow. She was a former uniformed police officer from Osaka who, after five short years on the job, couldn't take the grind or the institutional sexism, so she went into private security instead. It was a different kind of grind, boredom instead of bureaucracy, and the same sexism. If Saito asked her to fetch him a cup of green tea one more time, she might throw it in his face.

"It's Saturday, sir," she said, trying hard not to sound condescending. "The marketing department doesn't work on weekends."

"I don't care. Call them at home. This is very strange and I don't like it. In the meantime, keep an eye on those people." Saito pointed at the screen, which showed more guests putting on the replica watches that they'd taken off to go through the scanner.

"With respect, sir, you're talking about nearly everybody in the museum," Noriko said. "And we can't tell from here who is wearing the watches and who isn't."

"Then keep an eye on the Infinitum."

"We always do," she said.

"I mean a constant one," Saito said with irritation. "Do I have to spell it out for you? I want someone in here watching nothing but that watch all day."

The words were barely out of his mouth when Saito decided that the someone would be him.

Tamiko Harada wore a red jacket with a Gallery of Curiosities photo ID clipped to it and carried a ragged paperback copy of *Maekawa Kunio and the Emergence of Japanese Modernist Architecture* under her arm as she sat in a chair in the empty smoking area.

Her white blouse was opened one button too far down, showing a tantalizing glimpse of her cleavage. The open neckline appeared accidental rather than intentional, since the entire blouse was misbuttoned by one button, so it hung a bit lopsidedly on her, indicating she'd dressed in a hurry. It suggested to anyone who saw her that she was an absent-minded academic unaware of her casual sensuality. Of course, it wasn't an accident at all and there was nothing casual about her approach to her appearance, which was painstakingly premeditated.

She took out a pack of Seven Stars smokes from her inside jacket pocket, shook out the only real cigarette, lit it with a disposable lighter, and started reading the book. The rest of the cigarette carton contained an explosive device, courtesy of Sam Mertz. She had a second one in another pocket.

Within a few moments, several other red-jacketed, mostly Japanese employees came out of the secured door and joined her. She smiled and made eye contact with one of the men, who gestured to her book.

"Business or pleasure?" he asked. The name on his ID tag was Makoto.

"Excuse me?" Her ID identified her as Suki Yaguchi.

Makoto sat down in the chair next to her. "The book you're reading."

"Both. I love architecture and I'm curating an upcoming exhibit here on modernism in Japan. Mr. Mikitani is a huge fan of Le Corbusier."

"I didn't know that."

"So was Takamasa Yoshizaka, who designed the Inter-University Seminar House in Hachioji, which was the inspiration for this building."

"I didn't know that, either," Makoto said, his gaze falling into her cleavage. "Tell me more."

Tamiko continued her lecture on modernism so that if anybody in the security office had noticed her on camera, it would seem as if she were one of the group. More employees filed out of the building and soon someone wedged the rock in the door to keep it slightly ajar.

She was good to go.

After about ten minutes, some of the employees started snubbing out their cigarettes and slipping back inside to return to work. She was still lecturing Makoto about modernism as they walked through the door into the museum together, entering a long industrial corridor with unadorned walls and exposed ductwork and piping above their heads. By this point, though, Makoto was bored senseless by her monologue and even her cleavage wasn't enough to maintain his interest. He made an inelegant escape by dashing into the men's room.

She'd successfully entered the employees-only section of the museum without having to swipe her pass card at the door scanner, thanks to the propped-open door to the smoking area, but she couldn't be certain that the system hadn't detected and logged her presence anyway.

Tamiko slipped into the women's room, ditched the pass card in her pocket, and replaced it with one of the four other cards, with four different authentic codes embedded in them, that she kept in an RFID-reader-blocking envelope in her pocket.

Tamiko checked her watch, also an Infinitum replica. She had ten minutes to get down to level three, which was plenty of time.

She used her new RFID access card to get through the door into the employee stairwell, which also doubled as the fire escape, and then another card to open the door to the galleries, all to hide her movements from detection by a computer algorithm that might be tracking the path of individual employees through the building and flagging any unusual activity for immediate review by someone in security.

She slipped out into the third floor, moving among the museum guests, a big smile on her face.

Now the real fun would begin.

Danny was in the weapons exhibit, admiring a heavy medieval Indo-Persian war hammer with an iron head that was a blunt block on one end and a brutally curved spike on the other. Since his last visit, he'd read up on war hammers, in particular comparing their destructive force with a battle-ax, and there wasn't a clear answer about which weapon did more damage.

He was thinking about that, trying to come to his own decision, so it was easy for him to pretend not to notice Tamiko when she passed behind him on her way to the nuclear bomb display.

◆ ◆ ◆

Saito sat at a console, staring at the screen as guests passed by the Infinitum, some of them even holding their arms up to show off their replicas as they took selfies in front of one of the most valuable watches on earth.

Noriko came up beside him. "I reached some people in the marketing department. They told me the watch and ticket giveaway had nothing to do with them, but they wish they'd thought of it."

That made Saito only more uncomfortable. He could actually hear alarms ringing in his head. "Between the watches and the tickets, someone has spent a lot of money on this stunt, at least 800,000 yen on tickets alone, and I want to know why. What are they getting out of this?"

"Who did the gift shop sell all those watches to?"

"I asked them," Saito said. "They've never had a bulk purchase larger than four watches at a time. And since the watches are only sold here, whoever gave away these must have ordered them directly from the factory in China."

Which was run by bootlegging scumbags who had no problem supplying criminals with counterfeit goods at the same time they were creating souvenirs for museums and amusement parks.

"Can people do that?" Noriko asked.

"Obviously they can," Saito said. "We have at least a hundred people in here wearing them."

"I thought the Infinitum replicas were exclusive to our store. That's a big loophole in our contract."

"That's not what bothers me."

"On the other hand, the watches were given away," Noriko said, continuing her thought, "so it's not like someone is selling them out from under our gift shop, and the tickets the people wearing the watches used are legitimate, so the museum is actually making money. It's a harmless stunt."

He turned and looked her in the eye. "Is it?"

"It's probably a promotion by a watch company, a jewelry store, or some watch lover's society," she said. "Whatever it is, it doesn't hurt the museum. If anything, it brings us more attention."

Saito frowned, then shifted his gaze back to the screen, where more guests were filing past the watch in its indestructible round orb. The alarms only got louder.

"I want to shut down the time exhibit."

Noriko actually gasped. "Because a hundred people are wearing the replicas we sell in the gift shop?"

"Yes. It's too odd."

"Do you really think that argument is going to convince Mr. Mikitani to close the exhibit? Every guest has been thoroughly scanned. Nobody is carrying any weapons or tools and the watch is in an impenetrable case. What harm can possibly be done?"

The more she talked, the more anxious he felt, the alarm in his mind suddenly becoming so loud that it nearly drowned out her voice. Saito pushed his chair back from the console and stood up.

"I'm going down there."

And that's when he noticed, to his astonishment, that *everyone* was reacting to the alarm he was hearing.

Because this alarm was real.

A second earlier, Tamiko tossed her explosives, contained in the two cigarette packs that Sam gave her, under the nuclear bomb and walked away just as it exploded with an earsplitting roar.

The bombs generated a lot of sparks and an enormous amount of smoke, setting off the fire alarms throughout the museum and activating the ceiling sprinkler system, drenching everyone with water.

But the explosives were harmless, designed to make a big sound and generate clouds of smoke, and were no more dangerous than a Fourth of July sparkler. Before anybody could realize that, and to help the panic spread, Tamiko began yelling in Japanese and English:

"It's the nuclear bomb! It's going to blow! Run for your lives!"

That led to sheer pandemonium, and people ran screaming to the fire exits, where frightened staff members were directing them quickly out the doors, as if getting out of the building would save them from a thermonuclear blast.

But that's the thing about chaos—nobody thinks clearly, and that's what Danny was counting on.

He grabbed the medieval war hammer, which was heavier than he thought it would be, and ran against the current of fleeing guests, along through the black hole of time, and into the chamber full of watches in their glowing orbs atop their slender plantlike pedestals.

He hoped the reedy stands were as fragile as they looked.

Danny planted his feet in front of the Infinitum and swung the war hammer at the pedestal, bending it in half, setting off another alarm that blared at an entirely different pitch from the fire sirens.

He swung at the pedestal again and it snapped, the orb dropping with a heavy thunk to the ground. The curved-top base of the pedestal was still stuck to the bottom of the orb. So Danny put one foot down on the basketball-size orb to hold it steady and gave the piece of pedestal another serious whack, snapping it off.

The whole process had taken a little over a minute.

He scooped up the orb and turned to the emergency exit door, nearly tripping over an unconscious red-jacketed man on the floor right behind him.

Danny took a step back, looked up, and saw Tamiko standing there, a Taser crackling in her hand and a sly grin on her face.

She said, "He was creeping up behind you with this. I twisted his arm and he zapped himself."

"I didn't notice any of it," Danny said.

Tamiko switched off the Taser and tossed it. "You were occupied."

That was no excuse, Danny thought. He'd never been so inattentive. It was a nearly catastrophic mistake that could have put him back in prison. Perhaps he should have stayed retired, but it was too late for that now.

Tamiko led him to the employee access door, which opened for them thanks to the security card in her pocket.

Once they were in the hallway, emergency lights flashing all around them, Danny handed her the orb and quickly took off his jacket, which he turned inside out. The reverse side was red, and when he put the jacket back on, it was an exact match for the museum staff uniform. He removed his belt and twisted the prong in the center of the buckle, which slid off like a cap to reveal a tiny lockpick inside, hidden in plain sight from the X-ray scanner.

"Give me the orb," Danny said.

She handed it to him. He rolled it upside down to reveal a tiny keyhole at the base, like the bottom of a piggybank, and worked his pick inside.

Tamiko was surprised. "How did you know that lock was there?"

"Because the watch is ticking. The orb may be indestructible, but there still needs to be a way to get inside it to service the watch."

Danny easily picked the lock, removed the Infinitum replica on his wrist, swapped it for the real one in the orb, and sealed it again. It would look like the indestructible orb had confounded the would-be thieves, who'd left empty handed. The trick wouldn't fool museum staff for long, but it would buy them some time.

As they ran up the stairs, Danny peeled the goatee and prosthetics from his face so he was a different man, a Gallery of Curiosities employee, when they arrived at the top floor and joined the panicked mob of guests and employees fleeing across the lobby to the exits.

◆ ◆ ◆

Saito witnessed the theft unfold on the screen in front of him in disbelief and profound shame.

Each day, his security staff examined the guests and their belongings with the most sophisticated scanning tools on earth to prevent anyone from bringing in the tools necessary to vandalize the exhibits or steal any of the treasures.

But what was the point of that if the museum also offered easy access to a wide variety of equipment necessary to destroy or steal their most valuable objects?

How had he not realized that before?

But he had no time to dwell on the idiocy of the situation. He had to act fast.

Saito couldn't lock down the museum to prevent people from leaving, not with fires possibly raging inside, but he could do the next best thing.

He yelled out to the room: "Alert the police. Lock down the island. Nobody leaves. The ferries stay docked until I say they can go. I want everyone searched for the watch."

Noriko said, "Almost every guest is wearing one."

"Confiscate them all," he said.

"But who do we arrest?"

"Whoever is wearing the real one," he screamed at her. "Isn't that obvious?"

"How can we tell which watch that is?"

Saito was so frustrated by her stupidity that he wanted to strangle her. "We'll leave it to the experts in charge of the exhibit to tell us."

"It's Saturday. None of them are here."

He got in her face and yelled at the top of his lungs, spraying her with spittle. "Get them here!"

Hundreds of confused, wet, and frightened guests and employees were crowded outside the Gallery of Curiosities, waiting for someone to tell them what was happening, or what to do, or where to go, while they were also keeping a wary eye on the museum, fearing it might explode in a nuclear mushroom cloud at any second. Nobody noticed Danny and Tamiko as they hurried up the trail that led to the peak, where a stream of hikers flowed down to see what all the excitement was about.

They hiked up the mountain for the next three hours, frequently looking over their shoulders to see if anybody was chasing after them, but nobody seemed to be. Or if they were, they were far behind the pair.

When they reached the top, Tamiko cleared away some bushes, revealing the two backpacks and the large gym bag that she'd stowed there earlier. They unzipped everything and unloaded a wingsuit, a parachute pack, two helmets, and a tandem harness for Danny.

It wouldn't have been possible for Danny to learn, over just a few weeks, how to jump off a cliff in a wingsuit, which was much more complex and dangerous than skydiving, which he'd also never done. That was a problem, because before anyone could be taught how to wingsuit-fly, or allowed to even buy one of the webbed nylon suits, they had to prove that they'd already made hundreds of free-fall skydives.

Danny didn't have the time or the suicidal personality required for that. He didn't have to. He had Tamiko. And she'd assured him that tandem wingsuit diving was no big deal, that rich tourists in France did it for fun all the time. She suggested that they do a practice jump off a cliff she liked in Italy, but Danny refused.

He was willing to take this risk only once. And that time was now.

Tamiko stripped down to a bikini top and bottoms, leaving her clothes behind, then zipped herself into the wingsuit. He handed her one of the helmets. "I really don't get the point of the these."

"It's in case we have a hard landing."

"If that happens, we'll be dead."

"Don't be a worrywart." She strapped on her parachute while Danny strapped the tandem harness on himself.

Damn right he was worried.

He'd watched dozens of YouTube videos of wingsuit fliers hurtling through the air at over a hundred miles per hour, skirting cliff edges and treetops by inches. And almost all those daredevils he'd watched were now dead, killed in a jump gone wrong, due to a parachute failure or a split-second miscalculation. He'd even watched some of them die from their own points of view, the footage recovered from the GoPro cameras on their mangled corpses and posted to YouTube for one last, posthumous effort at viral success.

His harness had straps on the shoulders, chest, belly, and legs. Two straps dangled from the back of his shoulders and hips. Everything fit tight, but it didn't make him feel secure. He put on his helmet and took a deep breath, trying to calm himself down.

Tamiko came up behind him and snapped the straps from his shoulders and hips to rings in the same spots on her own harness, then pulled the straps in until he was tight against her body, his head pressed against her chest.

"Is the watch waterproof?" she asked.

"I don't know," he said. But what he was really thinking was: *I should have stayed retired. What the hell am I doing jumping off a cliff?*

"It costs $40 million," Tamiko said. "At that price, it should be."

"It's not a watch you buy to wear surfing or skydiving."

"So it doesn't have an altimeter, either?"

"We're about to jump off a cliff," Danny snapped at her, "and you're worried about the watch's features?"

"Only because I forgot my altimeter," she said. "Oh well, too late now."

He hoped she was joking.

They lowered their goggles and shuffled awkwardly toward the edge of the cliff, the vast inland sea and the isles of the Geiyo archipelago stretching out in front of them, the museum two thousand feet below.

Danny wished he'd packed a blindfold.

"Keep your arms at your sides and your legs together," Tamiko said. "And don't crap yourself."

"I'll do my best."

"Are you ready?"

"Not yet," he said, his heart pounding so hard it felt like it wanted to escape. "What's the count?"

She jumped.

He screamed.

They were falling, but also flying forward at an astonishing speed. It was exhilarating and terrifying at the same time. He tried to convince himself that this was just an amusement park ride, to enjoy the experience, to have fun.

But then Tamiko zeroed in on the upside-down pyramid, getting them so close he was afraid they might hit it, and he heard himself screaming again.

Proximity flying wasn't part of the plan.

In an instant, they were out over the water, streaking over the police boats and ferries, and speeding toward the next island, an uninhabited rock, two jagged crags jutting hundreds of feet up from the sea.

Tamiko suddenly straightened out into a midair standing position and pulled the rip cord. They were yanked up hard. He felt her shudder

155

against him and let out an orgiastic cry, which he wasn't sure was real. Then she quickly unzipped her arms from the wingsuit, grabbed the toggles behind her, and began steering them down.

She edged them around the curve of the island, getting dangerously close to the spiky outcroppings, and then he saw a boat below them that was hidden from view by the peaks on Surudoikiba.

The boat was an open-decked 33-foot, 740-horsepower Aquariva with a hand-carved mahogany deck inlaid with maple on a sleek fiberglass hull. It was the Rolls-Royce of cruisers and he could see Sam Mertz was at the helm.

She brought them down low, their feet almost skimming the surface of the water, before she made a gentle pinpoint landing with surprising grace on the cruiser's broad aft lounging deck, making it seem not only easy, but natural.

They were immediately met by Sam, a nautical cap on his head, who helped Danny, who was trembling, unstrap himself from Tamiko. She removed the parachute from her back, stepped out of her wingsuit, and let it all slide into the ocean. Now she was just a woman sunning herself on her yacht.

Sam said, "I'm surprised you two weren't pursued by helicopter gunships."

"You watch too many stupid movies." Tamiko took off her helmet and tossed it in the water.

Danny did the same with his helmet, watching them sink. He was still too shaken to speak. He stripped out of his clothes, down to the T-shirt and bathing shorts that he wore underneath, and kicked the discarded garments into the sea.

Sam nodded at Danny. "Let's see it."

Danny showed him the Infinitum on his wrist. It was ticking, which was a big relief.

"Nice," Sam said. "Now sit down."

Sam hurried to the steering wheel in its resplendent mahogany, silver, and leather dashboard, looked back to make sure Danny and

Tamiko were sitting on the cushioned bench seat, and then punched the throttle, the boat surging forward at forty-one knots northeast toward Osaka.

Tamiko rested her head on Danny's shoulder. He slipped his arm around her. Now they were a wealthy couple out enjoying the water on a beautiful day on their $600,000 luxury cruiser, nothing like the nondescript vehicle a thief would be expected to use for a smooth getaway.

She said, "Was it good for you?"

"We're both alive, so it was wonderful," Danny said, finally breathing normally. "But I never want to do that again."

"That wasn't what I was talking about." She gave his earlobe a gentle tug with her teeth and then whispered: "When I was pressed against your body and pulled the rip cord, my climax was so sharp and intense, I almost passed out."

"I'm glad you didn't," he said.

"Is that as close as we are ever going to get for the two of us . . . ?" Her voice trailed off.

"Absolutely," Danny said. "I could never match on solid ground what you felt today in the air." If she'd actually felt anything at all.

"You don't give yourself much credit."

"I'm pragmatic," he said.

"If that was true," Tamiko said, "you never would have jumped off that cliff with me."

"On the contrary. I know your experience and your skills, otherwise I wouldn't have trusted you with my life."

"Maybe that was the real reason my orgasm was more intense than ever," she said. "You surrendered yourself completely to me."

Danny looked at her. They were close enough to kiss, their lips practically touching, but he didn't feel any sexual tension, any magnetic pull, and he was sure that Tamiko didn't, either. She was studying him with scientific curiosity.

"You're right, *Brian*." She kissed his cheek and then put some friendly space between them. "On solid ground, you could never truly surrender yourself like that to anyone."

Tamiko said it without any malice. He was glad that she understood, because it was something that he'd accepted about himself long ago.

CHAPTER FOURTEEN

September 8

Andrew Walker, Eve Ronin, and her partner, Duncan Pavone, stood in Monte Murphson's garage, looking up at the Caltrans inspector's bloated, rotting body, which was swarming with flies and dripping fluids onto the floor.

This was Eve and Duncan's first look at the corpse since they'd arrived at the house on the fetid shores of Lake Lindero. Deputies were cordoning off the house with a string of yellow tape and the crime scene unit and medical examiner were on the way.

"I am having a serious case of déjà vu," Eve said to Walker. "We met you for the first time outside a house like this, investigating a man's probable suicide."

"At least this house isn't in ashes," Walker said.

Duncan smiled at Eve, who was both half his age and half his weight. "But maybe you can still dress up as Wonder Woman and save the world again."

She scowled at him, but otherwise ignored the comment. "This is a very expensive house for someone living on a Caltrans inspector's salary."

The three of them walked out of the garage and into the main house, though it didn't diminish the stench by much.

Duncan said: "How do you know what their salary is?"

"I don't but I know how much houses go for in Agoura and Calabasas," she said. "Your average civil servant doesn't make that kind of money."

"Unless they get a TV series," Duncan said.

Walker thought about his own situation. "My wife inherited our house. Maybe he inherited this one."

"Or maybe he got a TV series," Duncan said. "*Monte Murphson: Caltrans Inspector.*" He looked at Eve. "You're lucky he died, or you could have had some serious competition."

Walker's phone vibrated with a notification. He took it out and checked the screen as he said: "I looked around the house while I was waiting for you. I didn't find a suicide note, but I also didn't see any signs of a struggle or a break-in."

"A lot of people kill themselves," Eve said. "He could be one of them."

Duncan said, "If that's true, it means you probably won't have the opportunity to shoot anybody or be rushed to the ER."

"That's fine with me," she said, then gestured at Walker. "I'm still healing from the last case we worked with him."

Walker gave her his best smile. "Your nose looks great to me."

"You can't see the deviated septum. My left nostril feels like it's plugged with concrete."

"That reminds me," Walker said. "What happened to that Wonder Woman outfit?"

Duncan said, "She's wearing it under her clothes right now. When there's trouble, she spins around, her clothes fly off in a thundercrack, and she's ready for action. It's something to see."

Eve was not amused. "I'll wait for the crime scene unit outside."

She walked toward the splintered front door, irritated at both of them.

Walker turned to Duncan. "Where's her sense of humor?"

"It was last spotted in Pacoima," Duncan said.

Eve was already out the door when Walker called after her. "Don't you want to execute the search warrant?"

Eve stopped at the door and turned around to look at him. "What search warrant?"

"The one that was just granted and sent to my phone allowing us to toss this place, get his phone records, and dig into his financials."

Walker held up his phone to show off the document he'd been texted.

Eve came back into the house. "You contacted a judge for a search warrant before you called us to report the homicide?"

"Sharpe did. Murphson wasn't going to get any deader and I wanted to keep the investigation moving."

Duncan said, "What did you and Shar-Pei want to talk to Murphson about?"

"The businesses on the Caltrans property were violating every fire code ever written but Murphson didn't write up a single tenant," Walker said. "In fact, most of the tenants shouldn't have been there at all. They were in blatant violation of the regulations regarding the kinds of businesses that could be located under a freeway but he didn't report any of them."

Eve said, "So either he was a fool or he was paid to look the other way."

Walker glanced back at the garage. "Which means either he killed himself to avoid prosecution and shame or he was murdered to keep his mouth shut."

"I can see why a judge granted the warrant so fast and why you were in such a hurry to get it," she said.

"It's your warrant now," Walker said. "I'm drafting you both into the illustrious Los Angeles County Sheriff's Department Freeway Fire Investigation Task Force. FIT Force for short."

Duncan said, "That doesn't spell 'FIT.'"

161

"It does if you combine the *F*s in 'Freeway' and 'Fire' into one, because if we use and pronounce both *F*s in the acronym, it will sound like you're stuttering."

"Good point," Duncan said.

Eve sighed. "It doesn't matter what it's called. You're a detective, you don't have the authority to reassign us."

"Actually, I do. Lansing told us we could have whatever resources we want. We want you two. Let us know what you find out about Monte Murphson and his cause of death." Walker tipped his hat at her and headed for the door.

"Where are you going?" Eve said.

"Southland Premier Properties. They're the people who leased the land from Caltrans that was razed in the inferno."

"They're also the people most likely to have bribed Murphson and, if this wasn't a suicide, to have him killed," she said, calling after him. "You want some backup?"

Walker turned at the front step and gave her a smile. "I'll be fine. I don't think there's going to be a shoot-out."

"Yeah," Duncan said, "they'll probably just hang themselves when they see you coming. In fact, Shar-Pei told me he was tempted to do that himself the first day you showed up."

Eve said, "It was the hat."

Duncan looked at Eve, then at Walker. "What do you know, her sense of humor made it back safely from Pacoima."

"That wasn't a joke," Walker said. "It was a fact."

Southland Premier Properties was on the fifth floor of a half-vacant office building in Warner Center, across the street from the dead Promenade shopping mall that had been empty and slated for demolition for years.

The last Walker heard, it was going to be razed for a ten-thousand-seat arena.

Walker introduced himself to the young bottle-blond receptionist, who seemed irritated that he'd interrupted her from the screenplay she'd been reading, and told her he wanted to speak to whomever was in charge of the company. She said his name was Dwight Gordy and that she would see if he was busy.

"He's not," Walker said with a smile. "You can tell him I said so."

She wasn't charmed. She picked up the phone, told Gordy who was there to see him, listened for a moment, then hung up and looked at Walker.

"He will see you now in the conference room. It's down the hall, to your left."

Walker thanked her, walked past two empty offices, and into the conference room, which had a long table, six chairs, and two occupants, one of whom was an attractive woman in a designer pantsuit who looked physically ill when she spotted him. She recovered quickly, shifting her gaze to the legal pad in front of her and making a meaningless note on it with her Montblanc pen. He knew her and was delighted by her reaction.

Dwight Gordy was a tanned, physically fit man in his late forties who must have been going gray, since his eyebrows and hair were a color Walker had never seen on a human being or in nature. He also looked like he'd just come from the golf course or was on his way there, wearing a bright-red moisture-wicking Callaway polo, a white logo cap, a white belt, and blue slacks. Gordy stood up and offered Walker his hand.

"Perfect timing. I was just finishing up a meeting with our lawyer."

Walker shook Gordy's hand, which had a firm grip, and smiled at the woman. "Hello, Sheryl."

She gave him a curt nod. "Walker."

Gordy instantly picked up on their shared animosity. A goldfish could have detected it. "You two know each other?"

Walker said, "We've run into each other a few times. She's not a bad criminal defense attorney. Have you committed a crime, Dwight?"

Sheryl replied quickly. "Don't answer that, Mr. Gordy."

Walker took a seat across the table from them. "I know she's won some cases, Dwight, but not the eight times she's defended people that I've arrested."

Gordy sat down and glanced with some worry at his lawyer. She answered the look on his face.

"Seven. It's only been seven."

"Oops." Walker smiled at Gordy. "Maybe I was looking into the future."

Sheryl's face tightened up. "You should know, Mr. Gordy, that Walker is notorious for being a sneaky, obnoxious prick."

Gordy looked back at Walker. "I gathered that from the cowboy hat. What can I do for you, Detective?"

They were off to a great start, at least as far as Walker was concerned. He was going to enjoy this interview. "We're investigating the cause of the fire on your property."

"Then you're at the wrong place. The cause is obvious."

"People keep telling me that, but I don't see it."

"It was the deadbeats who were renting from us," Gordy said. "We've been trying to broom them out for months, but that's not easy. The laws in Los Angeles favor the lessee. It's a laborious process to get evictions and these people know how to game the system."

"That's funny," Walker said. "Because your lessees say you were strong-arming them to pay exorbitant rent for a patch of dirt and no access to basic utilities like water and electricity."

"They would say that," Gordy said. "We demanded that they upgrade their units to avoid the risk of fire . . . or get the hell out. Instead, they stopped paying us. They are no better than the squatters defecating on the sidewalks outside our fences."

"So you sent Big Mike to collect from your renters or force them to go."

Gordy cocked his head, trying to convey bewilderment. "Who is Big Mike?"

Walker wasn't fooled, but he played along.

"Maybe this will help." He reached into his shirt pocket and pulled out the piece of paper towel with Farhad's sketch of Big Mike on it. He unfolded the paper towel, smoothed it out on the table, and passed it to Gordy.

Gordy's receptionist might have been an actor, Walker thought, but her boss certainly wasn't.

"I don't recognize him," Gordy lied and passed the paper towel to Sheryl, who took a quick, dismissive glance at it.

"Wow, you've really gone high tech at the sheriff's department," she said. "Is that red hair on Fred Flintstone or ketchup?"

Sheryl slid the paper towel back to Walker.

He tucked it into his pocket and shifted his attention to Dwight Gordy.

"The renters say Big Mike is your collector, and if they don't pay on time, there's 18 percent daily interest, then Mike gets violent, and if that doesn't work, he sets their place or their vehicles on fire."

"That's ridiculous," Gordy said. "I don't have a collector. I'm a real estate investor, not a loan shark."

"Getting $25,000 a month in rents on a property you're leasing from the state for $6,000 is quite a profit."

Sheryl said, "When did it become a crime to make money?"

Walker held up his hands in mock surrender. "I was just admiring his business acumen. Let's get back to the fire."

"Which my client had nothing to do with."

"He just said that he knew his renters were violating fire safety codes."

"What he said, Walker, was that he was *concerned* that they were and that he demanded that they immediately bring their units into compliance."

"Okay." Walker turned to Gordy. "So how did you know they weren't in compliance?"

Gordy shifted in his seat and looked at the table, signaling to Walker that a lie was coming and it was going to be a good one.

"I went down there and saw it for myself. I left outraged and deeply concerned for the well-being of our community."

"You didn't learn about the problems from Monte Murphson?"

Gordy tried that bewildered look again but still couldn't pull it off convincingly, though Walker enjoyed seeing the effort. "Who is Monte Murphson?"

"The inspector responsible for making sure all the people leasing Caltrans property are following the rules, Dwight."

"I've never heard of him," Gordy said.

"You didn't think it was odd that Caltrans never contacted you about what was going on down there?"

"Why should they?"

"Oh, I don't know," Walker said. "Maybe because it was a blatant firetrap that you illegally subleased to businesses that aren't allowed to be operating under a freeway."

Sheryl jumped from her seat, as if making an objection in court.

"That's a totally unsupported and outrageous allegation. Caltrans regularly inspected the property and was well aware of the sublessees and the businesses that were operating there. They can't pretend now that they didn't know."

Walker looked up at her. "Unless they were never told."

"You'll have to talk to their inspector about that."

"I'd like to," Walker said, "but he's dead."

Sheryl sat down. She knew this interview had become a lot more serious for her client. "What happened?"

"His body is hanging from a rafter in his garage," Walker said.

Gordy shifted in his seat again and cleared his throat. "He clearly realized the extent of his responsibility for this catastrophe and was unwilling to accept the consequences, leaving me to be victimized by the legal system for his mistakes."

Walker pretended to mull that argument for a moment and hoped that he was a better actor than Gordy. "Do you have a Ouija board or happen to know any good mediums?"

"I'm afraid not," Gordy said.

Walker pushed his chair from the table and stood up. "Then I'll have to find out what I need to know another way."

Gordy stood up, too. "Good luck with that."

Walker started for the door, then did a Columbo, turning back to Gordy. "Oh, one more thing. You say the fire was caused by your renters. Aren't you liable for the damage?"

Sheryl answered for him. "You're forgetting that Mr. Gordy is a renter himself. The State of California owns the property, not him. They are the ones who are liable and insured and yet they will undoubtedly attempt to blame him to excuse their own failures."

"Like renting the land to him and not watching what he was doing with it."

"I wouldn't look at it that way," she said.

Walker smiled. "That's why it's going to be eight, not seven, times that I've beaten you."

Walker was on the street outside the building, walking to his truck parked in the red zone, when he got a call from Eve Ronin.

"Unless everybody has hung themselves at Southland Premier Properties, you should get back here," she said. "CSU and the ME are taking down the body for a preliminary examination."

"I'm on my way," he said.

"Did you find out anything we need to know?"

He briefed her as he got in his truck, headed west on Oxnard Street, north on Topanga, then west on the Ventura Freeway toward

Agoura Hills. He finished his story as he approached an overpass under construction that would soon be the world's largest wildlife crossing, a bridge of trees and grass for animals between the Santa Monica Mountains and the rest of California. Soon nobody would have to drive around the carcasses of deer, coyotes, and mountain lions that tried to cross eight lanes of traffic to mate outside of their gene pool. It would take all the adventure out of driving on the freeway.

Eve said, "It sounds to me like Murphson's death is very good news for Southland Premier Properties."

"At least they had the decency not to pop open champagne and throw confetti while I was there. What have you learned?"

"Monte Murphson was forty-seven, single, and probably an alcoholic."

"Probably?"

"He has opened and unopened liquor bottles in every room in the house, including the bathroom."

"Those must be the bottles for medicinal use."

"He also had enough empty bottles and cans in his trash to open his own recycling operation."

"Maybe he had a party recently."

"Not according to his neighbors," Eve said. "The only visitor they noticed was a four-door dually parked in the driveway beside his truck two nights ago."

Walker took the Reyes Adobe exit and then turned right. "What is a dually?"

"How can you wear a cowboy hat and not know that? It's a one-ton pickup truck with two tires in the front and two on each side in the back."

Walker made a left onto Canwood Street, which curved back down toward the freeway and then ran parallel to it. "Did the neighbors see anybody?"

"Nope. And they can't tell us the brand or color of the truck, either."

Walker was almost at the house. "Not much to go on."

"Well, we did find $78,280 in cash hidden in a secret compartment behind his medicine cabinet."

"Why didn't you start by telling me that?" He turned into the cul-de-sac, which was now crowded with official vehicles from LASD and a morgue wagon. Neighbors stood on their dead lawns, watching the Tyvek-suited forensic technicians go in and out of the house.

"I like to leave the best for last," Eve said. "See you in the garage."

He parked, got out of his truck, and went through the house to the garage, where CSU head Nan Baker and Deputy Medical Examiner Emilia Lopez were crouched beside Murphson's body, which now lay on a plastic sheet on the floor. Nan took pictures of the body, while other members of her crew were taking pictures of everything in the garage. Duncan and Eve stood across from Nan and Emilia.

Nan looked up at Walker. She was a big-boned African American woman in her forties who wasn't intimidated by anyone. Even the sheriff knew not to cross her.

"Thanks for the chopper, Walker. I could get used to that."

"Me too," Emilia said. She was short, in her thirties, and wore glasses that were too big for her round face. "It would have taken us hours to get here without it."

"It just shows you that this case is a top priority for the sheriff and that he expects quick results," Walker said. "Anything you can tell us here and now, even if it's an educated guess, will be helpful, starting with whether this is suicide or murder."

Emilia used her gloved hands to carefully lift the hose up from the man's bloated neck, revealing the bruising underneath.

"The bruising around his neck is angled upward, which is consistent with being hung. He doesn't appear to have any broken bones, bruises, or lacerations."

Eve crouched beside her to get a better look. Walker didn't want or need one—he'd take Emilia's word for it.

"So no signs of a struggle," Eve said.

169

"I wouldn't say that." Emilia pointed to his mouth, which was in a grotesque grimace. "Ordinarily, you can't read anything into a corpse's grimace. It's a common and natural postmortem occurrence."

"But not this time," Eve said.

Emilia pointed to his protruding lips. "There are teeth marks inside his lips and dried blood on his teeth, which is something I often see when someone is smothered."

Nan said, "The killer came up behind the victim, held a pillow or something else over his face, and held him tight against his body until it was over."

Eve looked over at her. "How do you know that?"

Nan held up some hairs in a pair of tweezers. "There's dog hair all over the victim's back, but nowhere else on his body. Does the victim have a dog?"

Duncan said, "Nope."

Eve squinted at Nan's tweezers. "How do you know it's dog hair?"

Walker and Duncan cringed and braced themselves for Nan's reply.

"Because hair is the most common biological evidence found at a crime scene and I've been doing this job since you were in diapers."

"You can tell the difference between human hair and dog hair on sight?"

Walker and Duncan cringed again. Eve just didn't know when to stop.

"Walker asked us for our best educated guess, which is what I am giving you," Nan said. "But I will, of course, confirm what I believe under a microscope and try to have the breed identified by our forensic hair expert."

Duncan leaned down toward Eve and said, "Ask her how she knows that the hairs didn't come from a cat, a horse, or a bear. That would be fun to watch."

Eve suddenly realized that she'd crossed a line, not once, but twice. She stood up and offered Nan a weak smile. "I'm sorry, I was just curious. I didn't mean to imply that I question your judgment. I have total faith in your experience."

"I'm thrilled to hear that." Nan bagged the hairs and took some more photographs of the body.

Walker said, "Murphson was smothered, and then hung to make his death look like a suicide." He waited to see if anyone would disagree.

Emilia said, "It's possible he was smothered into unconsciousness and then hung, but yes, in general, I think that's what happened here. But I won't be able to confirm it until I do my autopsy."

Duncan turned to Eve. "Congratulations. It looks like you may get to shoot someone and end up in the hospital on this case after all."

Walker gestured to Duncan and Eve and headed back into the house. They followed him into the living room, where more forensic technicians were taking photos and dusting for prints.

Walker said, "Obviously, Southland Premier Properties has a strong motive for killing Murphson."

"If they were bribing him," Duncan said.

Eve said, "He didn't get this house and that $78,000 in cash from selling Girl Scout Cookies."

"He may have been taking bribes from other Caltrans lessees," Duncan said. "Maybe one of them killed him out of fear of what he might say if he was questioned after the big fire."

"I suppose that's possible," Eve said. "We'll need to get a list of every property Murphson was inspecting."

"I can get you that," Walker said.

"And if you're the kind of QAnon conspiracy wacko who believes that our government is controlled by pedophile lizard people pretending to be humans," Duncan said, "then it's possible that Caltrans had him killed to cover the agency's total lack of oversight of the properties that they lease out."

Eve frowned. "I don't see Caltrans hiring killers to hide their laziness."

"You don't see that the president is a lizard, either," Duncan said.

"It's not so far-fetched," Walker said.

Eve shot Walker a look. "That the president is a lizard?"

"The Caltrans angle," Walker said. "Instead of the agency itself being the bad guy, it could be a single bureaucrat who is getting kickbacks or bribes on a statewide scale from companies to lease them properties and then look the other way when they sublease."

Eve sighed. "I guess we are on your task force now, whether we like it or not."

CHAPTER FIFTEEN

Walker drove to the Lost Hills sheriff's station in Calabasas and parked his truck in the back lot, where an LASD patrol chopper was waiting for him. The TFO and pilot were the same crew who'd ferried Nan and Emilia, and later Nan's team, over from East Los Angeles. The two officers weren't thrilled about their new jobs as chauffeurs, and Walker pretended to sympathize, but he didn't really care. He intended to take advantage of the helicopter as much as he possibly could during the traffic nightmare.

The flight to LASD headquarters took him over the gridlocked Los Angeles freeway system in minutes instead of hours and he wondered how long it would take for the people stuck in their cars down there to riot in the streets or realize they should just stay at home until I-10 was fixed.

LASD HQ was east of downtown and directly across the 1-10 freeway from California State University, Los Angeles, where the crime lab was located. The LASD shared a campus with the headquarters for the Los Angeles County Fire Department and a former women's jail that was now rented out as a location for movies and TV shows. Walker wondered how the sheriff would feel if *Ronin* was ever shot there, right outside his office window.

Once the chopper landed, Walker realized something he'd forgotten to do. He made a quick call to the assistant sheriff and then headed into the building.

Getting from the door to Sharpe's office to his desk required winding through a maze built of teetering stacks of overstuffed binders, instruction manuals, bulging files, and newspapers topped with fax machines, typewriters, boots, and assorted components from improvised explosives. One wrong move and a man could be buried alive. Perhaps some already were. It was not something Walker was eager to investigate, though on some hot summer days, it smelled to him like there could be a corpse in there somewhere.

Walker found a way through, but every few weeks, an old stack would topple or a new one would appear, forcing him to forge a new path. Thankfully, this was not one of those days, and he made it quickly to the desk, where Sharpe was leaning back in his duct tape–covered chair, his feet up on his doodle-covered blotter, watching videos of the freeway underpass on his desktop computer, which was covered with sticky notes going back a decade.

Sharpe spoke without taking his eyes off the screen. "Is it suicide or murder?"

"Murder."

Walker took a seat in one of the two guest chairs, which was one too many, because he was the only guest Sharpe ever had. Anyone else who came to see him called out to him from the safety of the door.

"Whodunit?"

"My money is on Southland Premier Properties," Walker said. "Or the lizard people at Caltrans."

That got Sharpe's attention. He lifted his feet off the desk, hit the space bar on the keyboard to pause the videos, and leaned forward.

"Lizard people?"

"You'll have to ask Duncan Pavone about that. It's his theory. Have you learned anything from the videos?"

"The security camera and TV news videos were useless. The fire was too far along. But the videos from the trucks and rideshare drivers really paid off. We have some shots, from different angles, of the property before the fire and then the early moments of the blaze. It's almost like time-lapse photography."

"Is it an accident or arson?"

"Arson," Sharpe said.

"Whodunit?"

Sharpe grimaced and sighed and scratched his cheek.

Well, well, Walker thought. He leaned forward, intrigued. "I wasn't really expecting an answer, but you already know who set the fire, don't you. And you don't like the answer."

"It's not definitive."

"Can you see the arsonist in the videos?"

Sharpe grimaced, and sighed, and scratched his other cheek. "Not in the flesh, but perhaps in the method."

"Perhaps?" Walker said. "Stop being so evasive. Who is it?"

Sharpe swung around to face his computer and tapped a few keys. "Let me show you what I've seen and then you can tell me."

Walker walked around the desk, careful to avoid a tipping coatrack burdened with a pile of clothes, to look over Sharpe's shoulder.

"This is a time-lapse video of sorts, compiled from the dash-cam footage recovered from big rigs leaving the logistics warehouse, that starts shortly before the fire."

The videos were jittery and jumpy, due to the editing and the movement of the vehicles, but the images themselves were surprisingly sharp. They were street-forward views from big rigs passing southeast under the freeway on West Washington Boulevard, the Caltrans property on the driver's side.

The property was surrounded by cyclone fencing topped with razor wire, bits of trash bags and strips of paper caught in the blades and fluttering like flags. Behind the fencing, the asphalt was jam-packed with trucks, cars, barrels, shipping containers, sheds, and tall stacks of wooden pallets and tires that reached nearly to the freeway's underbelly.

Sharpe pointed to the screen.

"Look here. As the trucks pass the property, you can see glimpses of a beat-to-shit Nissan Altima parked right between a huge pile of pallets and tires."

He could see the Altima through the bases of the pallets. It was like looking outside through a set of open blinds. "Yeah, I see it."

"We don't see the fire being set, but ten minutes later, the cameras on the passing trucks captured this." Sharpe fast-forwarded the footage to the moment he wanted and froze the image. Flames were coming up from under the Altima. "You see those flames?"

"Of course I do," Walker said.

Sharpe hit the + key on his keyboard repeatedly, zooming in on the car. The image got blurry and pixelated, but Walker could see that the fire was rising from two dark rectangular shapes beneath the car's gas tank. The shapes were burning primarily at both ends, which wasn't natural. But it *was* familiar.

"Those are Duraflame logs," he said. "You think Toniel Novar, our fugitive serial carport arsonist, did this."

"I didn't say that."

"You don't have to." Walker got out his phone and opened the browser.

"Are you going to Google Earth to see if any of Mateo Bonilla's graffiti was on the freeway?"

"Yes," Walker said.

"That won't be necessary. It's there. The truck and rideshare videos captured the graffiti, too."

Sharpe tracked back on the video and zoomed in on a spot that captured some pillars and walls covered in graffiti. And there, amid the many gang signs and crude depictions of male genitalia and topless women, were Bonilla's distinct bloated people. His style was unmistakable.

"Bonilla really got around Los Angeles," Walker said.

"But Bonilla's work obviously hasn't been painted over, because we're looking at it," Sharpe said. "There's no motive here for revenge."

"Or that's his only remaining art under the freeway and the rest was painted over."

"By whom?" Sharpe said. "Do you really think Southland Premier Properties or Caltrans or any of these sublessees would bother? And if they did, wouldn't they start with the gang signs and penises instead of one of his cartoon characters? Do you see any painted-over patches anywhere under that freeway? I don't."

"I'm sure a blank space gets covered fast with new graffiti."

"There's something else that bothers me," Sharpe said. "There are dozens of cars, trucks, and vans parked on the property but he picked this cheap little Altima to torch."

"Why does that bother you?"

"Because the car is parked among the tallest stacks of pallets and tires under the freeway."

"He obviously didn't want to be seen from the street setting fire to the car."

"I'm sure that's true, but that's not the main reason," Sharpe said. "I think he was using the car fire to ignite the pallets and tires and create an inferno. It's called 'laddering fuels,' something only a skilled arsonist or firefighter would know."

"Maybe he lucked into it," Walker said.

Sharpe shook his head. "It's a level of expertise he hasn't shown before."

"Maybe he figured it out after setting two dozen fires over two nights," Walker said.

"And where are the sixteen-ounce Coleman propane tanks he was using before?"

"Maybe he didn't want to risk the tank blowing while he was still around." Walker sat on the edge of the desk so he could look at Sharpe. "Are you going to tell Scruggs and Caffrey about this?"

"Hell no."

"Because you don't want them getting credit for solving both the serial carport fires and the I-10 freeway catastrophe when they arrest Toniel Novar."

"Because we don't have any proof that the fire was started by a Duraflame log. We already have synthetic logs on our minds and saw what we wanted to see. Those rectangular objects could be something else."

"You know they're not," Walker said. "You'd bet your badge on it."

"That's not enough," Sharpe said.

"It will have to be. All of the evidence is gone."

"Maybe not," Sharpe said and tapped his computer screen. "We know roughly where the car was parked under the overpass. If a synthetic log was used, the chemicals in it will have seeped into the asphalt and the fill underneath."

Walker found that hard to believe. "Even after the thousands of gallons of water that were sprayed on the fire?"

Sharpe nodded. "We just have to dig up a sample and have it analyzed. That will be our proof." He checked the time on his phone. "It's too late now. It will be dark in two hours. We'll go to the site first thing tomorrow."

"Fine," Walker said. "And if it is a Duraflame log . . . ?"

"We'll take over the carport fire case from those idiots Caffrey and Scruggs and use all the resources of the Los Angeles Sheriff's Department to track down Toniel Novar."

"What about the murder of Monte Murphson?"

"Solving that is a job for Duncan Pavone and Eve Ronin," Sharpe said. "You know, the *homicide* detectives."

"Who are now assigned to FIT."

"What's FIT?"

"Our freeway fire investigation task force," Walker said. "The two *F*s are counted as one *F* and 'taskforce' is often used as one word, so the *T* totally works."

"When did this become a task force?"

"When I drafted those two. It's official. I cleared it on the phone with the assistant sheriff on my way over here."

"Nice of you to let me know," Sharpe said.

"It didn't come up until now," he said. "So the homicide is officially part of our investigation."

"I don't see how if we determine that it's Toniel Novar who set the freeway fire. We catch him and FIT with one *F* is closed."

Walker wasn't so sure about that. "Did Monte Murphson file any reports with Caltrans citing Southland Premier and the businesses underneath the freeway for their numerous fire code violations?"

"Not that Caltrans can find, assuming they haven't put them in a shredder to cover their asses."

"Then we are only doing half our job if our task force doesn't solve the murder, too."

"How do you figure that?" Sharpe asked.

Walker stood up and began pacing in front of Sharpe's desk, working himself up for what he had to say.

"Because I'm sure it's connected somehow to that fire, if not to the arson itself, then to the conditions that allowed a simple car fire to become a ten-hour-long inferno that shut down the busiest interstate freeway in the nation. All the politicians care about is the horrible traffic and impact to our economy. Sure, that's bad, but that's just the big picture. There was an entire community of struggling individuals and families living under that freeway who barely escaped with their lives and lost everything they had. The blaze also destroyed the livelihoods of dozens of hardworking, uninsured people who toiled in the shadows and are now left with nothing. Yeah, I know how they lived and worked was a big reason why the fire was so intense, but that's because nobody in a position of power or responsibility did their jobs to make it safe. Those people under the freeway were ignored or exploited instead. They are the victims of this crime, more than anybody else, and they deserve justice for what they've lost."

Walker sat down, out of breath and taken by surprise that he had so much to say once he got started.

Sharpe clapped a few times. "Wow, that was quite an impassioned speech."

Walker caught his breath, and said: "I'm passionate about justice."

"No, you're not. You're passionate about arresting people, especially if they make a run for it first."

"That goes without saying."

"That speech could've gone without saying," Sharpe said.

"Did I convince you?"

"Nope," Sharpe said, "but while you were blathering on and on, my mind wandered and I realized that there is an important reason for us to stay involved in the murder investigation."

"Which is?"

"If I am wrong about the asphalt, it might be the only crime we are able to prove in the freeway fire."

CHAPTER SIXTEEN

September 9

Danny Cole leaned against a $400,000 chrome-plated McLaren Artura hybrid supercar that was parked in the spot closest to the front door of Pacific Breeze Rejuvenation Clinic on Second Street in Santa Monica, California. It was Danny's first visit back to the United States since the Malibu fire heist and only a couple of weeks after the theft of the Infinitum, which had made news worldwide. But he didn't feel like a man on the run. In fact, he felt completely relaxed, certainly more than he ever did while sitting in a hot spring bath, listening to water drip into a buried three-hundred-year-old pot.

He wore a light-brown $7,000 Brunello Cucinelli suede biker jacket over the designer's $1,000 textured-stripe white Panama shirt and $2,000 double-pleated crepe cotton double-twill trousers, along with a pair of Hiro Yanagimachi beige $1,700 handmade African kudu-skin sneakers that he'd picked up in Tokyo before heading back to California. It was a decadently casual outfit chosen to instantly communicate his wealth and appear nonthreatening to a fellow member of the 1 percent like Roland Slezak, who was inside the clinic that morning for his regular three-times-a-week visit.

Slezak was forty-eight, but identified as thirty-five, claiming it was an accurate reflection of his "epigenic age," which was determined not by his birthdays but by regular measurements of genetic markers in his blood, which he had performed as part of his rejuvenation treatment.

The treatment consisted of many things, including injections of platelet-rich plasma from sixteen-year-old athletes (who were paid $100 an hour and signed NDAs), "red light cap therapy" to stimulate his hair follicles, and an array of skin creams derived from gorilla sperm, snail mucin, and argan oil extracted from nuts eaten by wild Moroccan goats and gathered from their droppings. As a result, Slezak boasted that he had the heart of a twenty-five-year-old, the skin of a ten-year-old, the lung capacity of a nineteen-year-old, the gum inflammation of a seventeen-year-old, and the nighttime erections of a fifteen-year-old.

But despite the robust physical health that Slezak bragged about, there was a blue DISABLED PERSON placard dangling from the rearview mirror of his chrome-plated McLaren, which was parked in the spot reserved for people with permanent physical disabilities that made it difficult or impossible to walk. The placard allowed him to park in the reserved spot without getting a ticket.

Danny was still leaning his back against the McLaren when Slezak came bounding out of the clinic wearing $3,000 Versace black-and-gold barocco-pattern silk pajamas and matching satin slippers. Slezak was a short man with strangely rubberlike skin and synthetic-looking hair that made him seem to Danny like a wax figure of Joe Pesci come to life.

"It's not for sale," Slezak said in a nasally voice that sounded like two kazoos were lodged in his nostrils.

"You don't look disabled to me."

"I'm in a minority," he said.

"Which minority is that?"

"The 1 percent of the 1 percent."

Danny stepped away from the McLaren. "Being obscenely wealthy doesn't qualify you for disabled-person parking."

"It qualifies me for whatever I want."

"Ah." Danny nodded. "I suppose hubris could be considered a disability. I stand corrected."

Slezak gave him a once-over. "You don't look like a parking enforcement officer to me."

"I'm not a cop. I'm the opposite." Danny lifted up his sleeve to display the Infinitum on his wrist.

Slezak froze, like the magic spell that had brought him to life had worn off, and he was back to being a Joe Pesci wax figure again. "So you visited the Gallery of Curiosities and bought yourself a souvenir. Is that supposed to impress me?"

"I didn't buy this, Roland. I took it."

"You expect me to believe that's the real thing?"

"Nope." Danny reached into the pocket of his suede jacket and tossed Slezak a jeweler's loupe. Slezak caught it. "You can examine it and decide for yourself. But this isn't the place. Let's take a walk."

Danny headed for the street. It took Slezak another second or two to recover from his shock and come alive again. He hurried after Danny, stumbling into stride next to him as they walked toward Santa Monica Boulevard. It wasn't easy running in bedroom slippers.

"Let's assume it's real," Slezak said. "Why come to me with your stolen goods? Aren't you worried I'll start screaming for the police?"

"There aren't many people who can afford the Infinitum, even at a significant discount, and your interest in rare and expensive watches is well known," Danny said. "As is your lack of respect for ethics, morality, or the law, so you won't be screaming for the police."

"I'm seeing our meet-cute now in a different light."

They turned left onto Santa Monica, heading toward the ocean, the salt-air breeze carrying a chill that made Danny glad he was wearing the overpriced suede coat. "I wanted to confirm your character for myself."

"Or lack of it," Slezak said with surprising self-awareness. "If that's the genuine watch, it's worth $30 million."

"Forty," Danny said.

"Whatever. You're taking a big risk walking around with it on your wrist without protection. Someone could punch you in the face and take it from you."

"What makes you think I'm unprotected?" Danny stopped and glanced at Slezak's chest. Slezak looked down at himself and saw a red laser-targeting dot over his heart. As Slezak watched, the dot moved slowly down his body and settled on his groin.

Danny hoped Tamiko would resist the temptation to shoot Slezak just to prove that she could.

Slezak looked up, trying to spot the sniper among the office buildings across the street, but he couldn't see anyone behind a window or on a rooftop holding a rifle. He turned back to Danny and smiled.

"Where are we going?"

"Not far, to that table over there." Danny pointed to a pastry shop with outdoor seating.

"You want to stay out in the open."

"It's the best place to hide and the light is better."

"And your sniper can keep his eye on me in case I try to take that watch from you."

They went inside the pastry shop and Danny used cash to buy them two regular coffees without asking Slezak what he wanted. The coffees were just props anyway. They went outside with their drinks and sat opposite each other at a table.

Danny held out his arm. Slezak leaned down, put the loupe to his eye, and examined the watch for a long time, so long that Danny was able to finish his cup of coffee.

Finally, Slezak slowly sat up straight. His hand was trembling as he passed the loupe back to Danny. "Holy shit. It's the real thing. You must have balls of steel."

"You didn't hear them clanking as we walked?" Danny took his arm off the table and tugged his sleeve back down over the watch.

"How much do you want for it?"

"One dollar and a favor."

Slezak reached into the pocket of his pajama pants, hesitated when he noticed the red dot on his chest, and very slowly pulled out a wad of cash held together with a money clip, holding it up for a second so the sniper could see it.

"I only carry hundreds." He peeled one of the bills off and slid it across the table to Danny. "Keep the change. What's the favor?"

Danny slid the bill back to Slezak. "I want you to permanently lower the price of Xylaphram to a number that's affordable to everyone, with or without insurance. When the price cut is done, I'll sell you the watch for one dollar. You have forty-eight hours."

Slezak took the money and slipped it under his money clip. "What's in it for you if I lower the price?"

"Epileptic seizures run in my family and your medication is the only one that works for them," Danny said. "I want to be sure they can afford the medication."

"So why not sell me the watch for a few million dollars? That would cover your family's prescription costs forever."

"I want to be sure that everyone else who has the affliction can afford it, too."

"That kind of sentimentality is a fatal weakness if you want to get rich and stay that way."

Danny shrugged. "Everybody has a flaw."

"How do you know I won't raise the price on the pills once I get the watch?"

"Because I'll steal it back," Danny said, then looked at the dot. "And then I'll kill you."

"Good to know." Slezak grinned and held out his hand across the table. "We have a deal."

Danny knew they would. It was a small price to pay for an otherwise unobtainable watch. He shook hands with Slezak, then stood up, taking his empty coffee cup with him. He wasn't going to leave any DNA behind for anyone to find.

"I'll be in touch once the price has dropped. Stay here and don't use your phone until the red dot on your chest disappears. Or you won't need rejuvenation, Roland, you'll need resurrection."

Danny walked away. Five minutes later, Tamiko, who was positioned with her MK13 Mod 7 sniper rifle in a vacant office in a building across the street, flicked off the laser sight. But later, when she met up with Danny in the lobby of the Fairmont Miramar Hotel two blocks away, she told him that Slezak remained sitting there, just staring at the tabletop for another half hour.

What was Slezak thinking about, Danny wondered? Was he running the numbers on the deal, trying to figure out how much the Infinitum would end up costing him in lost Xylaphram profits?

Or was he thinking of a way to get the watch for nothing?

While Danny was pondering that question, the only lawman who'd ever caught him drove from his home in Reseda to the Lost Hills station in Calabasas, where a helicopter was waiting to take him downtown to LASD headquarters.

Andrew Walker was crossing the parking lot to the helipad when Eve Ronin arrived in her Ford Bronco, pulled up beside him, and rolled down her window. "What are you doing here?"

Walker motioned to the helicopter. "Getting a ride to work."

"You're kidding me."

"This is a high-priority case and I'm the co-commander of the FIT," Walker said. "I can't waste hours in traffic. My time is critical."

"I can't believe Lansing is letting you get away with this," Eve said. "You must truly be his Hail Mary shot at becoming mayor."

"He hasn't asked you, his big TV star, for an endorsement?"

"Of course he did," Eve said.

"And you refused?"

"I don't want to get involved in politics."

Walker laughed. "You are the most political person I know. It's how you got your homicide badge and how you've kept it. Refusing to endorse Lansing was a political decision that could end up biting you in the ass. If he wins, you'll have an enemy in the mayor's office."

"I have enemies everywhere," Eve said. "I am more concerned about who becomes the next sheriff."

"Are you thinking about running?"

"I'm twenty-six years old, Walker. I'm too young for the job."

"You're too young for the job you're doing."

"Speaking of my job, Emilia has confirmed that Murphson was murdered. He was already dead when he was strung up," Eve said. "And Nan says the hairs she found on his back were from a Doberman."

"Have you discovered any new suspects besides Dwight Gordy at Southland Premier Properties?"

"Maybe. We discovered that most of the Caltrans properties that Murphson was inspecting are subleased by companies like Southland Premier and are covered with flammable and toxic materials," she said. "He didn't write up any of them for their violations, either."

Walker said, "Duncan's Caltrans lizard people theory is looking better, unless Sharpe has already solved the case."

"He found something?"

"We'll know soon," Walker said, and headed over to the helicopter.

The ride to HQ was fast, and Sharpe was waiting for him on the helipad, his evidence kit in hand. Sharpe climbed inside and they flew back to the Santa Monica Freeway fire scene, landing again on the Toberman Park baseball field.

They walked down to the freeway, where they were met on Toberman Street by George Petroni, who had a big smile on his face, which Walker thought was unusual given how Sharpe had treated the man on their last visit. "You just love that chopper, fellas."

"What's not to love?" Walker said. "I'm using it now just to go grocery shopping."

"Isn't that misappropriation of official resources?"

"A cop has to eat and wear deodorant, doesn't he?"

Petroni laughed, a little too hard, then shifted his attention to Sharpe, who was glowering at him.

"What can I do for you, Detective?"

"We've identified the origin of the fire," Sharpe said.

Petroni held his arms out wide. "See? Clearing the site wasn't a problem after all."

"I wouldn't say that."

"You figured it out anyway, didn't you? So, was it an accident or arson?"

"Arson," Sharpe said. "A car fire ignited the surrounding pallets and tires."

Petroni snapped his fingers. "That'd do it. The fire that brought down part of the I-794 in downtown Milwaukee was over an illegal storage lot of scrapped tires. It burned incredibly hot, like an erupting volcano."

"That's why there shouldn't have been tires here, either," Sharpe said. "Or the wooden pallets to feed the flames."

"I agree with you," Petroni said. "People never learn, especially bureaucrats. I thought Milwaukee was a fluke, but here I am, on my third freeway fire repair job in a decade."

Petroni was clearly begging to be asked more about his history with freeway fires, offering an opportunity for the men to bond over some common ground, but Sharpe wasn't interested in establishing a new, friendly relationship with him.

"We need to collect a sample of asphalt under the overpass where the fire started," Sharpe said. "We'll also need some of your equipment to do it."

"Sure, no problem," Petroni said. "Show me where you want to dig and we'll handle it."

Toberman Street became a dead end at the Santa Monica Freeway, then resumed on the other side, where it intersected with West Washington Boulevard, which passed all the way under the span.

Sharpe led them purposefully under the freeway and across the Caltrans property toward the portion right above the intersection of the northbound terminus of Toberman Street and West Washington.

Hundreds of construction personnel were hard at work all around them and Walker noticed they'd made a lot of progress. Steel girders now underpinned the freeway between the existing pillars, and all of it was shored up by elaborate wood framing.

As they walked, Petroni began talking to fill the time.

"A few years ago, some ecologist had the bright idea to recycle waste by making a highway in New Mexico out of old, shredded tires. It caught fire shortly after it opened and became the highway to hell. Miles and miles of flames and toxic gas. Whole neighborhoods had to be relocated. It may still be burning when your grandchildren get their driver's licenses."

Walker said: "It's probably the state's biggest tourist attraction now."

Petroni laughed and clapped Walker on the back. "You see the bright side of everything, don't you."

"I try," Walker said.

Sharpe stopped by a section of badly damaged concrete pillars that were now surrounded, several feet in all directions, by wooden struts that were also supporting steel crossbeams. He pointed to an area between the two columns.

"Under there is where we need to dig."

"Got it." Petroni took a pen from his breast pocket, a notebook from his pants pocket, and made a notation. "We'll be glad to get that sample for you."

For the first time, Sharpe seemed to warm up to Petroni a little, his glower ebbing away. "Thank you, we appreciate it."

"My pleasure. Come back and see me in three or four months. I'll have the asphalt and dirt gift wrapped for you."

Sharpe's glower came back fast. "We need it now."

"The struts and beams you see here are what is supporting the overpass," Petroni said. "If we take that all down to dig your little hole, we won't be able to open the freeway for weeks."

"The evidence we need to catch the arsonist is there."

"I get it. I get it." Petroni held up his hands in surrender. "I really do. But here's the thing. The Los Angeles economy is losing a hundred million dollars every day that this freeway is closed. What do you think is more important to the governor, the mayor, and the people of this city? Catching the arsonist quickly or opening the freeway as soon as possible?"

Sharpe said, "Justice delayed is justice denied."

"But it costs a hell of a lot less," Petroni said. "I am not moving any of this support structure until the overpass is not only open to cars again but totally repaired. You can dig your hole and catch your arsonist then. Sorry, guys."

Petroni walked away to confer with some nearby construction workers, probably about nothing, before Sharpe could argue with him any further. Walker couldn't blame him for wanting to make a quick escape.

"We're done. Case closed," Sharpe said and started walking back toward Toberman Park.

Walker almost had to sprint to catch up. "I don't see why."

"Because without that dirt, we have no evidence that the fire was set by a synthetic log."

"We can still do it."

"How?" Sharpe asked as they emerged from under the freeway onto the northern continuation of Toberman Street. The air was full of the aroma of hickory smoke coming from behind Duke's BBQ.

"I don't know, but I think better on a full stomach." Walker sniffed. "Do you smell that?"

"It's not even 10:00 a.m. Duke's isn't going to be open for lunch yet."

"Who said anything about lunch? I'll bet that Duke opens at dawn now to serve breakfast to the construction crews. He'd be crazy not to."

Walker didn't wait for an answer and simply started walking toward the restaurant, Sharpe tagging along.

The front door was open, so Walker invited himself in. There were no customers at the tables, but Duke and the kitchen staff were busy working, cutting cooked meat and seasoning uncooked meat for the smoker. Duke's apron was already covered with stains, which meant he wasn't wearing a fresh one or he got dirty very fast.

Walker approached the counter. "You're right, Duke, the aroma is irresistible. Please tell me you're open."

"We serve breakfast until 11:00, then we switch to the lunch menu."

"What's the difference between the two menus?"

"On the lunch menu, you can't order our breakfast special, the LA Loco Moco," Duke said. "Brisket with fried eggs and hash browns."

That sounded delicious to Walker. "I've never had brisket and eggs."

"You haven't lived," Duke said.

"A breakfast special with coffee for me and the same for my partner."

Sharpe held up a hand. "No, thanks. I'll settle for a cup of coffee and a piece of toast."

"Coming right up," Duke said. "Find yourselves a seat."

Walker glanced up at the menu board for the price, put a twenty-dollar bill on the counter, and then he and Sharpe went to the nearest table and sat down.

"The whole dirt thing was a long shot anyway," Walker said. "You'll figure out another way to get proof."

Sharpe shook his head. "All the evidence that wasn't washed away was hauled off to the dump."

"Brilliant! That's where we'll go. Call Carter and ask her to find out which landfill has the rubble, and which state or local agency oversaw the removal." Walker smiled at him. "See, that wasn't so hard. I knew you'd solve the problem."

"I don't think you understood what I was trying to say."

"I got it. All the rubble that was under the overpass is now out at the dump," Walker said. "That should make it easy."

"Easy?"

"It has to be easier than removing the supports for an overpass so we can dig up some dirt that may, or may not, contain chemicals left over from the ashes of a burned log, even after being soaked with water and bulldozed."

"The dirt is still at the crime scene," Sharpe said. "The rubble is not."

"Humor me," Walker said.

"What do you think I've been doing since the day we met?"

The woman they'd met before brought over a coffeepot and two mugs, poured them each a cup, and as soon as she walked away, Duke brought over a breakfast special for Walker and a big hunk of hot buttered corn bread for Sharpe.

"I ordered toast," Sharpe said.

"That's our toast," Duke said, then waved a hand over Walker's plate: two fried eggs on top of two slices of brisket on top of a generous portion of hash browns. "Be sure to put barbecue sauce all over that."

"Yes, sir."

Duke left and Walker slathered sauce over everything, then used his knife and fork to take a big bite. He looked at Sharpe, who was staring at him.

"My God," Walker said. "I think I'm in heaven."

"The dump is not going to be any easier. At least with the dirt, I knew exactly where to go and what we were looking for." Sharpe used a knife to smear the pat of melting butter over the top of his corn bread, then picked it up to take a bite. "The rubble at the dump is going to be in one big pile, like your breakfast, except mixed in with all the other trash in the neighborhood from the last few weeks."

Walker talked while he ate. "You don't know that. Maybe the agency that oversaw the cleanup was smart enough to map the scene of the fire into numbered grids and then dump the rubble in a segregated area of the landfill and in separate sections marked with corresponding numbers."

Sharpe studied him. "Where did you learn about that approach?"

"It was in a documentary I watched on the plane to Green Bay," Walker said, though it was actually on the flight to Japan. "It was about the investigation into the sudden collapse of an apartment building."

"I'm impressed that you watched it and that it sank in." Sharpe tore off a piece of paper towel from the roll on the table and handed it to Walker. "You've got sauce on your cheeks."

Walker took the paper towel and a thought occurred to him. He wiped off his face and called out to Duke, then waved for him to come over.

Duke ambled up to their table. "Something wrong?"

"No, this is fantastic. Perfect for a big man with a big appetite. Which makes me wonder . . ." Walker reached into his shirt pocket and pulled out Farhad's sketch of Big Mike. "Has this guy ever come in here?"

"Sure."

Sharpe was stunned. "You recognize him?"

"He's a hard man to miss."

Walker said, "Do you know his name?"

"Nope," Duke said.

"Do you remember the last time he was in here?"

"A couple of days before the fire. Had a late lunch. Two whole racks of ribs. The man eats like it's his last meal."

Walker said, "Does he pay with cash?"

"Credit card."

"Do you think you could track down the transaction for us?"

"Sure." Duke went back to the kitchen.

Walker smiled at Sharpe. "I think our luck is changing."

The woman came over a few minutes later, freshened their cups of coffee, and handed Walker a receipt. "Duke said to give this to you."

Walker thanked her and he scanned the receipt. The man's name was Mike Nuchin. He handed the receipt to Sharpe. "When you call Carter about the dump, ask her to run this name through the DMV, get the make of his vehicle and his address, and see if he's had any run-ins with the law."

"Maybe I could pick up your dry cleaning, too," Sharpe said.

While Walker finished eating, taking his time to savor his meal, Sharpe went outside to make his call.

When Sharpe returned, Walker had finished off his meal and the rest of Sharpe's corn bread.

Sharpe sat down, noticed the crumbs on his plate, but didn't comment on the disappearance of his food. "The rubble, 597 metric tons of it, is out at a landfill in Sun Valley, and I can't believe I am saying this, but it was saved in locations that correspond to the state fire marshal's map of the scene. Carter has the paperwork. It was buried among the papers delivered to us when we started the case."

"You may have to send the fire marshal a gift basket," Walker said.

"How about I solve the fire for him instead?"

Walker smiled. "Now *that's* the Sharpe I know."

"Even if we find something tangible out there," Sharpe said, "the chain of evidence was destroyed the instant everything was bulldozed and moved from the crime scene to a distant, totally unsecured location. It will be useless in court."

"Screw the chain," Walker said. "Let's catch the arsonist and worry about the rest later."

Sharpe sighed. "And that's the Walker I know."

"Did Carter have anything on Big Mike Nuchin?"

Sharpe pulled a notebook out of his pocket and referred to some pages. "He drives a white 2019 Dodge Ram 3500 Mega Cab and lives up Castaic."

A dually, Walker thought. "If he has a Doberman, then we've just found Murphson's killer. Does Big Mike have a record?"

Sharpe glanced at his notes again. "He's been arrested for drunk and disorderly conduct, assault and battery, and assault with a deadly weapon. He did three years in Corcoran State Prison, got out about a decade ago, and has been clean ever since."

He won't go down nicely, Walker thought. *This could be fun.*

"How about you go to the dump in Sun Valley and see what you can find there while I track down Big Mike?"

"How about you investigate the arson with me at the landfill while Eve and Duncan, the *homicide* detectives, track down the murder suspect?"

"Your search could take days, but I can have Big Mike handled in a few hours," Walker said. "Take Carter along with you. She might learn something."

"How about you come along with me and learn something?"

"I'll read the CliffsNotes," Walker said. "It's how I graduated from college without ever attending a class."

"That explains a lot," Sharpe said.

CHAPTER SEVENTEEN

Walker flew back to the Lost Hills sheriff's station, where he met with Eve and Duncan in the parking lot, briefed them on the latest developments, and showed them Mike Nuchin's DMV photo.

"I'm going out to Castaic right now," Walker said.

"Not without us you're not," Eve said.

"I wouldn't think of it," he said. "You're the homicide detectives. I'm just a mere arson investigator."

Duncan added, "I'll call for a couple of uniformed deputies to meet us there for backup."

"That's overkill," Walker said. "We're just going to have a talk with the guy."

"Who has a history of violence and is probably a murderer," Duncan said.

"When I was a US marshal," Walker said, "I'd handle a guy like this on my own."

"That's why you're covered in scars from being beaten, stabbed, and shot while I'm fat, happy, and have the skin of a newborn baby."

"You want to come along, fine," Walker said. "But nobody else. This isn't a party."

Duncan looked at Eve for support, and she said: "I'd feel safer without two deputies I don't know standing behind my back."

"That's because you think most of them want to kill you," Duncan said.

"They do," she said.

"But they won't try if we're there, too."

"I guess you've never heard of friendly fire," she said.

"Forget the backup," Walker said. "If the three of us law enforcement professionals can't handle one man, we should be in a different line of work."

That settled that.

After some discussion, they decided to go to Castaic in two cars. Duncan and Eve took a plain-wrap LASD Explorer and Walker rode in his pickup truck.

The trip was a straight shot up Interstate 5, where they dealt with ordinary traffic hell, not the ninth circle of traffic hell that everyone on freeways around Central Los Angeles was experiencing because of the overpass fire.

The ride took an hour.

Castaic was a suburb forty-five miles north of Los Angeles with a split personality created by the interstate that bisected it. West of the freeway, it was a bedroom community of housing tracts. To the east, it was an aging truck stop of gas stations, fast-food places, and dreary motels that was also the gateway to the Castaic Lake Lagoon, the bottom of the overflow spillway and recreation area below the massive earthen dam that held back the Castaic Lake reservoir.

They got off I-5 at the Lake Hughes Road exit, facing a McDonald's restaurant, and turned west, traveling under the freeway onto Stone Canyon Road, where Walker pulled into a weedy vacant lot on the right.

Walker got out, pulled an overstuffed duffel bag out from behind his seat, and carried it to the back of his truck, where he dropped the tailgate.

Eve and Duncan pulled up beside his truck as he put the bag on the opened tailgate and unzipped it.

"What are we doing here?" Duncan asked.

"Seeing if Big Mike is home before we show up at his front door." Walker took a palm-size drone out of the bag, set it on the ground, then took out a control unit with a built-in color screen. He launched the drone and sent it flying across Stone Canyon Road and over the neighborhood to the north. It was a 1970s-era housing tract of identical one-story homes. The developer simply flip-flopped the floor plans and changed the exterior materials on the facades, like stone versus brick, in a failed attempt to break up the monotony.

Eve and Duncan stood on either side of Walker and looked over his shoulder at the controller screen as he hovered the drone over Big Mike's house.

There were no vehicles parked in the driveway, which was beside a well-maintained green lawn with a nicely trimmed hedge that lined the path up to the front door. The backyard wasn't as nice. It was full of weeds and contained a fishing boat on a trailer, a concrete patio, a barbecue, and a doghouse.

Walker zoomed in on the doghouse and saw a Doberman lying beside it. "Big Mike is our killer."

"The drone doesn't have the juice to stay up there all day," Eve said. "We're going to have to stake out the house until he comes home."

"We could do that," Walker said. "But I'm worried about his neighbors noticing us and either warning him or calling the law on us."

"We are the law," Duncan said.

"I have a plan." Walker handed Eve the controller and his Stetson, unbuttoned his shirt a little, and pulled it off over his head.

Duncan saw the scars on Walker's back and looked at Eve. "See? That's what happens when you don't have backup."

"He got those scars saving my life," Eve said. "And we had backup."

Walker sorted through some clothes in the bag, pulled out a brown United Parcel Service shirt, and pulled it over his head. The color didn't match his LASD green tactical pants, but it would have to do.

Duncan said, "You carry around costumes?"

Walker removed his gun belt and handed it to Duncan. "They come in handy when you're fugitive hunting."

"You're not a US marshal anymore."

"I'm nostalgic." He reached into the bag again and came out with two magnetized UPS logos.

Eve smiled. "You are full of surprises, Walker."

He closed the tailgate, then slapped one of the UPS logos on the truck's passenger door and the other on the driver's side, then climbed into the cab. He took off his Stetson and put it on the passenger seat. "I'll be right back. Keep an eye on me."

Walker drove out of the lot and across Stone Canyon Drive onto Bobcat Way, then pulled up in front of Big Mike's house. He rooted around behind the passenger seat for a padded UPS envelope, grabbed it, and got out.

The Doberman was going insane in Big Mike's backyard, barking and growling, so the whole neighborhood probably knew Walker was there even if they hadn't seen him drive up.

Walker carried the envelope to the front door and rang the bell. While he waited for a response, he bent down, pretending to tie his shoe, and hid himself behind the hedge from any watching neighbors.

He opened the envelope and quickly removed a tiny camera with a clip on the back, a burner phone, and a mobile hot spot, turned on all the devices, and crammed them into the hedge, attaching the camera to a branch so it faced the front door.

Walker rose, left the empty envelope on the doormat, and went back to his truck, where he sat for a moment to pull up the surveillance app on his phone to make sure he was getting a good signal from his hidden camera. The image was crooked, but that was fine.

He drove back to the empty lot where Eve and Duncan were waiting. He got out, stripping the UPS logo from the door as he did.

"What were you doing on the porch?" Duncan asked, offering him back his gun belt. "Eve couldn't get a clear view of you from the drone."

"That's good, because that means probably nobody else could see me, either." Walker tossed the logo placard in the truck bed, took the gun belt from him, and exchanged it for his phone, which showed Big Mike's door on the screen. "I put a camera on the house."

While Duncan and Eve looked at the phone, Walker buckled up his gun belt, walked around the front of the truck, and stripped the UPS logo off the passenger-side door.

"I like it," Eve said. "We can park over in the shopping center across the street and wait for him to show up."

Walker dropped the tailgate, tossed the other logo into the bed, and pulled off his UPS shirt.

Duncan shook his head. "I saw a McDonald's at the freeway off-ramp. Let's go wait there instead."

"Do you ever think about anything besides food?" Eve said.

"I'm thinking about what makes the most tactical sense," he said. "We can stay there as long as we want and they have Wi-Fi, air-conditioning, and bathrooms."

Walker stuffed the UPS shirt into the duffel bag, then pulled his LASD uniform shirt out and put it back on over his head. "It beats sitting in our cars."

So that's what they did, right after Eve brought the drone back and landed it in Walker's open palm.

The three of them sat in the McDonald's at a window booth with Walker's phone propped on the table between them, the screen showing them a live view of Big Mike's front door. Walker kept his eyes on the screen while he nursed a Coke.

Duncan used his McDonald's app and points to get two Quarter Pounders for the price of one, large fries, and a large drink and was happily devouring it all across the table from Walker. Eve sat beside

Duncan and nibbled on six chicken nuggets while reading something on her phone, shaking her head in disapproval the whole time.

"What are you reading?" Walker asked.

"The next *Ronin* script."

"How is it?"

"Awful." She set her phone down. "They keep trying to turn me into T. J. Hooker."

"I loved that show," Duncan said.

Walker asked, "Do they have your character wearing William Shatner's toupee?"

"It's all the ridiculous action," she said. "They have her jumping onto the hood of a fleeing bad guy's car or leaping from a bridge into a fleeing bad guy's speedboat or grabbing the landing skid of a fleeing bad guy's helicopter and flying off with him."

"You haven't done any of that?"

"I make them cut those scenes in every script but they aren't getting the message," she said.

"Which is?"

Duncan answered with his mouth full. "She wants the show to be so dull that it's canceled."

"I just want it to be realistic," she said.

"That'll be exciting." Duncan swallowed what he was eating. "The climax of every episode will be the two of us writing reports in our cubicles."

Walker looked out the window at the drive-through line.

A Dodge dually was arriving in the line, two cars away from the menu board. The man behind the wheel of the truck was built like the big orange stone guy in *The Fantastic Four* cartoons.

"You're not going to believe this," Walker said.

Eve and Duncan followed his gaze and saw the dually as another car pulled in behind it.

"That's him," Eve said. "Mike Nuchin."

Duncan said, "This is what I call a Happy Meal."

Walker grabbed his phone and slid out of the booth. So did they, leaving their food behind.

Eve said, "How do you want to handle it?"

"Like a routine traffic stop," Walker said.

Duncan smiled. "I have a better idea."

◆ ◆ ◆

Big Mike's huge six-wheeled Dodge dually pulled up to the menu board. There was a Kia Forte in front of it and a Lexus ES behind. He was pinned.

Walker cautiously made his way up the line from behind, approaching the truck on the driver's side with one hand on his holstered weapon, while Eve did the same from the passenger side.

Duncan's cheery voice came out over the menu's speaker: "Welcome to McDonald's!"

Big Mike leaned his blocky head out of his open window. "I'd like a Double Quarter Pounder meal, large fries, and a large Coke."

Walker crept closer, seeing himself reflected in Big Mike's driver's side mirror. He touched the side of the truck with the palm of his hand, a reflex from his days as a US Marshal. It had been drilled into him in training. Always leave your fingerprints on any car you pull over in case things go to shit, you get killed, and the assailant drives off. Out of the corner of his eye, Walker saw Eve doing the same thing. Deputies and police officers were given the same training.

Duncan said, "Please turn off your ignition, put your truck in park, and place your hands on the dashboard where we can see them."

Big Mike stared at the menu board. "Why the fuck would I want to do that?"

Duncan said, "So you don't get shot by a sheriff's deputy."

Big Mike glanced in his sideview mirror and saw Walker approaching.

"Shit!" he roared, jammed the truck into reverse, and stomped on the gas.

The truck blasted backward, smashing into the Lexus behind him, then abruptly surged forward, smashing into the Kia in front like they were bumper cars, creating just enough space to escape to the right.

Walker impulsively grabbed the side of the truck and vaulted himself into the bed just as Big Mike sped out, clipping the corner of the Kia, spinning it around.

The truck made a sharp left turn, and Walker slid across the bed, his side slamming hard into the right wheel hub, pain shooting through his entire body.

Big Mike's truck flew off the curb into the street, nearly tossing Walker from the bed, and charged east on Lake Hughes Road toward the Castaic Lake Lagoon recreation area.

Walker crawled up to the cab's rear window and banged on it with his fist. "Police! Pull over!"

"Fuck you!" Big Mike swerved hard left and right, tossing Walker from one side of the bed to the other.

Walker heard a siren, looked back, and saw Eve's Explorer roaring up behind them.

Big Mike weaved through the traffic, purposely clipping every car he passed so they'd spin into the path of the Explorer in pursuit.

Walker had to stop him.

But how?

He leaned over the passenger side of the truck bed and looked at the left front tire, wondering if he could get a shot at it.

Something moved in his peripheral vision.

It was Big Mike twisting in his seat, holding out his right arm . . .

. . . *and pointing a .357 Magnum at him.*

Walker ducked just as Mike fired, blasting out the rear window like a cannonball had blown through it.

The truck swerved sharply and Walker slid across the bed again, bashing his back painfully against the left-side wheel hub.

But he was glad to be there because Big Mike couldn't get a shot at him at this angle. Or at least he hoped not.

Walker drew his Glock with his right hand, leaned over the edge of the truck, took aim at the front driver's side tire, and fired.

The shot missed and startled Big Mike, who veered hard to the right, nearly flinging Walker out of the truck bed, and then swerved to the left, flopping him back inside.

The truck hurtled into the Castaic Lake recreation area, the truck bouncing hard over the uneven grass.

Walker scrambled over to the driver's side, took his Glock in his left hand, got up, and swung his left leg over the side, straddling the panel between his legs and holding on tight to the rim with his right hand.

Big Mike saw him in the side-view mirror and swerved back and forth, doing everything he could to buck Walker off the side as the truck bounced along at high speed.

Walker's groin was being pounded into the metal, maybe hard enough to give him a Dodge vasectomy, the pain blurring his vision. He couldn't keep his arm steady, but he fired repeatedly at the tire in the futile hope that one bullet would—

Boom!

The tire exploded.

The truck lurched brutally to the left, spitting shredded rubber at Walker, a chunk smacking off his Stetson as he held on to the side with one hand, his left hand in the air, holding his gun. He was a rodeo rider trying to break a Dodge Ram and losing.

But so was Big Mike, who lost control of the truck, veering across the park and straight at Castaic Lagoon.

Walker jumped off just as the Dodge hit the water.

Smacking into the lake stunned Walker like a stiff slap in the face, but it was also reassuring, since feeling it meant he wasn't dead.

He instinctively straightened up out of fear of drowning and discovered he was able to stand, the water only chest deep.

The truck was a few yards away in deeper water and Big Mike was struggling to open his door.

Walker raised his left arm and was surprised to see that he was still holding his gun, which he shifted to his right hand and aimed at Mike just as Eve's Explorer came to a stop at the shoreline.

"You're under arrest," Walker yelled. "Leave the gun in the car and hold your hands out of the window where I can see them."

Eve and Duncan jumped out of the Explorer, their guns drawn. Mike took one look at them and knew he was finished. He did as he was told, thrusting his arms out the open window.

Walker said, "Now pull yourself out through the window and into the water."

Mike squirmed out of the window, nearly getting stuck, and then flopped headfirst into the water. He emerged sputtering and coughing, but he was able to find his footing.

"Put your hands on your head," Walker said, "and make your way to shore."

Mike followed Walker's instructions. Eve covered Duncan, who patted Big Mike down and cuffed him.

Walker holstered his gun and trudged carefully to shore, his ribs sore and the ache from his groin rising deep into his stomach.

Eve handed him his Stetson as he emerged stiffly from the water. "That was the dumbest thing I've ever seen. What were you thinking?"

That's a good question, he thought. What he'd done was incredibly stupid. Any of the shots he'd fired at the front tire could have ricocheted off the pavement into a pedestrian, a passing car, Big Mike, or his own face. The shredded rubber that took his Stetson off his head proved that.

"Consciously? I wasn't thinking clearly at all," Walker said. "Subconsciously, I was probably thinking of T. J. Hooker, thanks to you."

"I didn't hypnotize you," Eve said. "Don't try to blame any of that on me."

"I don't know how it happened," Walker said, watching Duncan put Big Mike into the back seat of the Explorer and then amble over to them. "One second, I'm trying not to get hit by the truck and the next I'm jumping inside."

"Thanks a lot, Walker," Eve said. "I can't tell the producers anymore that stupid shit like this never happens. Now they'll have my character doing it every week."

"On the plus side," Duncan said, "I'll finally be able to watch the show without falling asleep."

They took Big Mike to the Santa Clarita Valley sheriff's station, processed him, and then put him in an interrogation room.

Big Mike sat wet and handcuffed across the table from Walker, who'd changed into a T-shirt and a pair of jeans that he kept in his truck. Eve was in another room, watching them on a monitor. Duncan was out managing the collection of evidence at the crime scene—which encompassed the McDonald's, two miles of Lake Hughes Road, and the Castaic Lagoon—and doing everything he could to make sure that neither Big Mike's name nor any identifying details about him and his vehicle were released to the press.

This was Walker's first opportunity to see Big Mike up close. Huge Mike would have been more descriptive. He was built like a freezer. Or maybe Walker just had ice on his mind. He really wanted to put a bag of it on his crotch.

"Do you believe in reincarnation, Mike?"

"Nope."

"That's good, because if you did, I have some really bad news for you," Walker said. "We have you for murdering Monte Murphson, the attempted murder of a police officer, and so many other charges that you will not only be in prison for the rest of this life, but your next few, too."

Big Mike thought about it for a moment, then said: "What if I'm reincarnated as a bird?"

"It'll be a chicken and you'll be diced, battered, and served as nuggets. But you're missing the point."

"That reincarnation and karma are connected?"

"That the only chance you have of getting out of prison before you die is to make a deal with the DA to reduce your charges in exchange for something more valuable to her than you."

"Like what?"

"Giving up the people who hired you to kill Murphson."

"That's not going to happen," Big Mike said.

"Dwight Gordy will be so relieved to hear that."

"Who?" Big Mike said.

Walker gave him a long look, then sighed sadly, as if he'd just come to a decision.

"I'm sure that you won't have any problem taking the fall and rotting in prison while Dwight enjoys the good life, rich and carefree, eating gourmet food in Italy, gambling in Macao, sport fishing in Cabo, and practicing tantric sex in Bangkok, never once thinking about the man whose sacrifice made it all possible. You won't care, because you will have something priceless that he doesn't, something that will give your soul comfort as you sit shivering in your dark cell for decades—the pride of knowing that you are a man of selfless, unwavering principle. I can respect that, so I won't waste any more of your time."

Walker got up, turned his back to Big Mike, and hobbled in pain to the door. He was getting too old for this T. J. Hooker shit. But damn, how he loved it.

"Wait," Big Mike said.

CHAPTER EIGHTEEN

The Sun Valley landfill was sixteen miles south of Santa Clarita, a few miles east of the I-5. Walker got there in twenty minutes.

He arrived at the portion of the dump that had been set aside for the I-10 rubble and saw ten massive piles of blackened, twisted debris and a huge crane, under Sharpe's direction, plucking out the hulk of a burned Altima.

Walker got out of his truck, grimacing because his groin was still sore, and walked gingerly over to Sharon Carter, who wore a Tyvek jumpsuit smeared with black soot from crawling around in the debris. She was watching the crane drop the car in an open spot between some piles. She had goggles on top of her head and a gas mask dangled around her neck.

"How's it going?" he asked.

"It's been amazing, Walker. I've never experienced anything like this at the academy or on the job. Working with Sharpe is a master class in investigative techniques."

"Oh yeah, it's a thrill," he said. "Every day with him is a revelation."

Sharpe approached them, his suit even dirtier than hers, and pulled off his gas mask. "Glad you found time in your busy schedule to drop by, Walker. We were able to locate the Altima from its unique shape, and the damage is consistent with fire logs being placed underneath it."

"Great, so we're done here. Case closed."

"Unfortunately, it doesn't prove anything," Sharpe said. "The Altima's fender has melted away and we have to find it."

"Why?"

"Based on my examination of the Altima's undercarriage, I believe the fender molding melted early in the fire and may have dropped down on a portion of one of the logs, smothering the flames and sealing the chunk in plastic."

It seemed like a big long shot to Walker. "So you want to root through tons of rubble for a glob of melted plastic that may or may not contain a perfectly preserved chunk of Duraflame log."

Carter said, "This is what I was talking about. Incredible, isn't it?"

"Awesome," Walker said, then looked at Sharpe. "There will be all kinds of melted globs in that pile, and even if you manage to find the right one, there's no guarantee there will be anything inside. It could take weeks and lead to nothing."

"You're right," he said. "That's why I've ordered two dozen more deputies to come out here and help us search. They're on the way. And, to speed things up, a crime scene technician will be assigned here to open the globs as we find them."

Carter looked at Walker. "This is real detective work."

He smiled. "Yes, it is, and very exciting, too. Let me know how it goes."

Sharpe narrowed his perpetually sleepy eyes at him or, Walker thought, perhaps he was just exhausted. "Where are you going to be?"

"We arrested Big Mike and he's agreed to flip on Dwight Gordy," Walker said. "And the rest."

"The rest?"

"All the companies who were renting Caltrans properties under the freeway and bribing Murphson not to cite them agreed to chip in on the killing," Walker said. "Gordy was the point man. But Big Mike claims he had nothing to do with the fire."

"Great, the murder is solved," Sharpe said. "What's left for you to do?"

"The DA says that Big Mike's testimony is not enough. I'm setting up a sting for tonight to catch them all."

Sharpe sighed. "Why can't you just make a simple arrest anymore? Now they all have to involve a con. Danny Cole was a bad influence on you."

At the mention of Cole's name, Walker stiffened up, feeling a stab of guilt, and he hoped that Sharpe didn't see it. He forced a smile. "If you want to catch a crook, it helps to think like one."

"As long as you don't cross the line yourself," Sharpe said, making Walker wonder if he somehow knew about the trip to Japan.

Carter said, "Who is Danny Cole?"

Walker could tell from the look on Sharpe's face that he regretted mentioning the thief's name. It was like saying Voldemort out loud.

"Never mind, Deputy. We have real detective work to do."

Sharpe quickly led her back to the pile of rubble because it was a question that he didn't want to answer any more than Walker did. They both had good reasons to feel guilty when it came to Danny Cole.

Earlier that same day, the thief who shall not be named rented a Porsche 911 and drove out to Simi Valley, a middle-income suburban community fifty miles north of Santa Monica.

He found a small local bank, opened an account, and placed the Infinitum in a safe-deposit box. He'd picked the city and the bank because it was one that no serious bank robbery crew would find desirable. That's because Simi Valley was known for being home to more law enforcement officers than anywhere else in Southern California.

On top of that, the bank didn't have a high-dollar clientele, so there wasn't much cash on hand and probably nothing of significant value in the safe-deposit boxes until he'd shown up. The bank was situated in a busy shopping center several miles from the Simi Valley Freeway, making a quick escape unlikely. In fact, a bank robber might not even make it out of the parking lot before the police got there since so many off-duty officers were likely to be there shopping for groceries at any given time.

Danny returned to his Porsche 911, started the ignition, and just sat there. He had nowhere to go and nothing to do until Roland Slezak lowered the price of Xylaphram. That could happen any time in the next forty-eight hours.

What could he possibly do until then?

One idea occurred to him, and it was a great one.

He took out his phone and called Karen Tennant, his criminal defense attorney. Her secretary answered the phone. Danny introduced himself as Brian Lockwood and asked if Karen was available. A moment later, she came on the phone.

"Brian, what a wonderful surprise. What can I do for you?"

"I'm in LA and an important legal matter has come up."

"Already? We've only been talking for five seconds."

"I'm under a lot of pressure," he said. "I hope you aren't tied up in court."

"I am, but I'm free this afternoon. Can you hold on until then?"

"I will do my best," he said. "I'm staying at Shutters in Santa Monica."

"Take a nap," she said. "You're going to need it."

When Walker was growing up in the San Fernando Valley, the fanciest restaurant in the dark, dreary food court at the Topanga Mall in Woodland Hills was Hot Dog on a Stick. Now the mall's food court was the 55,000-square-foot, skylight-lit Topanga Social, a "food hall" for "food enthusiasts" that featured "eateries" by famous local chefs and popular food trucks that represented the "diverse culinary scene" of Los Angeles.

He missed the Hot Dog on a Stick.

Walker sat at a table facing Eve Ronin with a ridiculously expensive "artisan" pizza between them. His back was to Big Mike, who sat alone several tables away, devouring two ten-ounce cheeseburgers and a plate of fries from Amboy like it was his last real meal for years, which it probably was, even with the plea deal. Eve was able to casually watch Big Mike while appearing to talk with Walker, who'd left his Stetson in his truck and wore a T-shirt, jeans, and an unzipped hoodie that was long enough to hide the Glock clipped to his belt.

They both wore flesh-colored earbuds so they could stay in contact with Duncan, who was stationed in the mall's security office, where he could see every camera feed, and a dozen deputies were in the parking lot, sitting in their squad cars, waiting to be called into action.

"Stop bouncing your knee," Walker said to Eve. "You're shaking the table."

"I'm sorry. It's just that almost every time I've done one of these stings it's gone wrong."

Walker took a bite of his pizza. "How many have you done?"

"Five."

"And how wrong did they go?"

"Bad guys got killed in four out of five of them," she said.

"That's because you didn't have me along."

"Yes, I did," she said. "One of those stings was with you."

"I thought you weren't counting that one," Walker said.

"Why wouldn't I count it?"

"You said stings that *you* did, not stings that *we* did," Walker said. "That death was a fluke."

Duncan's voice crackled in their ears. "Dwight Gordy is here."

Walker saw Gordy entering from the mall concourse, wearing a windbreaker over golf clothes, as if he might squeeze in another eighteen holes before bed.

"I see him," Walker said.

Eve did, too. "Dressed like that he'd be hard to miss."

Gordy walked up to Big Mike's table and sat down. Big Mike was wired for sound, so Walker and Eve could hear every word.

Gordy said, "Why are we meeting here?"

"So you can't put a bullet in the back of my head instead of paying me off."

Gordy stole a fry and popped it in his mouth. "If I was capable of that kind of violence, I wouldn't have hired you."

"You've never been in this situation."

"I'm not in a situation, you are." Gordy swiped another fry. "You told me you were a pro, that nobody would question the suicide, and that there would be no investigation. Clearly, you were wrong."

Walker's eyes were on the rest of the food hall, and he spotted someone taking a keen interest in the conversation. The man was Black and wore a long leather coat and dark sunglasses when it was 8:00 p.m. and eighty degrees outside.

Big Mike said: "I don't know how the police got to my front door, probably some molecular forensics shit. I don't stay up on the science. I'm just lucky I wasn't home and they didn't see my hidden camera."

Gordy dipped a fry in ketchup before eating it. "A pro would stay informed of developments in criminal forensic science."

"Fuck you and keep your fingers out of my fries. Where's the gym bag? I don't take checks."

Walker reached for another slice of pizza and spotted a man sitting alone at a table where three people had finished eating and left their plates. He was also wearing a long coat and looking in the direction of Big Mike's table.

Gordy reached into the inside pocket of his windbreaker and pulled out a bulging envelope.

Big Mike said, "Unless the US Mint started making a $10,000 bill, that's not $250,000."

Gordy set the envelope on the table. "It's twenty-five K. On top of the twenty-five I already paid you. That's more than enough."

Big Mike took the envelope. "I can't start a new life on $25,000."

"Where is the other twenty-five?"

"In my fucking house," Big Mike said. "You want to go get it for me? But even $50,000 is too little. I told you to bring $250,000 or else."

Gordy laughed. "Or else what? You are in no position to blackmail me. I'm not the one who killed the inspector, you are."

Gotcha, Walker thought.

"The money isn't to keep me quiet," Big Mike said. "It's to keep me from killing you."

"I'm not worried," he said. "We've both seen how good you are at that. You aren't exactly Hannibal Lecter."

"I didn't say I was going to eat you."

"I'm saying you're a lousy killer," Gordy said. "You're lucky you haven't already been caught. Do you really want to push your luck with another bungled murder? I'm giving you this money out of pity. Run while you still can and don't ever contact me again."

Gordy took another fry, got up, and walked out the way he came.

Walker said, "Don't move in on Dwight until he gets to his car."

Duncan said, "What's wrong?"

"We aren't the only ones watching this little drama."

Duncan said, "You mean the two Black guys in long coats? They might as well be wearing pink bunny suits. It would be just as subtle."

Big Mike remained at the table and, as he was instructed beforehand, took out a pair of earbuds and pretended that he was searching for some music on his iPhone. The truth was, he was waiting for instructions from Duncan.

Walker said, "Duncan, tell Big Mike to pick up his drink and walk casually to the top level of the parking lot and not look back."

Big Mike got the message an instant later, picked up his drink, and started walking. Long Coat #1 got up and followed after him at a discreet distance and, after a moment, so did Long Coat #2.

Eve said, "What do you suppose they're carrying under those coats?"

"It isn't subpoenas," Walker said. "Duncan, tell Big Mike to go toward the furthest car he sees when he gets to the rooftop. If there isn't one, tell him to go look at the view."

Walker and Eve got up and followed the followers.

They all trailed Big Mike down the long concourse of first-floor shops toward a set of escalators and an elevator that went up to the second floor of the mall and the upper two parking levels. Big Mike took the escalator to the second floor and, the instant he stepped on the next escalator flight, the two Long Coats moved quickly up the first flight, but not so fast as to attract attention.

Walker said to Eve: "You take the elevator to the top, I'll stay behind them, one flight back, on the escalators."

That's what he did and was able to keep them all in sight as they went up the flights to the uppermost level. The Long Coats were totally focused on Big Mike and unaware of anything happening behind them. If they had looked back when they'd reached the rooftop, they would have seen Walker hurrying up the last flight, taking three steps at a time.

The two Long Coats stepped through the automatic glass doors to the rooftop parking, and Walker ran the rest of the way up, drawing his Glock as he did.

As he got closer to the door, Walker could see them through the glass, closing in on Big Mike from behind as he headed across the largely deserted parking area to a distant car.

Long Coat #1 held a knife at his side.

Walker came through the door in a firing stance and said: "Police. Drop the knife or I'll drop you."

Long Coat #1 froze, but the other man whirled on Walker, pulling out a gun in the same motion, his open coat flaring very cinematically.

Eve shot the gunman twice from the open elevator and dropped him before Walker could get a shot off himself.

Big Mike hit the ground, too, not because he was hit, but because he didn't want to be.

"Shots fired. Man down," Eve said for Duncan's benefit.

"We saw it all," Duncan said. "There are cameras everywhere."

Long Coat #1 hadn't moved. His knife was already on the ground. He'd dropped it during the shooting.

Walker came up behind him and kicked the knife away. "Put your hands on your head, drop to your knees, then lie face down on the ground."

The man did as he was instructed.

Walker looked over at Eve. "Thanks."

Eve nodded. With her covering him, Walker holstered his weapon, patted the surviving Long Coat down, and cuffed his arms behind his back.

Duncan said, "Paramedics are on the way."

With the Long Coat secured, Eve holstered her gun and went to the man she'd shot, who lay in a widening pool of blood and stared up at her with cold, flat eyes.

She squatted beside him and went through the motions of checking for a pulse, then looked over at Walker and shook her head.

"That's five out of six now," she said. "Two out of three with you."

"It was his fault, not yours." Walker turned over the would-be assassin, grabbed him by his handcuffed arms, and lifted him to his feet. He looked the guy in the eye. "Let me guess. Your pay for this hit is in Big Mike's pocket."

Long Coat said nothing.

Duncan said, "Dwight didn't go to his car yet. He's trying on shoes at Ecco."

"Hold back," Walker said. "I want him."

Dwight Gordy stood in front of a full-length mirror, checking out how he looked wearing a pair of $250 sneaker-style, concrete-colored golf shoes that had two big air vents, like something on a car dashboard, on each side of the sole and framed in bright yellow. They really stood out. He couldn't decide how he felt about them.

A sales guy approached him holding a shoebox. "You might want to try these. I think they're your style."

Classy and cutting edge.

"Thank you." Gordy took the box and then lifted one of his feet. "What do you call these vents on the side?"

"Ecco Exhaust Grids."

"Really? What kind of exhaust would that be?"

"Foot exhaust," the sales guy said. "It's for superior ventilation. Excuse me for a moment, sir, I am needed in the back room."

The sales guy went away.

Gordy looked at his reflection again and decided the Ecco Exhaust Grids were cool and that he'd buy the shoes. And maybe this second pair, too, if they also had a cool design feature, like maybe Ecco Chrome Tailpipes or Ecco Afterburners.

He opened the shoebox and didn't see a pair of shoes inside. What he saw was his envelope stuffed with $25,000 in cash.

Gordy whirled around toward the back of the store and saw Walker standing at the sales counter, smiling at him.

"It's a refund, Dwight, since your hit team didn't get the job done. Big Mike is very much alive and oh-so-talkative."

Gordy dropped the box and ran for the exit, but two uniformed deputies stood in the doorway. He stopped, his shoulders slumped, and turned to face Walker, who ambled over toward him.

"You're under arrest for murder, soliciting murder, and terrible taste in shoes."

"I want my lawyer."

"So do I," Walker said, taking out his handcuffs. "I can't wait to see Sheryl again."

It was after 11:00 p.m. when Walker finally headed home from the Lost Hills station, where ADA Burnside got Dwight Gordy to agree, in return for a reduced sentence, to flip on the other Caltrans property lessees, the landlords who'd sublet the land to the businesses under the freeways and who'd conspired with him on the bribery and murder of Monte Murphson.

The surviving long-coat assassin was Wendell Glover and the dead man was Malik "Slick" Wilson. They were both security guards in the same Woodland Hills office building as Southland Premier Properties, but Burnside told Walker that Wendell would walk.

Burnside couldn't make an attempted murder charge stick against Wendell because Gordy hired Malik to kill Big Mike, and Wendell claimed he didn't know anything about it. Wendell said that all Malik told him was that a big white guy owed him money and might try to hurt him when he went to collect. Wendell's story was that he was just at the mall to watch his friend's back. And Burnside had no evidence to contradict it.

Walker was unhappy about that, but all in all, he was satisfied.

He drove home and hoped that Carly would already be asleep when he got there. He didn't want her to see him shirtless and bruised, because there was no way he was going to tell her how it actually happened, and he didn't want to lie to her. Also, if she was awake, she might want to make love, but even the thought of that made his testicles ache, and not in a good way.

When he arrived at home, he was surprised to see that Carly's BMW was parked in the garage, but when he got out of his truck, he noticed that the FOR SALE sign was gone from the dash, which explained why.

The car was sold.

The house was dark when he came in, but not their bedroom. Carly was wide awake, sitting up in bed in a tank top, reading something on her iPad. She smiled when she saw him. For the first time in their marriage, and in the totality of their relationship together, he hoped she hadn't stayed up because she wanted some good loving when he got home.

"Nice to see you smiling." Walker came in and kissed his wife on the cheek. "You must have got the price you wanted for the car."

"I haven't sold it." Carly set the iPad down on her lap. "I took it off the market."

He went into the bathroom so he could take off his clothes and check for bruises on his body without her seeing him. "What about the big talk we had the other night?"

"It doesn't matter now. We don't have any more money problems."

"How did that happen? Did you win the lottery or did you meet a horny billionaire?" There was a nasty bruise on his left side, but his manly equipment, much to his relief, appeared unharmed. But it still hurt. He stuffed his clothes in the laundry basket, went into his closet, and pulled on a fresh pair of boxers and a T-shirt.

"What would a horny billionaire want with me?" she asked.

Walker walked out and slipped into bed beside her. "What did Robert Redford want with Demi Moore in *Indecent Proposal*?"

"I don't know, I never saw the movie."

"Sex," he said. "A married couple is having money problems and run into this billionaire who offers the wife $1 million to spend the night with him."

"Why would your mind go there?"

He wondered why, too, since sex was the last thing he wanted now, so he went with what she'd expect him to say in this situation. "You're a shrink and you have to ask?"

"No, I did not run into a billionaire," she said. "But I did run into a multimillionaire."

"Where?"

"Online. And I got *very* excited." Carly picked up her iPad and suddenly she was very excited again, but not in the way he was afraid of. It was more like she was a kid on Christmas morning, eager to open the presents around the tree.

She tapped the screen and showed it to him.

It was a YouTube video. And there was Roland Slezak, wearing a cardigan sweater that could've been stolen off Mr. Rogers' back. He was strolling through a park filled with happy kids at play.

Walker wanted to punch the screen.

"Look at all of these children," Slezak said into the camera, his face so unnaturally smooth that it made him look like a CGI creation. "They seem happy, peaceful, and safe. But it's a cruel illusion. At any moment, that precious serenity could be shattered by a danger that can't be seen and that lurks deep within their bodies. And when it strikes, these children will be twisted, convulsed, and contorted by the grueling, uncontrollable spasms of an epileptic seizure, leaving them dazed, drooling, humiliated, and in some cases, bloodied and soiled. But this can stop it."

Slezak held up a tiny pill, almost too small to be seen between his index finger and thumb.

"Xylaphram. Amazing, isn't it? And it's not some new breakthrough drug. It's been available for decades. So why doesn't every afflicted child have access to this little pill?" Slezak asked the viewer. "Because the greedy, heartless insurance companies that have a stranglehold on medical care in this country refuse to cover the cost, putting this pill out of reach for most families. It's reprehensible, and as the maker of Xylaphram, I won't stand for it any longer."

Walker couldn't believe what he was seeing.

The image cut to Slezak handing out lollipops to the children as their thankful, teary-eyed parents, a diverse group reflecting whites, Blacks, Asians, and even a woman in a hijab, looked on with joy.

"As of today, the per-pill cost of Xylaphram will be less than the price of a lollipop," Slezak said, holding one up for emphasis. "And far below the cost of every other anti-seizure drug on the market. That should teach the insurance companies something about humanity . . . and humility."

Oh my God, Walker thought. *Danny did it.*

The next shot was of all the children and their parents gathered around Slezak like he was Santa Claus, or Taylor Swift, or maybe Jesus Christ. They were all licking lollipops and wearing lollipop T-shirts, except for the woman in the hijab, who'd disappeared.

"Nobody wants to see a child suffer through the terror and discomfort of an epileptic seizure," Slezak said, his arms around the kids. "And now, they won't have to."

Slezak smiled into the camera. Even his teeth looked unreal. Were they whitened? Capped? Or computer generated?

Carly tossed the iPad on the bed and gave Walker a big hug. "Our troubles are over."

He wanted to believe it. Walker's dream was that Cody would never have to suffer another seizure again. But as much as he wanted to share Carly's joy, he wouldn't be able to truly feel it while Slezak was still free. The man had to go down, and that hadn't happened yet.

And there was another reason for Walker's hesitancy. He still remembered what Danny told him in Japan.

You'd better be ready if I need you.

That call or text could come at any moment and Walker didn't know what kind of help Danny would need . . . or how far he'd have to bend the law to do it.

"What's wrong?" Carly said. She didn't have to be a shrink to pick up on Walker's worry, but he couldn't tell her the truth.

But that didn't mean he had to lie to her, either.

"I'm so happy that we don't have to worry anymore about Cody getting the drug he needs to control his seizures. It's wonderful news," Walker said. "But I'm also angry."

That was true.

"About what?"

"Not a word Slezak just said was true," Walker said. "He's the one who jacked up the price of Xylaphram, not the insurance companies. He's the one who needs to learn about humanity and humility."

"Maybe he has," she said, "which is why he's lowering the price below the $10,000 a year it cost us before he raised it to $150,000."

Walker jabbed a finger toward the iPad. "How do you know those lollipops don't cost $1,000 apiece? They could be gourmet suckers from Sweden that probably only cost $10 until Slezak bought the candymaker and jacked up the price."

Carly put her hand on Walker's in a calming gesture. "Why can't you just be relieved that he's finally doing the right thing and that we can afford Cody's medication again?"

"Because it's only one of the dozens of once-affordable specialty drugs that Slezak's made astronomically expensive. That's his business plan. People are still going to suffer or die because they can't pay the inflated cost of his drugs."

"But not us," Carly said. "Why can't you just be happy about that?"

"I am. This is great." Walker brought her hand to his lips and kissed it. "But Slezak needs to go down."

That was true.

"What happens to him is something you can't control," she said. "So all you're doing by telling yourself stuff like that is stoking your anger and stressing yourself out for nothing. It's unhealthy."

"Is that Carly the shrink talking?"

"It's Carly your wife talking. Besides, maybe this is just the beginning of his moral epiphany."

"I hope you're right."

But that was up to Danny Cole and now Walker found himself hoping the call would come soon so he could play a part in Roland Slezak's downfall, regardless of the risk.

And that was true, too.

◆ ◆ ◆

Danny Cole was also in bed, and having a dramatically different experience from Andrew Walker, though his body was bruised and his groin was sore, too. He'd had more sex in one day with Karen Tennant than he thought he could be capable of without powerful drugs, vitamin cocktails, or months of physical training. They'd stopped their sexual Olympics only briefly to eat some lavish room service meals, finish off a few bottles of champagne, and shower twice, though they didn't really stop in there, either.

Karen was wrapped around him now, her head on his bare shoulder. Her body was warm and sticky, her breathing relaxed, and she was picking out cashews from a bowl of mixed nuts that she'd playfully dumped on his chest.

"You're just going to leave me the Brazil nuts, aren't you," Danny said.

"I've always wondered if anybody likes those or if they are just in there to add weight to the package."

"Have you ever seen a jar or bag of Brazil nuts at the grocery store?"

"Mystery solved," she said. "I just love the meaningful, insightful pillow talk that happens in our postcoital afterglow."

"Does this mean we're calling it a night?"

"Hell no." She brushed the nuts off his chest and rolled on top of him. "I'm just getting started."

"I didn't even get to have a Brazil nut."

Karen kissed him hard, then pulled back to study him. "I'm having a difficult time getting used to this new face. I keep waiting for you to peel it off, like those guys in *Mission: Impossible*, and reveal your real one."

"This is the real one from now on."

"How does it feel looking at yourself in the mirror?"

"Every time I pull off a con, I put on a new face," he said. "This time doesn't feel any different. I'm always the same person under the skin."

She regarded him now like he was in the witness stand, and he thought, *Uh-oh.*

"You used present tense," Karen said.

"It's a figure of speech."

"What con are you pulling off now?"

"That you're naked on top of Brian Lockwood and not the charred corpse of Danny Cole."

"That's not it," Karen said. "I think you're engaged in a criminal activity."

"I don't see how. You're a consenting adult and I honestly thought what you asked me to do a few minutes ago was legal in California."

"There was a big museum theft recently in Japan, where I happened to visit you, that had all the earmarks of a Danny Cole job. It was creative, daring, and insane."

"Danny Cole is dead."

That might have gone over better, and sounded more definitive and decisive, if his burner didn't start ringing the instant he said it. Only two people, Tamiko and Sam, had that number.

He smiled apologetically and said, "I need to get that."

Karen climbed off him. "Why would you, a retired thief and con artist, have to take a call when you have a lusty, naked lawyer on top of you?"

He rolled on his side and began rooting around in his clothes on the floor for his burner. There were nuts all over them. "It's probably my investment adviser requesting my permission to make a risky trade."

"The stock exchange hasn't opened yet."

"It has in London and it's only minutes before Shanghai closes." Danny found his phone and answered it. "Lockwood speaking."

"Have you seen the news?" It was Sam Mertz, calling from his room at the Fairmont Miramar in Santa Monica.

Danny glanced at Karen, who was lying on her side, resting her head on her hand, observing him with amusement. He chose his next words carefully so Karen wouldn't be tipped off about the scheme he was involved in. "No, I haven't been keeping up on the pharmaceutical market. What's happening?"

"Slezak just lowered the price of Xylaphram."

That was fast, Danny thought.

"Excellent, it's time to sell off our shares. Do what you need to do. I'll be in touch." He ended the call, dropped the phone on the floor, and turned on his side to face Karen. "Sorry about that. It's a lot of money on the line."

"That's the only part I believe. I'm guessing about $40 million."

"Relax." He kissed her on the lips. "You can trust me."

"I know that." She kissed him back, and put a little tongue behind it. "But I also know you only express this extraordinary desire and stamina in bed after you've spent years in prison—"

He interrupted her. "That only happened once."

"—or when you're on the brink of a major score."

"It's you, baby. You're the score." Danny kissed her and slipped his hand between her legs. "But you aren't on the brink yet."

She smiled, but grabbed his wrist, stopping him from moving his hand any farther. "You got away after your last job and that was a certified miracle. They don't happen twice."

"I don't need any miracles."

"I hope you're right, because if you get caught this time, I won't be there for you." Karen looked him in the eye, like she was trying to see if Danny Cole was behind that mask and if he understood the gravity of what she was saying.

He was and he did and she must have seen it, because she let go of his wrist, rolled onto her back, and said: "But I'm here now."

CHAPTER NINETEEN

September 10

Walker drove out to the Sun Valley landfill early in the morning, resigned to spending the day sorting through ashes and soot looking for Sharpe's glob of plastic. On the plus side, his groin wasn't sore anymore and he'd managed to get dressed without Carly seeing his bruises. With luck, they'd fade fast.

He arrived to see a CSU van, several patrol cars, and dozens of people in white Tyvek suits and gas masks picking through the rubble like the birds that were circled over the rest of the dump. Sharpe and Carter were among them.

Off to one side, a pop-up canopy had been erected over a tarp piled with chunks of melted plastic that had been cut in half. Nan Baker stood with another CSU technician at a folding table, photographing and then carefully cutting open blackened globs of melted plastic. The discarded pieces were then tossed on the tarp.

Walker got out of his truck, left his hat on the seat, and began getting into a Tyvek suit of his own as Sharpe delivered another glob to Nan. Sharpe spotted Walker and ambled over.

"I saw your sting on the news," he said. "An active shooter situation at a major shopping mall."

"That's an exaggeration and totally inaccurate," Walker said. "It went down on the vacant top floor of the parking structure, no shoppers were there, and the shooter was killed before he could be active."

"Did you shoot him?"

"Eve did. Two shots, center mass."

"Impressive," Sharpe said. "It would be even more so if nobody got shot or killed."

"It comes with the job."

"I've never shot anyone."

"You don't run into many armed bad guys in the ashes of a burned building." Walker zipped up his suit. "Or in a landfill."

"I arrested plenty of arsonists before you came along," Sharpe said. "I've drawn my weapon, but I've never had to fire it."

"Remind me to get you a ribbon to pin on your chest."

Nan called out from the canopy. "I think we've got something here."

Carter rushed over from the rubble pile to join Sharpe and Walker at the table with Nan, who carefully pulled apart the glob, her assistant filming it for the record. Inside was a portion of a manufactured fire log, the ends burned, but the rest was still in its wrapping, which was scorched at the edges.

Carter clapped Sharpe on the back. "You were right."

"I usually am," he said.

Walker was truly amazed. "Have you ever thought about playing the lottery?"

"This isn't luck, Walker. It's what happens when you follow science, rigorous investigative principles, and proven methodology."

"Die-hard lotto-scratchers say the same thing," Walker said. "I think it's a bit of both. But now we know how the fire started and who did it."

"Do we? Take a closer look at that log," Sharpe said.

"I see it," Walker said. Nan was leaning over the log, examining it with a magnifying glass.

"The wrapping on it is gray," Sharpe said, "and you can make out a few letters of the brand name."

Walker saw *UEFIR.* "Ew-Fir?"

Nan straightened up. "It's TrueFire. Those are just the middle letters."

Sharpe said, "I'm not familiar with that brand, but I know the carport arsonist only used Duraflame logs, which have a *yellow* wrapping and"—he looked directly at Walker now, because this comment was aimed squarely at him—"they say *Duraflame* on them."

Now Walker saw Sharpe's point, but didn't feel as stupid, which he assumed was the point.

Nan added, "There is also a distinct difference in the material composition of the two brands of artificial fire log."

Walker said, "Okay, so Novar ran out of Duraflames and bought these TrueFires. What difference does it make?"

"I don't like inconsistencies," Sharpe said.

"Life is full of them."

Nan bent over the log again with her magnifying glass. "I can see a lot number on the wrapper and there's a price tag sticker with a barcode. We might be able to use this to trace the log to the Schafer Brothers grocery store it came from."

Carter said, "How do you know it's from Schafer Brothers?"

"There's no trick to it," Nan said. "I shop at Schafer. TrueFire is their private brand, though the log itself is probably sold under a variety of different store-brand names and packaging. At Schafers, they have TrueGranola, TrueShampoo, TrueChocolate, TrueTissue, TrueBacon, you name it."

Walker turned to Sharpe. "Inconsistencies or not, you have to tell Lansing that it's likely that the same fugitive who torched all those cars in Hollywood also took down the I-10."

Sharpe grimaced. "I know. I just don't want him calling a news conference to announce the case closed until we're absolutely sure it's the same arsonist."

"We'll know once I catch Toniel Novar," Walker said. "You call the sheriff and I'll call Caffrey and Scruggs."

"That's the first fair division of labor that you've ever suggested."

Walker walked a few steps away, took out his phone, and called Scruggs.

Scruggs didn't say hello. What he said was: "I had a feeling we'd be hearing from you today."

"How did you hear about it?"

"Hear about what?"

"That we discovered the I-10 fire was arson, sparked by a couple of Duraflames under a car." Actually, they were TrueFires, but he didn't want to get into the niggly details.

"I didn't hear that," Scruggs said. "How did you hear about us?"

"What about you?"

"We're in a car headed up to Big Bear, where we're going to apprehend Toniel Novar in a joint operation with the San Bernardino County Sheriff and the US Forest Service."

"He's camping up there?"

"Yeah, he painted his van black and swapped out the plates."

"How did you find him?"

"His license plate got swept up in a passive read by an ALPR on a CHP patrol car," Scruggs said. "The plates came back as stolen."

Scruggs was referring to the Automated License Plate Recognition system that existed on all CHP patrol cars and on hidden devices located on freeways, overpasses, and signposts throughout Southern California. Walker wanted to get one in his truck but hadn't been able to swing it, legally or otherwise.

"We got a photo of the van," Scruggs continued, "which was the right make and year, but wrong color. So we guessed it was him."

"And you guessed where he was heading from the bald eagles, snowcapped mountains, and lake in the mural Bonilla painted on their wall."

The scene was on Walker's mural list, but he hadn't been able to identify the locale before he left the case to focus on the Santa Monica Freeway fire.

"You got it," Scruggs said. "We were working our way through all the locations on the wall anyway. Big Bear was on our list. This just sped things up. We had the rangers fly a drone over the campsite to confirm he was there and he is."

Walker was frustrated that he couldn't catch Novar himself and that it was too late for him to join the arrest. But at least they had him.

"That's good to hear. Congratulations, guys."

"Holy shit," Scruggs said. "I just realized why you called. You wanted back on this investigation once you figured out that Novar set the overpass fire, too."

That's right, Walker thought. But he wasn't going to come right out and say it.

"We don't know yet that these serial carport fires and the I-10 fire are connected."

But Scruggs wasn't listening, he was talking to Caffrey: "Hey, Pete, you aren't going to believe this. We've just solved the two biggest Los Angeles arson cases in decades!"

Walker yelled into the phone: "You had nothing to do with the I-10 investigation and Sharpe and I were the ones who tied Novar to the carport fire spree."

"Says who?" Scruggs said. "You ditched the carport case and ran off because you saw a sparkly thing that might do more for your careers."

"Sheriff Lansing reassigned us."

"Thank you for the courtesy call, Walker. We'll let you know when we need your files on the I-10 case to wrap up *our* investigation."

"*Your* investigation?"

But Scruggs had already hung up. Walker swore to himself.

Sharpe came over to him. "I just got off with Lansing. He was ready to declare the case closed and hold a press conference. I managed to get him to wait until we've had a chance to question Novar. How did it go with you?"

"Scruggs thanked me for my courtesy call. He and Caffrey are about to arrest Novar at a campsite in Big Bear and close their investigation into, and I quote, 'the two biggest Los Angeles arson cases in decades.'"

"They couldn't solve how a marshmallow got roasted over a campfire," Sharpe said. "We need to get up to Big Bear pronto."

The helicopter trip to Big Bear took forty-five minutes. They landed at the Big Bear airport, which was just a few runways at the edge of the lake for civilian aircraft and helicopter tours.

Sharpe and Walker were met by a deputy in a San Bernardino County Sheriff's Department patrol car, who took them back to the station a few short miles away. They got there just as Scruggs and Caffrey arrived with Novar in handcuffs and his van, now painted black, on the back of a flatbed truck for processing.

Scruggs took Novar inside to be fingerprinted and booked as Caffrey met Sharpe and Walker at the door.

"How did you get here so fast?" Caffrey said. "It's a three-hour drive on a good day."

"We ordered a chopper to take us," Walker said. "Think about how we got the pull to do that and what it means."

"He isn't that smart," Sharpe said, then got in Caffrey's face. "It's because the governor of the state of California, the mayor of Los Angeles, and the sheriff of Los Angeles County, and, as far as you're concerned, Almighty God put us in charge of this investigation."

Caffrey was more amused than intimidated. "God spoke to you, Shar-Pei?"

"I'm going to question the suspect," Sharpe said.

"You don't have to," Caffrey said. "He confessed."

"What do you mean by 'confessed'?"

"I mean," Caffrey said, getting into Sharpe's face now, "we read him his rights at the campground, he refused a lawyer, and admitted that he set all of the fires. What part of that don't you understand?"

"That's what he said, 'all of the fires'?"

"The carport fires, the Tower, and the freeway." Caffrey ticked them off with three fingers.

"He said that?"

"Well, no, not exactly." Caffrey took a step back from Sharpe, as if he'd suddenly realized they were nearly nose to nose. "Obviously, we knew 'all of the fires' wasn't good enough, so we made him drill down. We asked him if he set the car fires over the two nights at those apartment buildings, and he said yes. Then we asked him if he set fire to the car, the guard shack, and the Tower, and he said yes."

"And then you asked him if he did the freeway."

"That's right," Caffrey said.

Sharpe groaned and walked away, mumbling to himself and gesticulating angrily with his hands.

Caffrey looked at Walker. "What's his problem?"

Walker knew exactly what it was.

"Let me ask you a question, Pete. Before you and Scruggs became arson investigators, did the Los Angeles Fire Department give you any formal training in how to question a suspect?"

"We had an intensive, rigorous daylong course at the Marriott in Woodland Hills."

"That's it?"

"We're firefighters," Caffrey said, "not cops."

"If that wasn't obvious before," Walker said, "it certainly is now."

"We recorded the confession with our phones and informed him we were doing it, if that's what you're worried about."

"Novar's confession is worthless," Walker said. "What the recording will prove is that you told him what fires he set."

"And he admitted to them. Case closed," Caffrey said. "The only thing you're angry about is that he didn't confess to you, that we closed the case and you didn't."

Sharpe marched back over to Caffrey and looked like he might hit him. "What I am upset about is that you two may have just let the actual freeway arsonist get away with it."

Caffrey looked at Walker. "What is he talking about?"

That's when Scruggs came outside.

"Oh, there you are, Pete," he said, then he noticed Sharpe and Walker, but if he was surprised to see them, he didn't show it. "Thanks for coming all this way to congratulate us. It really wasn't necessary. Novar has been processed. Now we just have to wait for the San Berdoo cops to give us the paperwork so we can take him back to LA. It's going to take a bit longer to get his van towed back. But we can still wrap this all up today."

Sharpe walked up to the door and shouldered Scruggs aside. "Next time you have a suspect in custody, read him his rights and then shut up until an actual law enforcement professional can handle the questioning."

Sharpe went inside and slammed the door behind him.

Scruggs, dumbfounded, looked at Walker, who was beginning to feel like Sharpe's interpreter.

"What is he talking about?"

Sharpe sat across the table from Toniel Novar in the interrogation room. Novar was handcuffed and slouched in his seat, dark circles under his bloodshot eyes, a couple of days' worth of beard on his cheeks. He looked as if he hadn't slept much in days.

And so did Sharpe. He seemed to be wearing every single minute of his life on his shoulders. His hunched back was even more pronounced, the folds on his sagging face even deeper and saggier. He was the epitome of a man exhausted by his job, a man counting the seconds until retirement, which couldn't come soon enough.

"I'm Walter Sharpe, an arson investigator with the Los Angeles County Sheriff's Department," he said with a sigh. "Were you read your rights and are you declining counsel?"

"Yes."

"And you are aware I am recording this conversation?"

"Yes. I did it. I did them all." When Novar said it, he also glanced at the mirror on the wall so whoever was watching in the other room got it, too.

The watchers were Walker, Caffrey, and Scruggs, standing in front of the one-way glass, which was a real museum piece, maybe from the 1960s. Walker would've liked to find an authentic one, pulled out of a police station, for his house, for the novelty and the "wow factor" they always talked about on HGTV. But he didn't know which wall he'd put it in, maybe between the garage and laundry room, and he didn't think Carly would go for it.

"So I've heard," Sharpe said to Novar and made a notation on the yellow pad in front of him. "Tell me about the first one."

"It was on North Alfred Street. I lit a log under the car."

"Do you remember what kind of car?"

"A BMW," Novar said. "The rich fuck."

"What kind of log?"

"Duraflame."

"Why did you do it?"

"Because those assholes painted over Mateo's art."

"When did they do that?"

"I don't know," Novar said. "Five, six months ago."

"So why did you wait until now to do something about it?"

Novar gave him a long, cold stare. "Because they killed him."

But he couldn't hold the stare, because his eyes were welling with tears. Embarrassed, he turned his head and wiped his eyes on his arm.

"The owner of the BMW?"

Toniel shook his head. "The assholes who ran us out of the Tower and destroyed Mateo's masterpiece . . . and then him. This city was his canvas and they painted over it."

The last line seemed rehearsed to Walker, or at least repeated from someone else. It didn't sound natural coming out of Novar's mouth. Maybe it was Bonilla who'd said it, or their landlady.

"I don't understand," Sharpe said. "If you blame the people who own the Tower for Mateo's death, what was the point of torching all of those apartment buildings?"

"Those people are all the same. They don't appreciate art. So they kill it."

"I still don't get why you started fires in the carports of apartment buildings that Mateo tagged," Sharpe said, "and didn't go straight to the place where he was mortally injured."

"I needed time," Novar said.

"I am really confused," Sharpe said. "Time for what?"

"To burn down the Tower," Novar said. "I didn't want anyone to get there and put it out before it got going, but I fucked up. What kind of detective are you?"

"Old and slow." Sharpe held up his hand apologetically. "You're going to have to be patient with me."

Walker had never seen Sharpe use his body, or his natural hangdog expression, so effectively.

"I set the cars on fire to burn down the apartments and keep the firemen busy while I torched the Tower. You follow?" Novar said, waiting for a nod from tired, old Sharpe before continuing. "But I didn't know what I was doing. I wish I had an airplane I could have flown into it instead of just some camping logs. I couldn't take the Tower down, but I could destroy every other building that destroyed his art."

Sharpe raised his hands again. "Whoa, slow down. I'm having a hard time keeping up. Let's go back and start at the beginning. After that first apartment carport fire, where did you go next?"

And then Sharpe meticulously walked him through each apartment fire and on through to the Tower. It was tedious, slow, and methodical, but Walker knew that was the point. Sharpe was tiring out Novar and getting him to lower his guard.

Novar wasn't the only one getting tired.

◆ ◆ ◆

In the cramped little observation room, Scruggs walked away from the window, found a chair against the opposite wall, and sat down. "Wake me up when this over."

"You're missing the point of all this," Walker said. "He's getting Novar to confirm every aspect of the fires. He's building a case."

Caffrey took the chair next to his partner. "What case? He's already confessed."

"You'll see," Walker said.

◆ ◆ ◆

Sharpe ran Novar through every fire on the first day of his sprec, then took him through the second spree, one fire at a time, until they got to the last one.

"What did you use to set that fire under the Chevy?"

"Another log. How many times do I have to tell you? I always used the logs. And it was a Prius, not a Chevy."

"Right. Sorry." Sharpe scratched something out on his pad. "Okay. Well, I guess that wraps it up. Thank you for providing all those details, and I'm sorry about your boyfriend's death."

"You aren't sorry about his art?"

"Some of it still exists," Sharpe said.

"For how much longer?"

"I don't know." Sharpe took his notepad and stood up to leave.

"Aren't you going to ask me about the other one?"

Sharpe appeared confused. "What other one?"

"You sure you aren't senile?"

"To be honest, no, I'm not," Sharpe said. "I'm getting more and more forgetful and it worries me."

"The 10 freeway," Novar said. "That was me, too."

"It was?" Sharpe sat down again and placed his pad in front of him. "Why did you do that?"

"So the entire city would feel my pain."

"They certainly have," Sharpe said, making a note.

"Except you," Novar said. "You didn't feel shit."

"How did you do it?"

"Like all the others. I put a log under a car and lit it."

"What kind of car?"

"I don't remember."

"Was it a two door? A four door? An SUV? A truck?"

Novar studied the ceiling, as if it might be written up there. "It's all starting to blur. You should understand that, a man in your condition."

"I do, but you remembered what the other cars were. I thought you might remember this one, too," Sharpe said. "What about the log?"

"What about it?"

"Was it another Duraflame?"

"Yes."

"How many logs?"

"One or two. I don't remember."

Sharpe set down his pen and leaned back in his chair. "This is really confusing me."

"How can it be confusing you? It's the same as all the others."

"That's just it." Sharpe leaned forward now. His hunched shoulders were gone, his gaze piercing. "It's not the same."

Walter Sharpe was no longer the old, tired, confused detective worn down by life. He was a werewolf, hungry for blood. The instant transformation was startling and a bit terrifying for Toniel Novar, who instinctively reared back in his seat.

In the observation room, Scruggs and Caffrey got up and went to the window. They could feel the change, too. It was electric. But Walker knew all along that it was coming and it brought a big smile to his face.

Novar cleared his throat. "What do you mean?"

"It wasn't a Duraflame log," Sharpe said, going for the kill. "It was a TrueFire log."

"How do you know what kind of log it was if it burned up?"

"Because it didn't," Sharpe said. "We have a piece of it, still in the wrapper."

"I ran out of Duraflame logs. So what?"

"When did that happen?"

"After all those apartment fires, obviously," Novar said. "You really are a dumb fuck."

"Where did you get the log?"

Novar seemed to sense a trap. "It was in the van. Left over from one of our camping trips."

"One log or two?"

"I don't remember."

"If you had leftover logs," Sharpe said, "why did you have to buy all those boxes of Duraflames? We have you on video buying them."

"I forgot they were in the van and I had a lot of places I wanted to hit."

"With so many recent lapses in memory, maybe you should be worried about senility," Sharpe said. "Why did you pick that particular freeway overpass out of all the ones in the city for your fire?"

"The same reason I went to all the spots," Novar snapped at him. "Because they destroyed Mateo's art."

"So did you," Sharpe said. "If you burned that freeway."

"You aren't making any sense."

"The columns of that overpass were covered with Mateo's art. It was pristine. Full of vibrant color and life, maybe the best remaining example of his work outside of your apartment." Sharpe pointed a finger at him. "Until *you* burned it all away."

"That's not true," Novar said, but his voice wavered. "It was all gone. That's why I did the freeway."

Sharpe shook his head. "Other people painted over your lover's art, but you are the only one who burned it. Do you really want to take credit for that? Do you think you can live with the shame and the stupidity?"

Novar couldn't look at him. "I'm done talking."

"You've talked enough."

Sharpe stood up, took his notepad, and left the room.

CHAPTER TWENTY

Walker, Caffrey, and Scruggs were still standing at the window, watching Novar tremble, as Sharpe came into the observation room.

"Novar didn't torch the freeway," Sharpe said.

Scruggs said, "He says he did."

"If you hadn't asked him about the freeway," Sharpe said, "Novar would never have admitted to it."

Caffrey said, "He knew it was set with fire logs."

"He guessed it," Sharpe said.

"How?"

"It's obvious. Why else would you think he was good for it if the freeway fire didn't follow the same MO? But Novar got it wrong. That fire was caused by two TrueFire logs, not Duraflames."

"He explained that," Scruggs said.

"I don't buy it," Sharpe said.

"You mean you *won't*," Caffrey said. "You just hate that you didn't get the guy but we did."

Scruggs added, "On the other freeway fires, the arsonists never admitted to the deed. This time, one of 'em does, and *you* try to talk him out of it. That's how envious you are of our arrest. It's fucking pathetic."

Sharpe stared at him. "What *other* freeway fires?"

"The ones in Pittsburgh and Milwaukee," Scruggs said. "Don't tell me that you, the self-proclaimed arson expert, haven't heard about them."

"Of course I have," Sharpe said. "But how do you know the details?"

Caffrey said, "Because we're also arson investigators who like to keep up and there's this new thing called Google. You ought to try it."

"Plus," Scruggs said, puffing up his chest proudly, "we got the inside scoop from George Petroni."

That surprised Walker. "You know Petroni?"

"We worked with him on his first job, a few years back when that gasoline tanker hit the overpass on the Hollywood Freeway," Scruggs said. "We've been doing this a long time, Walker. Contrary to what you've been told, we know our shit as well as, if not better than, Shar-Pei."

Sharpe said, "Have you been in touch with Petroni since he moved back to LA?"

"Yeah, we're buddies," Scruggs said. "We go fishing with him on his boat. He thinks you're an asshole, by the way. We told him that's what *everybody* thinks."

Without saying a word, Sharpe turned and walked out of the room. Walker shot a look of disapproval at the two detectives.

Caffrey said, "Don't give us that look, Walker. You know it's true. Shar-Pei thinks he's channeling God. He came right out today and said it. You were standing there."

"You may be right about Novar, but you made some rookie mistakes in that interrogation," Walker said. "You could learn a lot from Sharpe."

"Fuck him," Scruggs said.

◆ ◆ ◆

Walker found Sharpe pacing in the parking lot. "That went well."

Sharpe didn't stop pacing. "Those two just solved the freeway arson and made fools out of us."

"That's definitely the way they see it. And then you marched in and tried to take the victory away from them to save face. I totally get why they're pissed at you. I would be, too. But I understand how you feel because I feel the same way. We solved it, not them. All they did was make the arrest."

"No," Sharpe said. "They solved it. We didn't."

"Now you believe that Novar torched the overpass?"

"Of course not." Sharpe didn't slow his pacing. "He's obviously lying. He's committed to the lie because people won't remember the car fires, but they will remember the man who brought down a freeway."

"I'm confused," Walker said. "If that's true, how did *they* solve the crime and not us?"

"Think about it." Sharpe stopped in front of him. "What's the one thing all the freeway arson fires in LA, Pittsburgh, and Milwaukee have in common?"

Walker did and he remembered something George Petroni told him.

I thought Milwaukee was a fluke, but here I am, on my third freeway fire repair job in a decade.

Walker had to find a bench and sit down. The magnitude of their mistake was too heavy to manage standing up.

"It's Petroni. He did it."

"That's right." Sharpe sat down next to him. "He's probably the most daring and destructive serial arsonist in American history. He not only set massive fires in multiple states, but he stuck around to rebuild what he destroyed. It's unprecedented."

"He's got balls, that's for sure."

"It's an obsession," Sharpe said. "Ever since Petroni's first success, rebuilding a crippled freeway here in record time, he's repeated the experience again and again so he can bask in the glory of being a city's savior."

"Or maybe he just liked the huge payday," Walker said.

"More reward," Sharpe said. "That's what this is all about. The hardest part for him must have been biding his time in each city until a serial arsonist came along that he could frame for a freeway disaster."

"I'm sure he used the time well," Walker said. "He cozied up to the local arson investigators, bought them steak dinners or took them fishing, and regaled them with stories about his experiences. That way, when a serial arsonist finally struck, he could get them to gossip with him about the details of the fires."

Sharpe jerked a thumb at the station. "Just like he got Dumb and Dumber in there to tell him about the carport arsonist using campfire logs. That was how Petroni was able to copy what Novar had done."

But Petroni didn't know that all the logs were Duraflames, Walker thought. And he went too far by layering fuels, choosing a vehicle that was close to tires and pallets, and displaying a knowledge of fire that Novar didn't have. Novar admitted as much to Sharpe.

I set the cars on fire to burn down the apartments and keep the firemen busy while I torched the Tower. But I didn't know what I was doing.

"Caffrey and Scruggs were unknowingly aiding and abetting an arsonist," Walker said. "They are going to be humiliated when they find out."

"That's true," Sharpe said. "But mostly, this is on you."

"How do you figure that?"

"I wanted to arrest Petroni the instant I met him for tampering with the evidence," Sharpe said, "but you stopped me."

"We didn't have a case against him then and we don't have one now."

"But I was right," Sharpe said. "Now we know why he did it. He was actively obstructing us from the start."

"You're saying it's my fault that we didn't realize until now that Petroni set the freeway fire and is the most daring arsonist the world has ever known."

"Yes, I am," Sharpe said. "Maybe this will teach you to never question my instincts in the future—that's assuming we ever work in law enforcement again after this staggering failure."

"Nobody is going to know how we messed up."

"We can't keep quiet," Sharpe said. "We can't let Novar be prosecuted for a crime he didn't commit, even if he's confessed to it."

"That won't be up to us," Walker said.

"So you're saying we should just keep our mouths shut and let Petroni get away with it again?"

"I'm saying nobody will know about our mistake because we're going to make up for it and put Petroni away for this," Walker said. "All we need to do, before Caffrey and Scruggs announce Novar's arrest and Lansing shuts us down, is tie Petroni to the TrueFire log and prove he was under that overpass right before the fire started."

As soon as the words were out of his mouth, Walker knew how to do it.

"How can we possibly do that?"

Walker didn't answer. Instead he jumped to his feet and caught up with a uniformed deputy who was crossing the parking lot to his patrol car.

"Excuse me," Walker said to him. "Could you give us a ride to the airport?"

"Sure," the deputy said. "Climb in."

Walker waved Sharpe over, they got into the back seat of the patrol car, and Walker told the deputy: "Use the lights and siren. We're in a hurry."

"It's only six miles away and this isn't LA," the deputy said. "You won't get there any faster than you would without the ruckus."

"It will make me feel better."

The deputy sped out, tires squealing, lights flashing and siren wailing, and it seemed to make him feel better, too, since he had a huge grin on his face. Walker figured the deputy didn't get many excuses to make a ruckus.

"All we have is our speculation," Sharpe said, as if there had been no interruption at all in their conversation. "It's not enough to convince a judge to grant us search warrants for the geolocation data from Petroni's cell phone or from his car or even to see if he used his credit card for an Uber on the night of the fire."

"It'd be a pointless waste of time anyway," Walker said. "Petroni is too smart to carry his phone with him to an arson or to get there using a rideshare or by driving a car that isn't analog."

"What kind of car is that?"

"An old one that doesn't have any electronic components that store or broadcast location data," Walker said. "But none of that matters now. We don't need warrants to get the evidence we need."

The deputy got them to the helicopter in four minutes. While it didn't make a huge difference in time, the lights and siren did startle the tactical flight officer and the pilot, who were sitting in the open cockpit, and make them snap to attention. That's what Walker wanted, to instill in the helicopter crew a sense of urgency.

Walker thanked the deputy and rushed to the chopper.

"Let's go," he told the crew. "We need to get back to LASD HQ fast."

"Roger that," the pilot said.

They all climbed into the chopper and buckled up.

Sharpe said, "I hope you aren't talking about a sting."

"Nope," Walker said. "Straightforward manhunting."

Once they were in the air, Walker contacted Carter on the TFO's satellite phone and told her to drop everything and find out where

Petroni lived, the cars he owned, where he kept his boat, and if there were any Schafer Brothers grocery stores near his home.

"Also find out where he is," Walker said. "Call his office and tell him we need to give him more details about the patch of asphalt we want to dig up."

The truth was, Walker wanted to confirm that George Petroni would be in his construction trailer at the overpass when they were ready to arrest him. To her credit, Carter didn't ask Walker why he wanted all that information.

Sharpe overheard Walker's side of the call, and when Walker was finished, he said: "Even if we can get video of Petroni buying a TrueFire log in a Schafer Brothers store shortly before the inferno, that's not a crime and it doesn't put him under the overpass in the minutes before the fire."

"Free-Breeze will," Walker said.

"What is that?"

"It's a Bluetooth device that snaps onto an asthma-relief inhaler and tracks every dose. It helps patients identify what locations, weather, activities, or other environmental factors trigger their attacks. Petroni has a Free-Breeze. I saw it light up when he used his inhaler the first day we met him. He won't go anywhere without his inhaler, not even to set a freeway on fire."

"The device tracks your movements?"

"Constantly, through an app on your phone."

"How do you know that?"

"My brother has asthma and uses one of those things."

"We'll still need a warrant to get his location data from Free-Breeze."

"No, we won't," Walker said. "All we have to do is ask for it."

"It's an invasion of privacy."

"One that all Free-Breeze users allowed when they accepted the app's terms of service, which nobody ever reads before they click 'I Accept,'" Walker said. "If they did, they'd notice the boilerplate clause granting the company and its partners the unlimited right to use and share your data, including geolocation, to better serve you. That same clause is buried in the user agreements for most apps, especially the free ones."

"Free always has a price," Sharpe said.

"The app makers sell that information to data brokers and will gladly share it with law enforcement if you ask them politely."

"That's scary."

"Not if you're an agent for the surveillance state like us."

"But we're still screwed," Sharpe said. "There won't be any geolocation data from that inhaler if Petroni didn't bring his phone with him when he set the overpass on fire. I guarantee you that he didn't. He's not that stupid."

"It doesn't matter," Walker said with a smile. "The Free-Breeze device automatically syncs its data with the app the next time the phone is turned on and the inhaler is nearby."

"That's diabolical."

"Or a smart convenience," Walker said. "Depending on whether you are a law-abiding asthma sufferer, a criminal, or a cop."

Sharpe said, "I'm getting a flip phone."

Carter was waiting at Walker's cubicle, which was located outside Sharpe's office, forty-five minutes later, when the two detectives rushed into the arson unit's squad room.

"Petroni is at home," Carter said. "He called in sick around 8:30 a.m."

Walker was troubled by the timing, which was roughly when Sharpe found the preserved piece of TrueFire log in the melted piece of plastic at the Sun Valley landfill. But he was even more troubled by what was on his desk. It was a small, gift-wrapped box with a ribbon around it.

"Where is home?" Sharpe asked.

"A condo in Marina del Ray. He's got a twenty-eight-foot Wellcraft cabin cruiser in a slip there, too. I've got the address for you. He's got two registered vehicles, a new Audi R8 that he's leasing and a 1974 Ford F-250 pickup."

What troubled Walker about the box was that the wrapping paper was a Japanese design, a mix of blooming cherry blossoms, colorful koi fish, and red torii gates.

"Digital and analog," Sharpe said, intruding on Walker's thoughts.

"What?"

"His cars," Sharpe said. "One has cutting-edge digital features and the other doesn't have a single computerized element. I'm going to see if I can find that truck in any traffic camera footage near the overpass on the night of the fire."

"Good idea," Walker said. "I'll call Free-Breeze."

"Who?" Carter asked.

"Long story," Walker said, "that I don't have time to explain."

"Okay," Carter said. "There's a Schafer Brothers grocery store in Marina del Rey, and I'll get on them about Petroni. I can't wait to hear how you jumped from Novar to Petroni as the perp, but I get the feeling that we're racing the clock."

"Your instincts are on target once again," Sharpe said. "Oh, one more thing. Find out if anybody at that Sun Valley landfill got a call from Petroni this morning, or vice versa."

Walker was pleasantly surprised that he and Sharpe had shared the same thought about the timing of Petroni's sudden illness.

Carter got up to make her calls at another desk, Sharpe went into his office to download the traffic cam videos, and Walker took the seat at his cubicle, staring at that gift box like it was a ticking bomb.

Danny Cole was here.

But Walker had priorities to deal with . . . and that damn ticking clock. They had to arrest Petroni before Caffrey and Scruggs announced Novar's arrest for the freeway fire.

Walker turned to his desktop computer, got online, and found the contact number for Free-Breeze, where he identified himself to the operator and was referred to business affairs. As soon as that exec got on the phone, Walker explained what he wanted. The exec said that before they went any further, he'd call Walker back at the sheriff's department to confirm his identity, which Walker thought was a good idea.

Walker hung up and started unwrapping the box, but before he could open it, his phone rang.

He snatched up the receiver and identified himself. It was the Free-Breeze guy, who, now that he knew Walker was really a cop, said he'd email him a link momentarily that would give him access to Petroni's past and present geolocation data from the inhaler device. Walker gave him his email address, thanked him, and hung up.

He opened the box.

It contained a wristwatch, a replica of the Infinitum, which Walker recognized from all the news coverage about the robbery.

There was a printed card with the watch. It read:

Be in Calabasas by 3 p.m. this afternoon. This will help you keep track of the time.

It was already 2:30, and he didn't need a watch to know he wasn't going to make it. He supposed he could claim he was sick himself and leave the endgame of this investigation to Sharpe and Carter. But without the chopper, in the traffic hell that Petroni created, it would take him two hours to reach the far end of the valley.

Besides, his priority had to be Petroni, not Slezak.

Walker couldn't let one of the worst serial arsonists ever get away again just so he could help Danny Cole, one of the greatest thieves ever, get away again, even if it was for something that Walker had put him up to.

Whatever the hell *it* was.

He tossed the wrapping, the box, the card, and the watch in his trash can.

His iPhone vibrated. The email from Free-Breeze had come in. He opened it and clicked the link.

It took ten seconds for Walker to find out what he needed.

He rushed into Sharpe's office so fast that he nearly knocked down an entire stack of binders, papers, books, and office equipment, which might have buried them both alive.

"We've got him." Walker went around Sharpe's desk and showed him his phone screen, with a display that was very similar to Google Maps. The image showed a dot at the intersection of West Washington Boulevard and Toberman Street at 2:30 a.m. on September 5. "Petroni was at the overpass right before the fire started."

Sharpe got up. "Let's go arrest the son of a bitch. Is he still at home?"

Walker refreshed the geolocation data and it presented a blinking dot where Petroni was at that moment.

"He's on his boat in Marina del Rey," Walker said.

"Is he moving?"

"Not yet," he said.

◆ ◆ ◆

Sharpe and Walker rushed out to the helicopter and piled inside.

The pilot looked back at them from his seat. The name on his jumpsuit was Barney Preat and he had a mustache that Tom Selleck would envy. It wasn't the same pilot they'd had before. "Where are we going?"

"To make an arrest in Marina del Rey," Walker said. "We need to land somewhere near this boat slip."

He showed Barney the phone, and the pilot said: "We can land in the Marina del Rey public parking lot on Bali Way. That will put you right in front of his slip."

"Excellent."

Walker sat back in his seat behind the pilot, and the chopper lifted off.

They'd be there in fifteen minutes. But he was antsy, shaking his knee, worrying about what could go wrong in Calabasas while he was making the arrest.

Walker thought about sending Eve Ronin a text. But what could he say to her?

He glanced down at his phone.

The dot was moving fast. It was already out of the marina and into the bay.

"Oh shit," Walker said.

"What?" Sharpe said.

"He's running."

The TFO said, "Let me see that phone for a second."

Walker gave it to her. The TFO's name was Lauren Kelsey, and she looked tough enough to wrestle bears.

After a moment, she reached around the gun mount and handed the phone back to him. "I see where we're going. If you tell me who we're chasing, I can get more details on the boat from the harbormaster and alert the coast guard. We can also track his AIS transponder if it's activated."

"It won't be," Walker said, but gave her the information anyway.

She got on the radio and made some calls. Walker switched his radio to the other channel so he could talk to Sharpe without hearing the chatter on Lauren's and Barney's radios.

Sharpe said, "What spooked him?"

"I might have."

"How?"

"By contacting Free-Breeze," Walker said. "Petroni may have received an automated message from his app notifying him that his location data was accessed. I didn't think to ask Free-Breeze to stop that from happening."

"Then he knows we have him," Sharpe said.

"We won't if he hits international waters."

"How far is that from the coast?"

"Twelve nautical miles," Walker said.

"Is that really a thing?"

He didn't know. But he said: "Of course it's a thing."

"What I am asking is if he really is untouchable by law enforcement once he crosses that invisible line in the water."

Walker didn't know that, either, since it had never come up in his days as a US marshal, so he said: "Do you really want to find out?"

The LASD helicopter was flying over Marina del Rey and out into the bay when Sharpe and Walker both got texts.

"Good news," Sharpe said. "Carter has footage of Petroni buying the log the day before the fire."

"How did she get it so fast?"

"Petroni has a Shafer Brothers loyalty card. It turns out they have terms of service just like Free-Breeze's. It took them five seconds to find the date and time of the purchase. What's your news?"

It was a text from Danny Cole, who needed him to act in the next few minutes. Walker couldn't be in Calabasas now, but he knew somebody who could.

"No news. I need to pick something up on my way home tonight."

He sent Eve Ronin a text.

"There he is," said Lauren. She was watching the water with her binoculars. "At two o'clock. He's going about forty-five knots."

Walker looked up from his phone. He could see a white dot on the water, a frothy wake behind it. "How far are we from international waters?"

Lauren answered, "Two miles, maybe less, though it's not like there's a buoy marking the spot."

"He'll know and so will his lawyer," Walker said. "We have to stop him."

The chopper flew low and got in front of the boat's path. Walker could see Petroni in the wheelhouse, standing at the helm, as the boat charged toward them.

Lauren got on the loudspeaker. "This is the Los Angeles County Sheriff's Department. Stop your boat immediately."

The boat kept going, passing right underneath the chopper. Walker saw several big, red gasoline cans on the aft deck. Petroni was planning on a long trip.

"He's not going to stop until he gets to Mexico," Walker said.

Sharpe said, "Where's the coast guard?"

"Five miles out," the pilot said.

"They won't make it in time," Walker said. "Pull up alongside the boat and get as low as you can."

"What do you intend to do?"

Walker took out his gun. "I'm going to stop him."

"That won't do the job," Lauren said, and reached her right arm back, dangling a key out to him. "Open the weapons mount and take the AR-15. It's a .308 and can blast through an engine block."

Walker unlocked the mount, removed the bracket holding the weapons in place, and pulled out the rifle. It was loaded—all he had to do was chamber a round.

"You sound like you've done it," Walker said.

"Once or twice," she said. "But I think you need to do this one."

"Right you are." He took off his hat and handed it to Sharpe. "Take care of this."

Lauren said, "Don't open the door until Barney gives you the go-ahead."

Petroni rocketed forward, his cruiser bouncing on the swells, but there was no way he could shake off a helicopter.

Walker knew Petroni's only hope was that they'd run low on gas and be forced to return to base or that he'd hit international waters before they could stop him.

"Okay," Barney said. "Go."

Walker slid open the passenger door of the chopper, buffeting the interior with a sudden rush of air.

Barney steadied the chopper and maintained his pursuit of the cabin cruiser, coming up alongside and to the rear of it.

Petroni looked over his shoulder, saw Walker and the rifle, and began making sharp, sudden turns.

Walker took aim at the moving target and fired, missing the outboards. He swore to himself and fired multiple times until he finally punched holes in the outboards and saw smoke billowing out of them.

The boat sputtered, lurching to a stop and rocking in the backwash from its own wake.

Barney circled the boat and Walker saw that not only were both outboards crippled, but two of the spare fuel tanks were spilling gasoline all over the aft deck.

His shots hadn't missed after all.

Lauren got on the loudspeaker. "George Petroni, you are under arrest. Come out with your hands up and prepare to be boarded by the United States Coast Guard."

At first the boat was still, but then the rear door of the wheelhouse opened and Petroni came out.

He was holding a flare gun at his side.

"Fuck," Barney said, pulling back hard, veering them away.

But the helicopter was a big, fat, easy target that would be impossible to miss if Petroni decided now to take the shot.

Walker aimed his rifle at Petroni, ready to put him down if he pointed the flare gun at them.

But Petroni didn't. He aimed the flare gun at his engines and the punctured gasoline cans and the fuel sloshing around on his deck.

"Don't do it, George," Walker yelled, but he was talking to himself. Petroni fired.

The boat exploded in a thunder-cracking fireball that consumed Petroni, obliterated the wheelhouse, and blasted fiberglass, wood, and body parts in all directions.

CHAPTER TWENTY-ONE

Thirty Minutes Earlier

The world's largest Rolex was in a clock tower above a jewelry store at The Commons, a shopping center in Calabasas that was designed to resemble an old Italian village. Danny thought it was the perfect place to meet with Roland Slezak and give him the Infinitum watch.

Between the jewelry store and the front parking lot was a circular patio, with some tables arranged around a statue that came from the garden of a French castle. Perhaps it was even from the same castle that Slezak had bought, dismantled, and shipped to Malibu to be rebuilt where the house once stood that Danny had burned down. The thought amused Danny, which was all that mattered.

An armed guard stood in the doorway of the jewelry store. He was there in case the same mob that had once swarmed and pillaged the Sephora next door and the Ulta across the street tried the same thing at the jeweler. Danny knew where all the cameras were around the patio, so he wore a Dodgers cap and sat at an angle facing the parking lot. His face wouldn't show up clearly on any video, assuming anybody ever looked at the footage. The same wouldn't be true for Roland Slezak, who parked his chrome-plated McLaren in the disabled-person spot, opened the winged door, and then strode up to the table, giving the cameras several unobstructed angles on his waxy, unnatural face.

Slezak wasn't alone. Upon his arrival, two men appeared at each end of the patio and sat down at nearby tables. They were undoubtedly armed, but they didn't worry Danny.

Slezak sat down across the table from Danny and took off his diamond-crusted Bvlgari sunglasses and stuck them in the breast pocket of his Prada Double Match bowling shirt, which had flowers on one half and yellow stripes on the other.

"I see you brought company," Danny said.

"I don't want to get mugged on the way to my car."

"Then maybe you shouldn't wear diamond-crusted sunglasses."

"Says the man wearing a $40 million watch," Slezak said.

"I'm not calling attention to myself."

"Because you're a wanted criminal," Slezak said. "I'm not."

Danny smiled. "Wanted or criminal?"

Slezak smiled back, removed a crisp dollar bill from his shirt pocket, and slid it across the table to Danny. The dollar bill was so new, it almost seemed fake.

"I don't usually carry dollar bills," Slezak said. "They're for people who buy corn dogs. I had to get it from the bank."

Danny picked up the dollar, slipped it into his pocket, and then pulled up his sleeve to reveal the Infinitum around his wrist. He removed the watch with care, far more care than someone who'd jumped off a cliff with it on his arm, and placed it gently on the table between them.

Slezak didn't let the Infinitum sit there for an instant. He immediately snatched it up and put it around his own wrist, then held it up in front of his face so he could admire it.

"It's a perfect fit, like it was always meant to be there."

"Enjoy it," Danny said, getting up. "I've got a dollar in my pocket and I'm craving a corn dog."

"Sit down, Danny," Slezak said. "We aren't finished."

Danny froze.

Obviously, the new face hadn't fooled anyone. Was it the way he moved that gave him away? He really should've worked on that limp. But that didn't explain how Slezak knew his name.

"My name isn't Danny."

"I don't know or care what the fuck your name is now, but you're Danny Cole," Slezak said. "You can sit down, or my friends can put you down, it's up to you."

Danny looked back and forth between the two sets of two men, all of whom had stiffened up, ready to come over and make him sit.

He sat down and said to Slezak, "I suggest you look at your chest."

Slezak did. There was a laser dot in the center of it. Tamiko was in a tree on the hillside behind The Commons with her rifle. She had Slezak in her sights.

Danny added, "There is another targeting dot on the back of your head."

Only there was no weapon involved with that laser dot. Sam Mertz sat in a car in the parking lot, aiming only the laser-targeting device at Slezak. He was a safecracker, an explosives expert, a firefighter, and a vintner, but not a killer.

"Oh, I'm sure there is," Slezak said. "I'd be disappointed in you if there wasn't. I want to tell you a story."

"I hope it has some action."

"It does. After the fire that destroyed my dream home, and everything I owned, I turned on the TV news and learned that two men, former members of a convict firefighting crew, plunged into the inferno to rescue two lost teenagers. One of those noble, selfless ex-convicts, Danny Cole, was killed in the valiant effort. Imagine my shock when I recognized the guy's face. It was the firefighter who'd forced me to evacuate my home. Then it all clicked together. I was robbed."

"I'm sorry to hear that."

"It's nice of you to apologize, since it was you," Slezak said. "I'll never forget that face."

"It's not mine."

"Not anymore," Slezak said. "But the eyes, and the cockiness behind them, are the same. I knew it was you the moment you showed me the Infinitum, which was taken in a bold daylight theft that only someone who'd burn down the Santa Monica fucking Mountains just to rob some houses would be ballsy enough to pull off."

"It wasn't about the houses."

"I know what it was about, Danny, and I don't give a shit. Your friend Arnie's life meant nothing to me then and it doesn't now."

This was not going the way Danny planned. Sam was right, he thought—it was impossible to anticipate everything.

"Is there a point to your whining, Roland? Do you want to kill me, is that it? Because that's not going to happen. Not here, not ever."

"I don't want to kill you, Danny. That would be a waste of your talent and the millions in profits I gave up lowering the price of Xylaphram."

"You did get a nice wristwatch out of it."

"I'm going to get a lot more," Slezak said. "There are a bunch of valuable things I want and you're going to steal them for me."

"Why would I do that?"

"The story goes that Cole got killed rescuing those sweet, stupid teenagers, but not that other courageous ex-convict firefighter. That guy got a medal from the governor and was hired by the Los Angeles Fire Department to be a real firefighter. His name was Bobby Logan. Did you know he has a wife and two chubby kids?"

Slezak took a phone out of his pants pocket and put it on the table. On the screen was a candid photo of Bobby and his family in a grocery store checkout line.

"You'll steal for me, Danny. You'll even do my laundry and wash my car, if that's what I want," Slezak said. "Because if you don't, if you disappear on me, I'll have them killed."

"You'd die, too. I'd see to that."

"But Bobby and his adorable family would still be dead and you'd have to live with it. I don't think you could. You couldn't even live with the death of that dipshit car thief on your firefighting crew. That's why you robbed me and burned down my house before. And that's why you've come after me again, this time to lower the price of a drug for retards." Slezak stuck out his tongue, tucked an arm against his chest, and mimed a seizure, then started laughing. "You're not going to kill me. You have a conscience."

"I could ease it by killing you now," Danny said. "All it takes is one subtle signal to my friends and you're dead in an instant."

"If I die, Bobby's family dies," Slezak said. "Do you think I'd come here and threaten you if I hadn't already made those arrangements?"

"What if you have a stroke?"

"They'll still die, so you'd better hope I live a long and healthy life." Slezak got up, but he left the phone on the table. "Take the phone, Danny. I'll be calling you. It might be tomorrow, next week, or next year, but you'd better answer and say 'yes, sir, how can I serve you, sir.' Or maybe it should be 'yes, master.' I'll have to think on that."

Slezak went to his McLaren, and once he was safely inside and backing out of his parking spot, his goons got up and left, too.

Danny sent a quick text on his own phone, then got up and walked away, leaving behind Slezak's burner and peeling off the waxlike coating from his fingertips that covered his prints.

Eve sat at her cubicle at the Lost Hills station, working her way through the mountains of paperwork on the Murphson murder, when she got a text from Walker:

Got a tip from a trusted CI: In five minutes, the buyer of rare stolen watch will be speeding on Las Virgenes Road in a chromed McLaren heading to Mulholland. Keep me out of it. I need to protect my CI.

There was a McDonald's on Las Virgenes, and it was five minutes away from the station. The timing was perfect.

Eve got up from her cubicle and looked over at Duncan, who was in his own cubicle, slogging through the paper, too. "I'm craving some McNuggets. Can I get you anything?"

"I'll come with you," Duncan said. "I'm craving a Double Quarter Pounder with Cheese, large fries, and a large Coke."

"You always are."

They walked out of the station, got into an unmarked Explorer, and drove east on Agoura Road toward Las Virgenes.

"I'm glad you're finally learning the importance of pre-gaming dinner," Duncan said.

"Six McNuggets is a snack," Eve said. "A Double Quarter Pounder with Cheese, large fries, and a Coke is dinner."

"It's 4:00 p.m. I don't have dinner until eight," Duncan said. "But pre-gaming gets the digestive machinery oiled and assures smooth absorption of the proteins, fiber, and nutrients. It's very important for good health."

"And if you don't eat a massive meal before your massive meal?"

"Severe constipation, of course. You don't want that."

Eve eased the Explorer to a stop near the intersection, preparing to make a left turn into the McDonald's drive-through on the north corner, just as the chromed sports car rocketed past on Las Virgenes.

She flicked on the flashers hidden behind their front grille, turned on the siren, and punched the gas.

The Explorer jerked forward, startling Duncan, who glared at her. "You've got to be kidding me."

"We can't just ignore a blatant speeding infraction like that."

"I can," Duncan said.

The Explorer couldn't possibly catch a McLaren that was going at full speed, which was about 250 miles per hour, but there were a few things going in her favor. The driver wasn't fleeing, the car was distinctive, and she was already close enough to read the plates.

The McLaren pulled over onto the shoulder. Duncan reached for the radio to call in the plates and ask for a patrol car as backup.

The patrol car also had a ticket book. They didn't.

Eve got out and approached the McLaren from the driver's side and touched the rear quarter panel, a habit from her days as a deputy on patrol, which weren't that long ago. She'd noticed that Walker did it when he approached Big Mike's Dodge dually. She hadn't known that US Marshals got the same training that deputies and LAPD patrol officers did.

The driver rolled down his window. She flashed her badge at him.

"Do you know how fast you were driving, sir?"

"Not fast enough," he said with a grin. "You don't look like a traffic cop to me."

"I'm not," she said. "I'm a homicide detective."

"I can assure you that I haven't killed anyone."

"You could at the speed you were driving," she said. "May I see your license and registration, please?"

He took out his wallet, fished out his driver's license, and handed it to her, giving her a glimpse of the most unusual wristwatch she'd ever seen.

"Isn't this below your pay grade?" he asked.

"My job is to enforce the law whenever I see a violation." Eve checked his driver's license, then glanced behind her to see Duncan standing outside the car, ready to assist if things got ugly.

Slezak said, "How are you going to prove there was a violation without a radar gun? I'll argue you singled me out because I have a fast car, but that doesn't mean I was going fast. It's a form of discrimination to assume that I was."

"You've been through this before, Mr. Slezak."

"Many times. The discrimination is pervasive," he said. "Take my advice, honey. Save yourself the trouble of going to court. I'll win. I always do."

Honey?

Eve glanced behind her, saw a patrol car rolling up behind the Explorer, and shifted her gaze back at Slezak.

She smiled. "Nice watch."

Slezak saw something he didn't like in her smile and stomped on his gas pedal.

The McLaren blasted away, showering Eve in a spray of dirt and gravel, before it became a chrome blur, speeding down the center of the road, weaving through traffic on both sides.

The patrol car peeled out after the McLaren, but she knew that a Dodge Charger, even with a 5.7 Hemi, was no match for a world-class supercar that could go from 0 to 100 in three seconds.

Duncan rushed over to Eve. "Are you all right?"

Eve was covered in dirt and had stinging nicks on her face from the gravel, but she was more angry at herself than hurt. She shouldn't have mentioned the watch.

"We'll never catch up to him on the road," Eve said. "Call for air support."

◆ ◆ ◆

The LASD chopper carrying Sharpe and Walker circled Petroni's burning boat and the coast guard cutter that had just arrived when they heard the dispatcher's request for an airship to aid in the vehicle pursuit of Roland Slezak.

Sharpe gave Walker a hard look. He knew the name for the same reason that Walker did. It was a secret they shared.

The dispatcher said that Slezak was fleeing a traffic stop in a chrome-plated McLaren and was last seen traveling at high speeds southbound on Las Virgenes Road in Calabasas.

Walker wondered if this meant that something in Danny's scheme had gone wrong or if everything was working out fine. He needed to know.

"Take the pursuit call, Barney," Walker said.

"We can't just leave the scene," Barney said.

"Yes, we can. The coast guard is here," Walker said. "Petroni isn't going anywhere now and we can catch this guy. He's on his way to Wishbone Canyon."

"How do you know?"

"Trust me," Walker said.

Barney nodded at Lauren, who radioed in. The chopper veered away from the flaming boat and headed northeast toward the Malibu Hills.

Walker saw Sharpe still giving him a look, the same one that he gave Toniel Novar after transforming from Sleepy Sharpe into Killer Sharpe.

"What's wrong?" Walker asked, feeling about as guilty and stupid as Novar probably did.

"We're together in a helicopter heading to Wishbone Canyon again," Sharpe said. "You don't find that déjà vu unsettling?"

"At least this time the canyon isn't on fire," Walker said.

A few minutes later, they were soaring over the Malibu Hills, much of them still blackened and eerily barren nearly two years after a raging, unstoppable firestorm destroyed every single home in its path except one—the Epitome, a 21,000-square-foot, $100 million mega-mansion on the eastern ridge of Wishbone Canyon.

The Epitome was a two-story, white-marble modernist house built to withstand both wildfires and earthquakes. The mega-mansion curved around a travertine-tiled circular motor court that followed the contour of a shallow moat that surrounded the property and acted as a firebreak.

The Epitome was also where Sharpe and Walker, two lost teenagers, and ex-convict Bobby Logan had sought refuge from the relentless inferno that claimed Danny Cole's life.

That was Sharpe and Walker's story, anyway.

And their secret.

Across the canyon, on the western ridge, an imported French castle was being reconstructed, carved stone by carved stone, on the same spot where Roland Slezak's mansion once stood.

Slezak was living in the Epitome in the meantime and Walker was certain that was where he was heading now in his McLaren, intending to lock himself in the same impenetrable safe room that had saved their lives. It was an irrational thing for Slezak to do, but it also made sense to Walker. Slezak was terrified and seeking safety.

As the helicopter neared the bright-white Epitome, which practically glowed against the desolate backdrop, Walker pointed to the huge motor court, which was more than big enough to work as a helipad. "Take us down there."

"Roger that," Barney said.

The instant the chopper touched down, Walker and Sharpe piled out, crouching low to avoid the blades.

Walker, still carrying the rifle, decided they would make their stand on the sleek steel-and-glass bridge between the long driveway up to the house and the motor court.

Sharpe came up beside him and handed him his Stetson. "Here we are again."

"It's a different situation," Walker said, putting on the hat.

"Then why does it feel like we're coming full circle?"

Walker felt it, too, but unlike Sharpe, he knew about Danny Cole's involvement in this situation.

The two detectives didn't have another second to dwell on their feelings because that's when Slezak's car surged up the driveway toward the bridge and came to a screeching stop on the other side. The driver's side door of the McLaren opened up and outward, toward the front of the car, shielding Slezak from the detectives' view and giving him cover.

Walker shouted, "Listen up, Roland. We're sheriff's deputies. It's all over. Come out slowly, with your hands up."

Slezak did emerge slowly, but not with his hands up. He was in the strangest pose Walker had ever seen. He was dangling the Infinitum from his left hand and aiming a gun at it with his right.

"Back off or I'll shoot the watch," Slezak shouted.

Sharpe looked incredulously at Walker. "Is he holding his watch hostage?"

"It's not just any watch," Walker said. "It's the Infinitum."

"The one-of-a-kind zillion-dollar one that was stolen in Japan?"

Walker nodded. "Uh-huh."

Sharpe considered that, then yelled back to Slezak. "We don't care. Put the gun down."

"I'm not bluffing, I'll do it," Slezak said. "I'll shoot the watch."

"Go ahead," Sharpe said. "But try not to blow your hand off, that would make a mess."

A patrol car and a plain-wrap Explorer pulled up ten yards behind Slezak. Eve, Duncan, and two uniformed deputies emerged from their vehicles, their guns drawn.

Slezak looked between the two sets of cops on either side of him. "Back off, all of you, and let me go home, or you'll be responsible for the destruction of this irreplaceable $40 million work of art."

Walker said, "We're not going anywhere, Roland, and we're certainly not letting you lock yourself in your safe room. We're resolving this situation right here, right now."

"You don't understand," Slezak yelled. "I'm holding the fucking *Mona Lisa* at gunpoint."

"We get it," Sharpe shouted back. "And we don't care."

Slezak stomped his feet, like a child having a tantrum. "I can't go to prison. Rejuvenation isn't possible."

Sharpe spoke low to Walker. "Did he say 'rejuvenation'?"

"I think so."

"Maybe he meant 'rehabilitation.'"

"He's nuts." Walker raised his voice. "Put your gun down, Roland."

Slezak shook his head. "It's Danny Cole you want, not me. He stole this. I can give him to you."

Sharpe spoke to Walker in a near whisper. "Now this whole crazy situation makes some sense. Danny should have stayed dead."

"I guess Danny had unfinished business," Walker whispered back.

"We really *are* coming full circle," Sharpe said.

Now Walker understood Danny's entire scheme and the trap he'd set for Slezak. Danny wasn't going to take down Slezak. He was giving that pleasure to Walker, who was giving it to Eve. But at least Walker would get to witness it.

Walker raised his voice so Slezak could hear him. "That's great, Roland. You have something to offer the DA that might keep you out of jail. But there won't be any deals if you destroy the watch."

Slezak thought about that for a long moment, then dropped the gun and raised his hands above his head. The watch still dangled from his hand.

"Get on your knees," Walker instructed, "and then lay face down on the ground, but be careful not to drop the watch."

Slezak did as he was told.

Walker nodded at Eve, and she said something to the two deputies, who hurried forward, patted Slezak down, handcuffed him, and lifted him to his feet.

Eve holstered her gun, went up to Slezak, read him his rights, and then told the deputies to take him to their patrol car.

Walker and Sharpe joined her, and so did Duncan. Up close, Walker could see that Eve's face was covered with little cuts, like she'd nicked herself shaving off a beard. She saw him studying her face and she touched her cheeks, examined her hands, and saw some blood on her fingertips.

"It could be worse," she said. "At least I won't need a hospital visit this time."

"Not even a plastic surgeon?"

"Is it that bad?" she asked.

"Your face is fine," Sharpe said. "Tell us how we got here."

"We were on our way to McDonald's," Eve said, "and this guy sped right past us."

"So naturally she had to chase after him." Duncan crouched, his knees cracking, stuck a pencil in the barrel of Slezak's gun, and picked it up.

"We're the law," Eve said to him.

"We're the hungry," Duncan said, and dropped the gun from his pencil into an evidence bag. "We still are."

"We pulled him over and I asked for his ID." Eve took a pair of disposable gloves out of her pocket and slipped them on. "When Slezak handed me his driver's license, I recognized the watch and he bolted."

"Unbelievable," Sharpe said, in a tone that suggested he didn't believe it at all. "It's like winning the lottery."

"I'm sure that's not how Slezak sees it," Walker said. "This will make headlines around the world."

"Oh, great," Duncan said. "Just what Eve needs. More publicity."

"No, I don't. I have had enough for a lifetime." Eve picked up the watch, took an evidence baggie out of her pocket, and slipped it inside. "Who is this 'Danny Cole' that Slezak was ranting about?"

"An ex-convict who ended up being a hero," Sharpe said. "He died in the Malibu fire saving the lives of two teenagers."

She said, "Slezak seems to think Cole survived."

"He's also afraid he can't rejuvenate in prison," Walker said. "I don't think he's mentally sound."

"I suppose we'll find out," Eve said, then looked directly at Walker. "Thanks for the assist."

"We were in the neighborhood," Walker said.

"Doing what?"

"Catching the freeway arsonist."

"Not exactly," Sharpe said. "He blew himself up before we could arrest him."

Duncan sighed. "I guess he didn't think he could rejuvenate in prison, either."

◆ ◆ ◆

The clock hadn't stopped ticking for Walker and Sharpe at the Epitome.

They still had to notify Lansing that they'd solved the case and stop Caffrey and Scruggs from making a humiliating mistake by going public with their arrest.

Sharpe called Lansing and Walker called Caffrey.

Walker got Caffrey on the second ring, who said: "Calling to apologize for Shar-Pei?"

"You haven't announced Novar's arrest yet, have you?"

"We just called our chief," Caffrey said. "He's setting up a press conference in an hour so he can do it, the publicity hog. Is this when you start begging for some credit?"

"Cancel the press conference or he's going to fire you tomorrow."

Caffrey laughed. "Why would he do that?"

"Novar didn't do the freeway arson," Walker said. "And the guy who did just blew himself up to avoid arrest."

"You're shitting me," Caffrey said.

"Even worse, you and Scruggs share the blame for the freeway fire. You could even be considered accomplices."

"Now I *know* you're shitting me."

"The arsonist was George Petroni," Walker said.

"Bullshit."

"We can tie him to the fire logs and put him at the freeway when the fire was set. He knew that we could, too, and that his other arsons would be revealed, so he made a run for Mexico on his boat. But we caught up to him first."

"What other arsons?"

"He brought down the freeways in Pittsburgh and Milwaukee, too."

There was a long silence. Caffrey's voice was weak. "What does any of this have to do with us?"

"Petroni used the details you and Scruggs gave him about the carport arson spree to torch the freeway and frame Novar for it. You two were fishing buddies with the worst serial arsonist in American history. If that comes out, it'll be a scandal that rocks the entire LAFD. You and Scruggs will be lucky if you're only ridiculed and fired and not prosecuted, too," Walker said. "But we're going to take pity on you and say that we don't know where Petroni got his inside information, that he took his secret with him to hell."

"What's the catch?"

"There is none," Walker said. "We all make mistakes."

He wasn't going to tell Caffrey that they'd also inadvertently solved the freeway arson case, making fools of Walker and Sharpe, who up until that point had no idea that Petroni was involved. Petroni might have gone on for years, repeating the same arson and becoming obscenely wealthy along the way.

So yes, Walker knew about making mistakes and had genuine sympathy for his colleagues.

"Thank you," Caffrey said. "I suppose you want the Novar arrest now, too."

"Nope, you and Scruggs are the face of the carport investigation. It's all yours," Walker said. "But you might want to drop the Shar-Pei crap from now on."

"Sure. I appreciate this, Walker. We've never had any problem with you. You're a stand-up guy. But Sharpe, he just has this way of . . ." Caffrey didn't finish his thought. "I've got to go and stop the chief."

Caffrey ended the call.

Sharpe came over to Walker. "Lansing is so happy that I think we're a lock for those certificates of appreciation."

"I'm thrilled." Walker was sure now that he wouldn't have to worry about being disciplined for using department helicopters for his commute. "Did you tell him about the connection between Petroni, Caffrey, and Scruggs?"

"Nope," Sharpe said. "I'm not telling anyone."

"I'm glad you feel that way, because that's what I told Caffrey we'd do," Walker said. "It's nice to know that you and I, at least this time, are on the same wavelength."

Sharpe looked over at the driveway. The chromed McLaren was still there, but Eve, Duncan, and the deputies were already gone. The helicopter was powered down, Lauren and Barney both wandering around the property, talking on their cell phones. The two detectives weren't alone, but they had privacy.

"I've just got one question," Sharpe said. "Why did you and Danny do this?"

Walker knew that the look Sharpe gave him on the helicopter had more behind it than just the feeling of coming full circle on the incendiary event that brought the two of them together.

"What makes you think I was involved?"

"You got Eve Ronin to be at the right place at the right time because you couldn't be there yourself," Sharpe said. "That was the frantic texting you were doing in the helicopter. It was Danny Cole who stole the watch and set up Slezak to be arrested. I'm assuming it was more payback for the convict firefighter who got killed protecting Slezak's house. The only thing I can't understand is why you're helping him."

"We're helping each other," Walker said. "Cody has epilepsy. There's only one drug that stops his seizures."

Sharpe considered that for a moment, then nodded. He must have seen the news about Slezak's unexpected, drastic cut in the price of Xylaphram.

Walker said, "Are we okay?"

"I'm a cop, and my duty is to enforce the law," Sharpe said, and Walker felt a horrible rolling of apprehension in his gut. "And this feels like justice to me."

They were okay.

CHAPTER
TWENTY-TWO

September 11

The next morning, there were three back-to-back press conferences on the steps of Los Angeles City Hall.

First, the chief of the Los Angeles Fire Department, with Caffrey and Scruggs standing behind him, announced that his arson investigators, whom he introduced by name, with the cooperation of the Los Angeles County Sheriff's Department, had arrested the arsonist responsible for "two days of terror" in Hollywood. He went on to explain the details of the crime without ever mentioning Walker and Sharpe, who were also outside city hall, standing alongside Eve Ronin and Duncan Pavone.

The chief was followed at the podium by Sheriff Richard Lansing, who announced that a task force that he'd assembled had identified the freeway arsonist, who he was "horrified and appalled" to announce was George Petroni, the contractor hired by the mayor and governor to oversee the repair of the I-10, the same freeway that he was actually responsible for damaging.

The sheriff shook his head in dismay after he said it, as if the governor and mayor should have known what a monumental mistake they were making.

The two politicians were still standing on the step and smiling. There wasn't much else they could do. But Walker knew they had to be enraged by Lansing's brutal cheap shot. It was Lansing's declaration of war, in the same way that the surprise attack on Pearl Harbor was Japan's.

Lansing explained that Petroni killed himself rather than face responsibility for the 1-10 arson, as well as the freeway fires he'd set in Pittsburgh and Milwaukee, where the companies he'd worked for had been paid "tens of millions of dollars" in early-completion bonuses, in which he shared a significant percentage of the proceeds.

"This makes George Petroni the most successful and insidious serial arsonist our nation has ever known," Lansing said. "He would still be terrorizing and embezzling from our cities if not for the determination and skill of the detectives under my command. But the horror doesn't end there."

This last comment startled the governor and the mayor, who didn't think there could be anything worse than what they'd already heard today from the sheriff, a scandal-plagued political adversary they'd long ago written off as a threat. Obviously, they were wrong.

"Our investigation has revealed rampant corruption and gross mismanagement at the California Department of Transportation, which directly contributed to the highly combustible conditions that allowed Petroni's arson to become such a destructive inferno," Lansing said. "That deeply troubling and shocking aspect of the investigation, which is still ongoing, has resulted in the arrests of a dozen property managers, who've leased state land under our Southland freeways, for the bribery and murder of a Caltrans inspector."

The news sent a palpable ripple of excitement through the audience of reporters, a pause Lansing used to beckon Walker, Sharpe, Eve, and Duncan to the podium, where he thanked them by name for their "exceptional and relentless detective work" that set a "new gold standard" for law enforcement.

At that point, Lansing introduced the governor and the mayor, who had a big announcement of their own.

The governor and mayor, both looking deeply uncomfortable, stepped up to deliver what they'd thought would be, and should have been, the biggest and best news of the day, which was that the Santa Monica Freeway would be opening in three days, ending the traffic nightmare months earlier than anybody ever imagined, though repairs would be ongoing for a while.

But their big announcement came off like an afterthought, a limp effort to distract from their failures in oversight. It didn't help them that the unspoken reason the freeway was opening so fast was because of the work done by the arsonist responsible for the disaster.

In fact, the first question from the press to the governor and the mayor was whether Petroni's company would still be getting their early-completion bonus.

Things went downhill fast from there, the reporters bombarding the two politicians with questions about the corruption, malfeasance, incompetence, and murder surrounding Caltrans and the freeway fire, much to Lansing's barely disguised delight.

And when the governor and mayor finally found cheap, desperate excuses to leave the steps, the media wanted to hear from Eve Ronin. Her astonishing recovery of the stolen Infinitum had already made her a media sensation from Los Angeles to Japan and everywhere in between by that morning. They had a lot of questions.

She politely declined to answer them.

But she had a question of her own she wanted answered, and it wasn't from the press.

As everyone dispersed, she made sure to come down the steps alongside Walker, who she deftly edged away from everyone else so they could speak in private.

She asked, "Why didn't you want any credit for recovering the Infinitum?"

He'd been expecting the question and had an answer ready. "I owed you one for Wonder Woman."

"That's not why you did it."

"As I told you before, I'm also protecting a valuable CI," he said.

"And now, so are you."

"Are you talking about yourself or this mysterious informant?"

"Both," Walker said, and then, as Sharpe and Duncan came down the steps beside them, close enough now to hear them talking, he asked: "How did things go with Slezak and the DA?"

Eve said, "Slezak told us a wild story about Danny Cole, a con man and thief that we later discovered that *you'd* arrested and put in prison."

"What a small world," Walker said.

"What a stunning coincidence," Duncan said, clearly skeptical. "You forgot to mention that yesterday."

"I was still a bit dazed," Walker said. "We'd just witnessed a man die in a boat explosion."

"And the arrest is meaningless trivia," Sharpe said. "What was Slezak's wild story?"

Eve said, "Slezak claimed Cole approached him out of nowhere with the watch and offered to give it to him if he slashed the price of some anti-seizure drug."

"Slezak also mentioned something about a corn dog," Duncan said. "But it didn't make much sense."

"Of course you'd remember him mentioning food," Sharpe said.

"Because I'm starving," Duncan said. "It's almost lunchtime and I haven't pre-gamed."

"Pre-gamed?" Sharpe said.

Walker said, "None of this sounds like Danny Cole to me. He's a master thief who stole to make huge scores for himself, not for charity. What proof does Slezak have to back up his ridiculous story?"

"None," Eve said. "He says Cole gave him the watch at a table at The Commons. We pulled the security camera footage but we couldn't see the man's face. And the only fingerprints on the watch belonged to Slezak, so there's no corroboration there, either. The guy is a ghost."

"Danny Cole would have to be," Sharpe said. "He's been dead for two years. What did the DA say about all this?"

Duncan said, "Unless he gave up the real name of the person who stole the Infinitum for him, there would be no deals."

"Not that she's motivated to make any," Eve added. "We caught him with a stolen one-of-a-kind watch on his wrist. It's an easy, effortless conviction."

"It's nice when that happens," Walker said.

"That's the thing," Duncan said. "It never does."

Walker knew how to get Duncan's suspicious mind on a different track. "Have you ever tried an LA Loco Moco for breakfast?"

"What's that?"

"Two fried eggs on two pieces of smoked brisket on a huge helping of hash browns, all slathered in barbecue sauce."

"No and that's a crime," Duncan said, actually licking his lips. "Where do they serve that?"

"Duke's BBQ. It's ten minutes from here, but he stops serving breakfast at eleven," Walker said. "We might make it if we use our lights and siren."

"Of course we will," Duncan said. "That's what they were invented for."

Bobby Logan and his family lived in a picture-perfect house in a tree-lined South Pasadena neighborhood that was so picture perfect that there were film crews shooting movies, TV shows, and commercials on the street three days a week.

Bobby's wife and kids frolicked in the swimming pool, their golden retriever leaping in to join the fun, while Bobby and Danny Cole, dressed in T-shirts and shorts, relaxed on side-by-side chaise lounges, sipping beers and enjoying the sunshine. Hot dogs and hamburgers sizzled on the outdoor grill.

"This is the life," Bobby said to his old friend, who he'd introduced to his wife as a fellow firefighter, which was true. They were on the convict firefighting crew together and, not long after their release, had also burglarized several mansions in the middle of the Malibu wildfire, which they'd ignited themselves.

But he didn't tell her that part.

"I'm happy for you, Bobby," Danny said.

He'd called yesterday to warn him about possible retaliation by Roland Slezak, which he thought was a low risk but felt Bobby should know. Bobby responded by inviting him over for a family barbecue. That was Bobby in a nutshell. Danny warned him that he looked different, and that it might be a shock at first sight. But if it was, Bobby didn't show it at all when Danny showed up at his door. He gave Danny a big hug, brought him inside, and let the dog jump all over him.

And now here they were, in Bobby's backyard, posing for a Norman Rockwell painting.

"You can have this, too," Bobby said, gesturing with his bottle at the scene in front of them.

"It's not for me. I'd die of boredom."

"Your family will keep you too busy for that."

"I don't have a family."

"That's not entirely true. You have me, Sam, and Tamiko, and probably some people I don't even know about," Bobby said, watching his family splash around, the kids giggling, the dog barking with glee. "But yeah, it's not like this, and what you all do, that's not for me. Not anymore. I'm never going back to that."

"I don't blame you," Danny said. "You're so rich, if you never earn another dollar, you can keep this house, put your kids through college, and spend your retirement traveling the world with your wife, staying in the best hotels, eating the best food, doing anything you want."

"That's true, and I have you to thank for that," Bobby said. "And those two cops who let me go."

"So why do you risk your life fighting fires?"

"Because I love it. I think it's what I was born to do," Bobby said. "You said I have it all, but my family and the money are just three-quarters of it. The rest is firefighting. What's the point of living if you aren't being who you are and doing what you love?"

Danny finished his beer and thought about how happy his friend was. Bobby was living his dream, one that the recovering drug addict and ex-convict never really believed was possible to achieve.

And yet, here he was.

Danny had truly believed that he was living his own dream, his best life, traveling the world pulling off dangerous heists and elaborate cons, right up till the moment US Marshal Andrew Walker arrested him and sent him to prison.

It was an exciting, fun, and lucrative life, but Danny was never entirely satisfied. Something was missing.

Was it the challenge, the money, or the risk? Were none of them high enough? So he'd kept chasing scores, hoping he would discover what it was.

He didn't find it until after the Malibu fire job, when he felt an emotional fulfillment that he'd never experienced before and knew he never would again.

Which was why he'd retired, while he was still rich and free. He was safe, pursued by no one, ready to live a new life.

And yet, here he was.

He'd finished another heist and con, but not for the challenge, the money, or the risk. For something else. For *someone* else. And he was happy.

Truly, deeply, ridiculously happy.

Because he was feeling that fulfillment again. How could he walk away from this? But more importantly, how could he experience it *again*?

He'd have to think hard about that.

But he knew that it would mean following Bobby Logan's example, being who he was and doing what he loved.

And not getting caught.

Danny smiled at Bobby. "You're right. I can have this, too."

AUTHOR'S NOTE & ACKNOWLEDGMENTS

The story you've just read is entirely fictional, but many of the elements were inspired by Harry Burkhart's 2012 spree of carport fires, a case that was investigated by Ed Nordskog, a former arson and explosives detective with the Los Angeles County Sheriff's Department, and that he chronicled in his excellent book *The Arsonist Profiles: Analyzing Arson Motives and Behaviors*.

I am also indebted to Lauren Abernathy, a tactical flight officer and crew chief for the San Bernardino County Sheriff's Department, and Kelsey Parsons, a former deputy sheriff with the same department, for their advice and technical expertise. I also want to thank my cousin Joe Barer for giving me an education in the world of watch collecting.

You should blame me, not any of them, for any errors in forensics, horology, geography, gravity, or logic that probably occurred when I twisted pesky facts to fit my fiction.

The Gallery of Curiosities, the bizarre collection it contains, and the Japanese island it's on (or should I say *in*) are entirely figments of my imagination, but I was inspired by my visit to the amazing Museum of Old and New Art in Hobart, Tasmania, which obviously made a lasting impression on me. I'm eager to go back and visit it again.

The unnamed *ryokan* in Hakone, Japan, is based on an actual one I stayed in as part of my research for the settings in this novel.

Sam Mertz's winery on Waiheke Island, New Zealand, is a mash-up of several wineries I visited there, but primarily the idyllic Mudbrick Vineyard and Restaurant.

I didn't make it to Switzerland for this book and I certainly didn't jump off a cliff in a wing suit, but like Danny Cole, I watched a lot of videos and read many articles on the subject, which gives me the expertise and the chutzpah to make stuff up.

The asthma inhaler device that ultimately plays a key role in this story actually exists, under a different name, of course. In fact, I use one of those devices myself. (Does this mean I can write off my asthma meds now?)

The passive license plate readers mentioned in the book also exist and are *everywhere*. I was given an excellent demonstration, by the officers of a law enforcement agency in Southern California, of their use and how amazingly effective they are at tracking and identifying vehicles. The officers would rather I didn't mention their names or their agency, but they know who they are, and I thank them.

And, finally, if you'd like to know more about the personal information that law enforcement agencies can get about you without obtaining a warrant, I recommend the *Wall Street Journal* article "U.S. Spy Agencies Know Your Secrets. They Bought Them" by Byron Tau (March 8, 2024). There's a lot more information out there on the subject, but this article presents a great overview.

As always, I want to thank my publisher Gracie Doyle, my editors Megha Parekh and Charlotte Herscher, my agent Amy Tannenbaum, and my wife Valerie and daughter Madison, without whom there wouldn't be a third Sharpe & Walker adventure and I'd be taking your order now at Arby's.

ABOUT THE AUTHOR

Photo © 2024 Linda Woods

Lee Goldberg is a two-time Edgar Award and two-time Shamus Award finalist and the #1 *New York Times* bestselling author of more than sixty novels, including the Eve Ronin series, the Ian Ludlow series, the Sharpe & Walker series, and seven books in the Fox & O'Hare series, which he coauthored with Janet Evanovich. He has also written and/or produced many TV shows, including *Diagnosis Murder*, *SeaQuest*, and *Monk*, and is the cocreator of the Hallmark movie series *Mystery 101*. As an international television consultant, he has advised networks and studios in Canada, France, Germany, Spain, China, Sweden, and the Netherlands on the creation, writing, and production of episodic series. For more information, visit www.leegoldberg.com.